A WISH SO FREE

SLAVES OF SANDSPIRE

Z.R. ABADDI

CHAPTER
ONE

Reema's feet touched sand.

As she emerged from the mines, her gaze lifted to the canopy of stars overhead. If she were anyone else, she'd stop to marvel at them, letting the awe burn her eyes with tears.

But she wasn't anyone else. She was the Ifrit, gang lord of the mines. And she'd come back to the surface for one reason only: to undo the damage she'd done by releasing the Djinn into the world.

To her, the stars were only worth noticing for how they lit the night around her. They illuminated three small buildings made from sandstone, and beyond that, far in the distance, she saw the silhouette of Sandspire, the second greatest city in the desert of Sundara.

After a lifetime in the cramped tunnels, the ability to see so far felt strange. It left her feeling adrift, like she was dreaming.

Her attention shifted to a hand reaching out of the Hole. She helped Alaric to the surface, her eyes catching on the burn scar that striped across his face, from where the Djinn had removed the steel band that once obscured his eyes. But now, his brown eyes glowed as nearly as bright as the stars themselves.

"Finally," he breathed.

She nodded, looking back toward the nearby buildings. It had taken close to two weeks for the slaves to build their way out of the mines. It had been harder than she imagined.

Mining marble was easy; they had been doing it for as long as she could remember. But *building* something stable and tall enough to climb fifty feet out of the Hole? That was the tough part, and none of them were architects. Every time they failed, they lost several lives. And yet, each time, the miners picked up their pickaxes and went right back to work. They were used to collapses, to the loss of lives. They weren't about to give up when freedom was right at their fingertips.

Asif was the next to touch sand.

Like Reema, his gaze did not find the stars or the city in the distance, but rather the buildings nearby. His lip curled back over bared teeth.

"I've been waiting for this," he growled as he gripped his pickaxe in hand.

Reema narrowed her gaze. When she climbed her way to the surface, she expected to see sands burnt black from the Djinn's passing, or to see guards to come running with their swords in hand, ready to slaughter any miner who dared taste freedom. Instead, she was met with endless quiet and the calm that came with it.

It fueled her rage, hot enough that even the soft brush of desert air couldn't cool it.

Her fists clenched, jaw tight.

Renfri emerged from the mines, stepping between Reema and Asif. Unlike the others, she was speechless, her eyes wide with awe as she stared at the night sky. Reema studied her, surprised that the former gang lord would gawk at the sight.

"It's been that long, huh?" Reema asked.

"You have no idea," Renfri whispered.

"Then you can wait a little while longer. We've got work to do."

Renfri blinked, looking down from the sky to the fire burning in Reema's dark eyes and the shiv in her outstretched hand.

"Those buildings over there?" Reema gestured toward them. "That's where the guards stay."

Renfri's smile widened as she took the shiv from Reema. "Say no more."

While the rest of the miners climbed out of the Hole, the four of them raced across the sands, soft crunching underfoot.

Alaric was the fastest, still somewhat accustomed to the desert sands compared to the others who had spent a lifetime walking on solid stone.

He reached the first building, pressing his back against the rough sandstone as he peeked around the corner. He signaled it was clear to Reema, who stepped ahead of him, holding her relic pickaxe at the ready, gleaming with the Angel's magic. Renfri and Asif flanked them, their expressions mirroring hers. They, too, were thinking of all the times Captain Hamza had mocked and tortured them, reducing them to something less than human.

They slipped inside, brushing past a heavy fabric curtain blocking the doorway. She led the way, scanning the room, her heart deadly calm. Shelves lined the walls, stacked high with sacks of lentils and dates, dried meat, and jars of water. A lone lantern hung from the ceiling, casting dim light that made the shadows dance.

"Empty," she whispered, frustration clear in her voice.

"Look at all this," Asif said, lifting a sack of lentils. "There's so much food. And the bastards let us practically *starve* down there."

Asif tossed the sack aside.

She watched it land, feeling the painful emptiness in her stomach more than ever. She buried the urge to stuff herself full of dates and drown herself with water. There would be time for that soon enough.

They crept out of the building, moving toward the next one. The silence was unnerving, broken only by the soft whisper of the desert's howl. But Reema welcomed it. It covered the sound of shifting sand as they ran across it.

They approached the second building, and Reema signaled for them to stop. This building had a door. She pressed her ear against it and listened. She heard the soft rumble of a man snoring. After a moment, she nodded.

"Someone's inside," she mouthed.

The others readied their weapons as she pushed the door open slowly, the hinges protesting softly. They slipped inside, the room as dark as the mines. It was only with the glow of Alaric's eyes that they were able to see the Captain sprawled in his bed, his chest rising and falling in deep sleep.

Renfri stalked toward him, drawing the shiv back so that she could bury it into his neck. But Reema grabbed her arm, pulling her to a stop.

Renfri's eyes flashed with anger, but Reema shook her head.

"Not yet," Reema mouthed.

She passed her pickaxe to Alaric and took the shiv from Renfri's hand. She snuck forward, fighting the urge to plunge it into his chest, to see that glorious crimson blood paint these shadows red. The tension in the air was thick, threatening to snap at any moment. But this time, *she* controlled it.

She pressed the marble shiv's edge to the Captain's throat.

His lips curved into a frown, hands instinctively going to his throat as his eyes slowly opened. He drew a sharp breath, his eyes jolting wide open in fear. He reached for something in the shadows, but she pressed him back into the bed with the shiv. Blood slowly ran down his neck.

His gaze flicked from her to the others behind her, the whites of his eyes flaring with even more fear at the sight of Alaric's glowing eyes. Even if Alaric's stare wasn't terrifying enough, the glow of his eyes in the shadows was.

Reema lifted a finger to her lips. "Quiet, or I'll cut you open. Understand?"

Captain Hamza's tongue brushed across his trembling lips. Nervous beads of sweat ran along his brow. He nodded.

"Stand."

He shifted slowly, the covers falling away to reveal a pouchy stomach littered with burns. She suspected they were from sparks off his emberdust pipe.

He opened his mouth, but a firm press of the shiv silenced him.

"What'd I say?"

He swallowed, his throat bobbing over the shiv, drawing a small cut that made him wince.

"Turn around."

He obeyed, holding his shaking hands up. Reema wrinkled her nose at the bitter stench of piss. She glanced down; sure enough, his trousers were soaked.

She felt no pang of pity. She could only remember the time that he unzipped those same trousers, pulled out his dick, and pissed down the Hole while his guards laughed.

She looped her arm around his throat, holding the shiv to it still, and whispered in his ear, "Now walk."

Renfri, Asif, and Alaric flanked them as Reema led Captain Hamza to the third and final building. The Captain opened his mouth again, but she silenced him with a sharp jerk.

When they reached the building, she motioned for Asif to brush aside the heavy fabric covering the door. Asif drew it back, and with the Captain as her hostage, she entered.

She expected to hear the rumbling snores of sleeping

guards. Instead, she was greeted with shadowed rows of empty bunks and silence. The hairs on her neck rose, prickling fear spreading goosebumps along her arms.

Reema spun the Captain around and held the shiv to his throat again.

"Where are they?" Her voice boomed in the small space.

"They're not here," he said, his gaze focused solely on her and not the fuming Renfri and Asif. "That's what I was trying to tell you."

"Where are they?" she asked again, pressing the shiv deeper.

"The slave master called them back to the city!" he whimpered. "Left me here alone to guard the mines."

Sweat dripped off him. A spineless man without an ounce of dignity or kindness. He disgusted her. Killing him would be a mercy to the world. At the thought, her lips drew back over her teeth.

He shook, leaning forward despite the shiv pressing into his neck. Something sparked in his gaze. Hope?

"I know what you want, Reema. You want revenge. I can help you get it. Let me take you to them. I'll give you each and every man."

"You think you know me?" Reema asked, her voice low and soft. Somehow, that made the Captain only shake more. "If you did, then you'd know what's coming for you."

He opened his mouth to say something. She drove a punch to his face, hearing the satisfying crack of a broken nose. He cried out in pain as he fell back against one of the empty bunks.

"Renfri," she called, staring down at the Captain as he rolled on the ground, holding his hands to his gushing nose.

"Yes, Ifrit?" Renfri answered, a gleeful note in her voice.

"Take this dog back to the Hole and toss him down into the mines. Let's see how he likes the dark."

Renfri laughed. "Oh, it'll be my pleasure."

The Captain scrambled back, screaming for Reema to kill him, to show him mercy. But he asked the wrong person. Alaric was the one with goodness and compassion in his heart. Not her.

She turned toward Alaric and Asif. "Let's get the food. We have hungry miners to feed."

The Captain's screams followed her out the door.

CHAPTER
TWO

Reema sat by the crackling fire with her inner circle. Thanks to the starlight, they no longer needed it for the light, but after so long in the mines, it felt wrong to not have a fire nearby.

The twins, Omar and Ra'ad, scooped lentils into their mouths while Reema, Alaric, Asif, and Renfri rested with hands over their full bellies. It had been a long time since Reema didn't feel any hint of that biting hunger. She'd forgotten how sundamned good it felt to be free of it.

She glanced at the nearby fires, where miners circled around, eating their rationed shares of lentils and dates. Their faces lit with smiles, voices upbeat as they gazed up at the stars, still reveling in the taste of their newfound freedom.

She had a feeling that more than a few of them would soon wish that they'd stayed down in the mines.

"It's time we talked about what's next," Reema said.

Omar and Ra'ad exchanged glances, setting their

bowls aside. Along with the others, they gave her their full attention.

"When the Djinn removed the steel band around Alaric's eyes, he said that he wanted Alaric to see the city of Zareen burn when he takes the Seat of the Desert."

"He wants the Angel's throne?" Renfri asked.

Reema nodded, "That's what he said. If we want to stop him before he reaches Zareen, we'll have to be quick crossing the desert."

Her gaze passed over each of them.

"It's not going to be easy," she added.

"I could care less about that," Renfri said. "What I want to know is how we're going to do the Djinn in. You plan to kill him with *that*?"

Renfri motioned toward the relic pickaxe.

Reema considered the relic at her side. She lifted it, turned it against the firelight, watched the way that it gleamed. "I tried already. It didn't work."

"So how in the sundamned hells do you plan to kill him?"

Reema didn't have an answer.

Renfri blinked, glancing between Reema, Alaric, and the others. "Don't tell me that you want to chase after the *Djinn* and you don't have a way to kill him."

Reema turned to Alaric, who was focused on playing with a stick in the sand. He seemed to be lost in thought.

"The Commonborn Queen—" she started.

"Hold on, now you expect me to believe that there's a *Commonborn* Queen?" Renfri interrupted. She stood, shadows gathering around her as she clenched her fists at her sides. "Give me one reason why I shouldn't gut you here and now."

"Because it's the truth." Alaric's voice stripped the shadows away, his glowing brown eyes boring into her. "Much has happened since you became a slave, Renfri. Sit down."

Renfri glanced between Alaric and the others. Then she spat to the side and sat. "Let's hear it then."

"The Djinn told us that the Angel was dead. I don't know how or why the Queen did it, but that's not important. All that matters now is that she helps us bring an end to him. And she will."

"And why would someone capable of killing the Angel going to help *us*?"

"Besides the fact that her city's in danger?" The corner of his mouth lifted. "She owes me."

Renfri stared at Alaric in disbelief before shaking her head. "So we march these miners across the desert, beat the Djinn to the city of Zareen, and tell the bitch to kill the monster? If that's the plan, why do we need to bring the miners at all?"

"You're asking a lot of questions," Alaric said, his voice low and soft. Reema could sense the frustration in it.

Renfri's eyes narrowed. "Did you think I wouldn't?"

Reema sighed and raised her hand, silencing both of them. "Enough. We bring the miners because we know it's better to be prepared than not. Besides, something tells me the Queen will be more likely to listen to us if we've got a small army at our back."

Renfri grunted, knowing that Reema had a point.

"If we want to cross the desert with these miners alive, we'll need to ration the supplies," Reema said. "We also need people we trust watching them. Last thing we need is someone going missing. That'd be the death of us."

Renfri stood, scowling at them. She had clearly had enough of Reema and her gang. "I'll handle that."

She turned and headed toward some of her own gang from the mines.

"Asif?" Reema asked.

Asif grunted, pushing himself to his feet. "I know. I'll keep an eye on her."

He followed Renfri, leaving Reema and Alaric alone with the twins.

"Omar, Ra'ad?" she asked.

"Yes, boss?"

"Piss off."

A heartbeat later, they were gone.

Reema glanced at Alaric, who had returned to playing in the sand with a stick. The fire crackled, the only sound breaking the soft quiet as Reema waited for him to speak. But when he didn't, she sat next to him.

"There's something you're not telling me," she said.

His stick spun, tracing intricate designs in the sand. She followed the patterns, as if they might explain the thoughts spinning in his mind. But they offered no answers.

"What is it?" she pressed.

"What if she can't kill the Djinn? What if we show up, and there's nothing we can do?"

Reema's eyes flickered with concern as she absorbed

Alaric's fears. She scooted closer, her voice low and steady, though she hardly felt it. "You think it's a trap?"

Alaric stopped his drawing, his gaze locked on the intricate patterns in the sand. "It's not just that," he sighed, rubbing the bridge of his nose. "We know nothing about the Djinn—no weaknesses, no tendencies. We are marching blind into what could be our end."

"What other choice do we have?" she asked. "The only reason I even know about the Djinn is because I stumbled into an old man in the dark who knew of his myth. He's long gone, and it's not like there's a store of knowledge on the Djinn."

His silence stretched long enough that Reema looked at him again, her brow furrowing.

"Is there?"

He ran his hand through his tussled hair, looking more stressed by the minute. "There might be."

"So what's the issue?"

Slowly, he lifted his gaze to hers, tinged with worry. Her eyes went from him to the shadowed silhouette of Sandspire in the far distance, where the slave master ruled.

"Oh," she whispered, glowing blue eyes flashing in her mind, along with that cruel smirk and her sister's dying scream.

"There's a scholar in Sandspire, holed up in my father's library. If anyone knows anything about the Djinn, it'd be him."

Reema considered the idea, the firelight dancing in her dark eyes. She tried to keep the bitter hatred from rising, but it was hard when all she could hear were Hana's screams.

"It will not be easy. My father's palace is heavily guarded, and the guards will know my face. My punishment was rather... public."

"And your father?" she asked. "What if we run into him?"

"That's the risk," Alaric admitted, turning to face her, the firelight illuminating half his face, casting the other half in shadow. "But it's one we need to take. We can't keep flying blind, not with so much at stake."

She nodded in agreement as she stood, her silhouette etched against the flames, a queen in her own right as gang lord of the miners.

"I'll speak to Asif and the others—have them start leading the miners across the desert. We'll have to catch up to them, but it'll be easy with just the two of us."

"Eager to be alone with me again, huh?"

Her mind flashed back to the passionate kiss they shared in the dark, lost in the western veins, stumbling through the pitch black. She could still feel his hands on her, exploring her curves. Could still feel the heat throbbing through her. Her face flushed.

She stared at him out of habit, appreciating every part of him. Then her gaze locked with his, realizing he was staring at her the same way.

Her flushed face burned even hotter.

His smile inched wider.

Not trusting herself to speak, she walked away. But she got the feeling he was still watching, still appreciating.

CHAPTER
THREE

Reema's dreams left her more flustered than she'd been the night before. In them, she had returned to the dark quiet beneath the earth, finding it more hot than cold. But the heat had nothing to do with the earth, and everything to do with the man pressed against her. His kisses branded her. His hands scorched her. Her heart pounded like the goblet-shaped drums at Commonborn weddings, each thump pulling her deeper into him.

When she woke, her skin flushed against the cool desert morning air. It was that peaceful time when the sky softened enough to see, but the sun hadn't risen high enough to earn its curses.

She rose from where she'd made her bed in the sand, covered with leftover garments from the guards' quarters. A few miners were awake, keeping to themselves, soft smiles playing on their lips as they reveled in the first light of day. But most still snored in their makeshift beds.

She glanced at where Alaric had slept, brazenly close to hers. But his spot was empty.

"Finally awake, are you?"

Renfri sat nearby, poking at the dying coals with the stick Alaric had been using. Her sturdy linen tunic had been tossed aside, replaced by the soft cotton the guards wore under their armor. Her eyes were lined with kohl—where had she found that?

A sleepy grumble drew her attention to a man lying in Renfri's bed, naked except for the small linen scrap thrown over him. Scratches covered his torso.

Reema frowned, realizing how deeply she must have slept to not hear the former gang lord in the throes of passion. Renfri wasn't exactly known for being quiet, either.

"You've had a good night, then," Reema said as she sat beside her, glancing around again for Alaric. He was still nowhere to be seen.

"By the way you were moaning in your sleep last night, it seemed like yours wasn't too bad, either," Renfri said with a deep smirk.

Reema cleared her throat, fighting back the embarrassment. She couldn't let Renfri shake her so easily. If Renfri thought she was going soft, it was only a matter of time before she shivved her in the night.

She was starting to regret making Renfri her Second. Trusting your Second was crucial, and she didn't trust Renfri as far as she could throw her. But she hadn't had much choice; it was the only way to win the trust of the miners.

"I know you're worried about me," Renfri said. One

of the coals sparked before settling into the ashes around it. "I would be too."

Reema's hand drifted to the shiv she kept at her side. She'd been discrete about it, but Renfri's gaze caught on her hand.

Renfri's eyes narrowed, reading the tension radiating from Reema like heat from the fading coals. With a soft sigh, uncharacteristic of her usual gruff demeanor, she tossed the stick aside, its scraping sound punctuating the quiet morning air.

"You can relax, Ifrit," Renfri began, her voice gentle yet firm. "You look at me like I'm about to shiv you in the back, but hear me out."

Reema's hand stayed on her shiv, but she relaxed enough to listen.

"I made a promise to be your Second," Renfri continued, her gaze steady and sincere. "Far as I'm concerned, that means we're one gang now. Allies."

Reema blinked, her frown deepening.

Seeing the doubt on Reema's face, Renfri picked up the stick again, turning it in her hands. "Listen, we made a deal to unite these poor fools to stop the Djinn. That's bigger than any old grudges from the mines or any ... current distractions."

Her eyes flicked pointedly to Alaric's empty bed.

"You need to make a choice, Reema," Renfri's voice dropped, cutting through the earlier softness. "Either lay with him, or don't. But whatever you do, you need to move on. The world can't afford for your mind to be anywhere but here."

She leaned closer, her voice dropping to a conspiratorial whisper. "And if you can't sort it out, I will. Because if it comes to it, I'll hold you accountable—even if that means taking you out myself. Our survival hangs by a thread, and I won't let anything, or anyone, risk that."

Reema met Renfri's gaze, the severity of the threat sinking in. There was a raw honesty in Renfri's eyes she hadn't expected. She had thought she knew Renfri as a cold, heartless gang lord who discarded men for her pleasure. But now, Reema realized she might have misunderstood her. Slowly, she pulled her hand away from the shiv, letting it rest by her side.

"I hear you," Reema said after a moment.

Renfri nodded, a trace of respect flickering across her features. "We're in this together," she said. She pushed herself to her feet and tossed the stick aside. "Now, I'm going to get these lazy bastards up and ready. Long march ahead."

Reema watched as Renfri kicked several miners awake, her sharp voice cutting through the air as she spurred them into action. Her mind drifted, lingering on Renfri's words about Alaric.

"What was that about?"

She looked over her shoulder as Alaric approached, carrying two bags stuffed with supplies left behind in the barracks after Renfri and Asif raided them.

"Nothing to worry about. That everything we need for Sandspire?"

He nodded, "It should be. But we'll need to pick up more supplies in the city, get some clothing that'll keep us shaded for trip through the desert." He eyed the miners, dressed in their torn, dusty linen tunics. "The sun isn't kind to those who are not prepared."

Asif, Omar, and Ra'ad approached in time to hear Alaric's comment. Before dashing off to the barracks for any leftover clothing that might help shield them from the sun, they wished Reema and Alaric safe travels to Sandspire.

Asif's final, parting comment was a whisper in Reema's ear, "If you see that blue-eyed monster, do me a favor and twist the blade when you finish him. I want to know if he screams."

Reema smiled and agreed. Soon, she and Alaric were off, the clamor of the miners fading into the distance.

With a day's walk ahead, Reema kept her eyes on the horizon, her smile growing as the rising sun painted the sky in purples and blues. The desert wind was cool, each breath bringing fresh air. Though her thighs burned from climbing the rolling sand dunes, she enjoyed herself.

But that did not last long.

She soon discovered what kind of hell was in store for her as the sun reached higher into the sky, dispelling that magical painted sky to a cruel, cloudless one. The air grew blisteringly hot, its heat beating down on her as if it were attempting to drive her back into the mines. And if the Djinn wasn't roaming the earth free because of her, she might have actually turned back.

The small scar at the corner of her eye, where the Djinn had boiled a tear on her cheek, throbbed, stinging with every bead of sweat.

Alaric gazed at her sympathetically, knowing that the extent of the desert's cruelty was something that she must have forgotten about over her long years in the mines. He removed the cloth shielding his face from the sun and sand, passing it to her with a gentle smile.

Reema took it without hesitation. She wrapped it around her face, hoping to feel instant relief. Instead, the pain felt only marginally better. She wanted Alaric to speak, to draw her into conversation that might help her forget this pain. But with the way the sun shone down on them, their throats were left impossibly dry, making it so that every spoken word scraped their throats raw.

She adjusted the straps of the bag over her shoulder, wincing at how it dug into her shoulders. The covered relic pickaxe weighed awkwardly on her, making it difficult to walk. To this point, she ignored it, knowing its worth. But damn the deep if the thought didn't come to her to abandon it.

"How much further?" she grated out, her dark brown eyes catching on the distant city of Sandspire.

A single spire rose far above the other buildings, stabbing into the sky like a pillar of hope for distant travelers. But as the spire wavered in the sweltering heat, she found it more demoralizing than helpful. They'd been walking for what felt like an eternity, and seemed no closer than when they began.

"We're making slower progress than I thought we would," he answered.

A stream of curses spilled from her lips as she stumbled over a raised patch of sand and fell to her knees. She pushed herself to her feet with a scowl and reached for the jug of water attached to her bag. The heated water tasted like piss, but it did the job of making her feel a little less exhausted.

Her face twisted at the taste. With her mouth and throat less dry than before, she asked, "Any chance of reaching it today?"

While Alaric waited on her to finish drinking, he gazed out toward the city. "Sandspire's a strange city. It'll look like it's far away, then it'll appear in front of you all at once."

She capped the jug and slung it back into place. "Is that a yes or no?"

"It's an 'I don't know.' But I'd guess that it's not likely to happen. Not at the rate we're going. Normally I make the trip atop a camel."

She shook her head, "Of course you do."

"What's that supposed to mean?"

"It means you're Bloodlined. All you've ever known is a life of ease—silver spoons, feather-stuffed beds, camels to ride whenever you go anywhere because Angel forbid you touch your feet to the sundamned sand."

Alaric eyed her, surprised by her outburst. Truth was, she was too. The heat was getting to her in a way she hadn't experienced before, and the only escape from it was a city that didn't seem to be getting any closer.

"That's not all I've known," he said softly.

She thought of the scars lashing across his chest and shoulders. That was right. He'd known the harsh touch of a whip and had been made to face his father while he suffered.

"Sorry," she said, meeting his eyes. The words felt

strange in her mouth. She couldn't remember the last time she apologized, except by her sister's grave.

Alaric's features softened under the desert sun as he took in her apology, his voice calm against the quiet expanse. "It's fine," he said gently. "Let's keep moving. We have more ground to cover."

They resumed their journey across the desert, the city of Sandspire a constant, teasing mirage on the horizon. Its lone spire continued to mock them, with Reema vowing under her breath to destroy the sundamned thing once they reached the city.

The heat beat down on them, sapping their strength, narrowing their world to the simple act of putting one foot in front of the other. The silence between them grew, filled only by the shuffle of their feet and the occasional gust of wind stirring the sand. And in that silence, guilt gnawed at her. She wondered if people were dying even now, with the Djinn laughing above them as their ashes scattered across the sands.

She clenched her jaw, head bowed as she stared at her feet. She wished there was a way to go back and undo everything. But the world was cruel and linear. The only thing she could hope for was that the Djinn took his time assaulting the surface world, long enough for her and the miners to stop him.

It was with a jolt that Alaric's voice pierced the silence, yanking her from her troublesome thoughts.

"We should make camp now," he said.

"Now?" she asked, scanning the world around her. There was still daylight left.

His throat too dry to answer, he didn't bother

responding. Instead, he found a spot on a slight rise that offered them a strategic view of the surrounding desert and the ever-distant Sandspire.

She joined him, watching as he withdrew two bedrolls from the packs and set up a small, thin tent that offered some shade. She dropped her pack next to it and crawled in, a deep, satisfied sigh escaping her lips at the immediate relief from the cruel sun.

She closed her eyes for just a moment, surprised at the weariness in her muscles and bones. The trek across the desert had been harsher than she'd anticipated. She breathed in, breathed out, and—

Alaric gently nudged her. Her eyes jolted open, bloodshot and wide. She scrambled, trying to remember where she was.

The corner of his lips lifted. "Relax. You fell asleep."

She blinked her eyes clear, surprised at how fast sleep had come over her. Must have had something to do with the sun. Damn the deep, she was beginning to miss the mines.

"Come on," he said, offering his hand. "I have something I want to show you."

She stared at him skeptically but trusted him enough

to place her hand in his. He drew her to her feet and guided her out of the tent.

The sky stole her breath away.

The sun descended beneath the horizon, painting the sky in brilliant hues of orange, red, and purple. The stars burned into the sky, and beside them, the crescent moon hung low.

She found herself rushing up to a higher point on the rise, where the desert stretched out endlessly in every direction, its vastness underscored by the spectacular sunset.

Standing atop the dune, she was transported through time. She could feel Hana standing next to her, quiet and observing. A soft smile played at her lips as she stared at the sky unblinkingly, as if she was afraid to miss something.

Tears welled in her eyes.

Alaric joined her, keeping a respectful distance. His presence was a quiet comfort as they watched the sky catch fire with the dying light. They stayed even as the sun sank below the horizon, its final rays lingering like a caress on the rippling sands, transforming the harsh desert into something beautiful.

A warm hand slipped into Reema's. She looked up, meeting his gaze. The embers of the sunset reflected in his glowing brown eyes, casting them in a light that seemed to pull her closer, tethering her to him. She could not help but think that somehow, he was even more beautiful than the sunset itself.

Her heart was a steady thrum, a rhythm echoing into the peaceful quiet of the desert night. The world around them—the vast, unending desert, the brilliant hues of the dying day—faded into a backdrop for the two of them, alone on the dune.

His usual smirk was gone. His voice was barely above a whisper, reverent and awe-filled as he spoke, his breath mingling with the cool air.

"It never gets old," he murmured, his gaze locked on hers.

Sensing he wasn't talking about the sunset, her heart skipped a beat. She was suddenly glad that none of the other miners were there, especially the members of her gang. Because if they were, they'd see how this man—a Bloodlined who knew a life without labor—had *softened* the great Ifrit of the mines. They'd wonder how he had managed to cull her rage, her desire to see the world bleed red in revenge. And she would have no answer for them. There was something special about Alaric, and it had nothing to do with the Angel's blood running through his veins.

Seeing the emotion in her eyes, he lifted his hand to her face. It was warm, like fire against ice. She didn't trust herself to speak, fearing it would break the spell between them.

He stepped closer, closing the small gap between them. His other hand reached up slowly, deliberately brushing a stray lock of hair from her face. His touch was tentative, as if he were aware of her usual fierceness, her capacity for both warmth and wrath.

Like Reema, the desert held its breath—the winds paused, the sands settled. Time seemed to slow as Alaric leaned in, his eyes searching hers in a way that stripped her of any other thoughts or feelings, leaving her vulnerable and bare before him. Reema's heart pounded, a wild drumbeat urging her forward.

"I see you," he whispered, sending her butterflies into a frenzy.

Then their lips met.

The kiss was gentle, a soft brush that spoke of new beginnings, of walls crumbling and barriers breaking. It was a whisper against the roar of their past struggles, a tender merging of two souls who had found solace and understanding in each other. As they pulled closer, the kiss deepened, stirring a warmth that radiated through her, chasing away the thoughts of guilt. And damn the deep, it felt freeing.

Clinging to that freedom, she pressed against him, desire clawing through her like hot fire. Entranced by each other, they didn't bother going back down the dune.

She surrendered herself to the taste of his lips, to the smell of him that reminded her of pages from *Beneath the Sands of Sorrow*. And he surrendered to her.

Her fingers danced over the scars of his past, across his stomach and along his waist. His fingers tangled in her hair, pulling her closer as his tongue lit fires within her.

He lay her down against the warmed sands of the dune, and there, he sealed the bond they had forged deep in the black depths of the mines.

Above, the first stars began to twinkle in the deepening blue of the night sky, but they were invisible to Reema as she couldn't tear her gaze from the brilliant glow of his eyes, not even as her breaths tightened and quickened.

Her eyes drifted to the branded scar across his eye line, where the Djinn had heated the steel band and broken it away so that he could witness the destruction of everything he loved.

For a single beat, guilt returned, reminding her that she did not deserve this. Once this man saw the damage the Djinn had would do to the world—and was reminded of her role in it—he would want her no longer.

The guilt that flickered through Reema's mind was swiftly quelled by Alaric's touch, his hands pulling her back to the present. His gaze locked onto hers, intense and unyielding, and in his eyes, she saw not judgment, but a fierce desire that matched her own.

She built a wall in her mind thick enough to keep the assaulting thoughts at bay, trapping her in this moment with him. She pressed herself into him, burning hotter than the sun could ever hope to.

As they moved together, the desert sands warmed beneath them, cradling their forms. Alaric's lips traveled from her mouth down her neck, igniting small fires inside her, each kiss sealing promises they hadn't yet dared to voice.

And when they were spent, Alaric lifted her in his arms and carried her down to the tent, leaving their clothing atop the dune. She mumbled against his ear that she wouldn't be the one to climb the sand dune naked the next morning under the sun's fresh heat. His laughter echoed across the desert, drawing a rare smile from her.

Back in the tent, deep into the night, she lay beside him, listening to the gentle rumble of his snores. She rested her head against his bare chest, feeling it rise and fall.

One voice broke through the forming cracks in her mental wall: Renfri's.

Either lay with him, or don't. But whatever you do, you need to move on. The world can't afford for your mind to be anywhere but here.

Reema lifted her head, glancing at the beautiful man beside her, and knew she was in trouble.

CHAPTER
FOUR

The next morning, neither spoke. A strange tension lingered between Reema and Alaric as they traversed the desert. Alaric glanced at her from time to time, brows furrowed in confusion, wondering if he'd done something wrong. But Reema kept her eyes straight ahead, unwilling to meet his gaze for fear that she might confess the gnawing guilt inside her.

She tried to block it all out—the nearness of him, the brutal sun beating down on them, and the sundamned sands rubbing against her skin, collected in their linen miner tunics when they'd left them atop the dune. She tried to find a solitary place in her mind where she could steal a moment of peace.

But it wasn't working.

The only thing that seemed to help was focusing on the shining spire rising up out of the approaching city, dancing back and forth. Only when the sun reached its highest point and the heat became unbearable did the mirage break.

Alaric had been right. The city was suddenly right in front of them.

The air shifted, filled with the heavy aroma of spices mixed with subtle notes of sandalwood. The unmistakable tang of bustling markets wafted toward them, so different from the sterile, dry air of the desert.

Reema stopped.

The walls of Sandspire rose before them, built from towering blocks of red sandstone that glowed warmly under the sun. She sensed these walls had stood for a thousand years, etched with time and worn by desert sandstorms. And yet, they were still here.

But it wasn't the walls that held her gaze—it was the spire stabbing into the sky. There was a reason it shone so brilliantly against the sun, serving as a beacon to desert travelers.

It was made of white marble.

The same white marble that a thousand miners had died to mine, the same white marble that she had slaved her whole life to mine.

Its surface was smoother and cooler, more refined than the blocks they had mined. It reflected the sunlight in blinding flashes.

She clenched her fists, wanting nothing more than to tear the spire down. She glanced at Alaric and saw his furrowed brows and deep frown.

"What is it?" she asked.

"The city. It's quieter than normal."

She turned back to the city, listening to the distant clamor of shouting merchants, camel hooves on paved streets, and children laughing as they chased each other.

The sounds settled into a cacophony that was over-whelming and invigorating. How could *this* be any louder?

"Come," he said, making no acknowledgment of the sundamned spire.

She ignored it and followed him as he led her around the city, away from the arched gate.

As they neared the city, the spire's shadow fell over them. Reema couldn't help but look up, her eyes tracing the lines of marble that soared upward. She tried to calculate how many blocks it would've taken to build such a thing, but soon lost count. She wondered if anyone in Sandspire ever stopped to gaze up and mourn the lives lost to build it.

Somehow, she doubted it.

He picked up pace, and she matched it. Whatever tension had lingered between them vanished with the city's appearance. It was strange hearing the sounds of the city after a lifetime where silence ruled the mines. Here, men could shout and scream without fear that others would descend on them and kill them just to keep the quiet.

As they rounded the city walls, her eyes caught on a large building atop the tallest dune in the city. Her jaw dropped at the sight of the palace. It rose taller than the mansions surrounding it, its red sandstone dome warm from the sunlight. The walls were etched with swirling designs, crafted by masters. Even more stunning was the fact that all around it lay sprawling *green*, not desert sand.

"What is that?" she breathed.

"The palace gardens," he answered. "Fruits, vegetables, flowers in every shade."

She sputtered, trying to find the words. Only after a full minute did her brain catch up. "But how?"

"Sandspire was built atop an oasis," he said, as if that explained everything. Instead, it only left her with more questions.

He came to a stop, resting his hands on his hips. He made for a strange sight, with his unruly beard and marble-and-sand-dusted skin, while his eyes marked him as Bloodlined. "I read a story once, about how a boy and a girl from opposing families fled through a secret tunnel to the west of the city."

"And?"

He eyed her. "Well, we're *west* of the city."

Reema looked around, scanning the desert sand dunes rising around the city. But there was nothing—no signs of divots to mark an entrance, no red sandstone peeking through the golden sand. It looked exactly the same as the desert they'd been walking through for the last day and a half.

"Do you see anything?" Alaric asked.

"Why are you asking me? You're the one who read the book."

"I thought you might be able to spot a tunnel from a hundred yards away."

Reema scowled. "I'm used to being in the mines, not above them. I don't have a sundamned clue what a secret tunnel looks like."

He sighed, his voice clearly marked with frustration. Shaking his head, he said, "This was a foolish idea.

Maybe it's best that we try entering through the city gates instead of wasting our time trying to pick out the entrance from all of *this*."

An idea popped into her mind. She raised a hand, stopping him before he could turn back toward the city's entrance, and slung the relic pickaxe off her shoulder.

The last time she'd wielded its power, it had carved a tunnel with a single tap of its head against the marble. The quality of it was better than what could be made by having the help of even a dozen miners.

She wondered how capable it was. Could it shape a tunnel to a vague location?

She unwrapped it from the cloth, exposing its gleam to the sunlight. The handle was smooth, power resonating through her fingers. The weight was comforting, familiar yet charged with an anticipation she hadn't felt since she'd freed the Djinn.

Alaric watched her, curiosity in his gaze.

"Let's try this," she said, her voice carrying a certainty that she only partially felt.

She closed her eyes, taking a deep breath of the hot, spice-laden air. She pictured her goal and felt a magnetic pull to the right. The strange sensation in her mind told her where to position herself, and next, she pictured the layout of Sandspire in her mind, from the twisting alleys that she could see over the walls to the rising marble spire, and beneath it all, the hidden veins of the world beneath the city. She imagined the tunnel, not as a mere hole in the ground, but as a thoroughfare, shaped by her will and the pickaxe's magic.

She opened her eyes and lifted the pickaxe. The

ancient metal gleamed in the subdued light, magic thrumming down its shaft. With an explosive shout, she swung the pickaxe down.

The pickaxe struck the sand, and instead of the dull thud of metal hitting ground, there was a resonant chime, like the clear ring of a bell vibrating through the air. The ground trembled beneath them, grains of sand dancing as if alive, and then the earth began to part.

It was as if the desert itself obeyed her command, the sands shifting to create the opening she envisioned. The ground split with a precision no ordinary miner's tool could achieve, a perfect tunnel arching into the darkness below. The walls of the newly formed passage glimmered faintly, touched by the pickaxe's magic, reinforcing them against collapse.

Reema stepped back, her breath catching as she witnessed the full force of the Angel's gift. When she'd first seen the pickaxe in the black marble cave, she knew it was special, capable of freeing the Djinn from his specially crafted prison. But the reality of what it could do—the sheer power to reshape the world around her—was overwhelming.

She lifted it to the sun, her mouth parting in awe, imagining the life she could have lived in the mines if she'd had this relic back then.

Alaric moved next to her, his earlier doubt replaced by awe.

"Incredible," he breathed, his gaze fixed on the tunnel before them.

"Let's get out of this Angel-damned sun," she said,

her voice steady despite the adrenaline coursing through her.

"Wait," he called. "Leave your bags behind. We won't need them in the city."

She dropped the bag of supplies, a sour taste in her mouth at the thought of leaving behind perfectly good lentils and dates. But it would only slow them down. She dropped her bag beside his and led the way into the tunnel with her relic pickaxe in hand.

As they descended into the cool, beckoning darkness of the tunnel, the sounds of the city above faded into a distant murmur, replaced by the echo of their footsteps on solid sandstone. The sandstone was far softer than the marble she was used to, and though it wasn't exactly soft, her feet appreciated its solidness after hours of trekking over endless sand.

They walked through the perfectly shaped tunnel, the darkness lit only by the dull gleam of the pickaxe and the glow of Alaric's eyes. In the darkness, Reema instinctively moved closer to him, forgetting all the earlier tension.

Alaric glanced down at her, the corner of his mouth twitching into a smile.

"What?" she asked.

"You just keep surprising me, is all." His gaze flicked from her to the pickaxe in her hands. "That relic's nothing like I've ever seen, and have seen more than my fair share of relics."

"They're not all like this?" she asked.

"No, not even close. The Angel gifted different things to people—swords that could cut through anything, jewelry that could extend a man's life, I've even heard of a moving painting."

A moving painting? She tried to imagine a painting moving through one of the Bloodlined's homes on its own, but she struggled to picture it.

"But I've never heard of something that could shape the earth. Not like that." He pursed his lips, brows furrowing. "Make sure you don't lose it. If my father gets hold of it ..."

His voice trailed off, the shadows and silence rushing in to fill the void.

"What happens if he gets it?" Reema asked.

He gave her a dark look. "Then Zareen doesn't stand a chance."

CHAPTER
FIVE

After what felt like an eternity of walking through the shaped tunnel, they finally reached a junction where a wall had been blown out. Alaric exchanged a glance with her before stepping over shattered stone and into an ancient tunnel with marble-lined walls.

It didn't feel like home to Reema, though, because the marble was nothing like the dusty, rugged stone she was used to. It was refined, smooth, and polished. The glow of Alaric's eyes danced along its surface.

Reema's nose twitched as she struggled to keep from sneezing. The air smelled thick with dust, and it looked like no one had walked through this tunnel in centuries.

"This must be it," Alaric said, running his hand along the walls. He glanced over his shoulder, worry creeping into his gaze.

"What is it?"

"Are you able to close that entrance you made?"

"Why would you want to do that?"

"Because anybody can break into the city now. This tunnel leads directly to the palace."

"So?"

His gaze narrowed. "I do not think it is a smart idea for us to undermine the safety of the city's walls."

Reema scowled, but he had a point. With an exasperated sigh, she closed her eyes and pictured the tunnel collapsing. She tapped the pickaxe's head against the wall of the tunnel they'd come from.

A soft chime echoed before a deep rumble shook the earth. Reema clamped her hands over her ears as the tunnel collapsed, the quake ear-splitting. Alaric grabbed her arm and yanked her back as a wave of dust rushed toward them. It forced its way into her mouth and flaring nostrils, choking the air from her lungs. Her eyes welled with tears as she and Alaric struggled to catch their breaths. After a few moments of choking and coughing, they finally managed to draw a breath of fresh air.

Somehow, it felt even darker than before.

"Just like old times," he said, recalling when they'd fallen from the collapsed bridge into unexplored depths.

"Don't remind me." She placed a hand on his shoulder, knowing he could navigate the darkness better than she could. One benefit of having spent so long blinded by that steel band.

He led them deeper into the tunnels. The sound of their breathing and gentle footsteps echoing back at them was strangely calming. Reema's shoulders loosened as the tension lifted.

"Do you think you'll ever miss it?" Alaric asked.

"The mines?"

He nodded.

She was quiet for a long moment, sifting through her murky thoughts. "How could I not? It's home."

And it was, despite everything that happened in the mines. In the mines, life was simple: survive and mine. That was it. But here, on the surface, life was much more: making coin, politics seeping into everyday life, and that was just the start. She had a feeling that she would soon miss that simplicity of the mines. It was just ... easy.

But there was danger in that thought. She had seen her fair share of slaves give into that ease, and that more than anything was what kept them down in life. No one wants to make life harder for themselves, and it's easier to let others rule you. She couldn't let herself be content with that—not when men like Alaric's father held power.

"It's strange," Alaric said. "I think I'll miss it too."

Her brow rose. "Why?"

He paused, glancing over his shoulder, the glow of his brown eyes settling on her. "Because it'll always be where I met you."

Butterflies danced in her stomach, and she thought back to Renfri's words again. She needed to focus, because until she stopped the Djinn and undid everything, she could never be worthy of him, of *this*.

She cleared her throat, trying to dispel the butterflies in her stomach. "Let's keep going."

She could sense his smirk. Sundamned bastard knew the effect he had on her, and he was proud of it. But he said nothing as he turned and continued on.

"What's Sandspire like?" she asked, unable to keep herself from speaking.

"Compared to the mines?"

"Sure."

He was quiet for a long minute. Then he answered, "It's a beautiful city, perhaps even more beautiful than Zareen, depending on who you ask. It's not divided into different districts either. It's all one big market, with merchants lining nearly every street."

"That sounds awful," she said, thinking of merchants screaming out the prices of their wares, forever competing with each other.

"You would think so, but once you get used to it, it's ... nice. Sandspire specializes in spices, particularly saffron. Saffron's worth more than its weight in gold, if you didn't know. And the smell of it fresh in the morning is like nothing you've ever experienced."

"*Gold?*" Reema asked. "Why?"

"It's not easy to harvest, from what I am told."

"I don't know if I believe all this."

"Sandspire's sounding too good, isn't it?"

"With the way you're describing it, yeah."

He sighed. "On the surface, the city is that good. The citizens thrive, and while we do have the poor and homeless, they're at least not forced to live somewhere with glass-sharded sand that cuts their feet to ribbons."

"But?"

"But," Alaric continued, his tone darkening, "Sandspire has its own kind of rot. In Zareen, the Bloodlined see themselves as higher, sure, but in Sandspire, they see the Commonborn as less than human."

Reema's lip curled in distaste as she thought of how the slavers treated them, how the slave master had laughed when he murdered Hana without a second thought.

"The number of slaves has soared," Alaric went on, his voice laden with bitterness. "And the abuse... it's rampant. It doesn't matter if you're a wealthy merchant or a homeless beggar. The cruelty exists at every level of society."

"Except for the Bloodlined."

He nodded. "Except for us."

Reema's jaw tightened, her eyes narrowing with a mix of anger and sorrow. "Why haven't you tried to change it?"

"You think I haven't tried?"

Her anger softened, remembering the lashes across his chest. No, Alaric wasn't someone who would stand by and watch the Commonborn suffer.

"My father doesn't listen to me. He thinks I'm weak, a rare imperfection in the Angel's bloodline. That's why he sent me away from Sandspire. He's ashamed of me."

She saw a flicker of pain in Alaric's eyes, a glimpse of the torment that still ate away at him. But just as quickly as it appeared, it was gone.

Reema didn't know what to say. A disturbing silence settled around them as they navigated the old tunnels. At first, she worried they'd come across a fork in the tunnel and be forced to choose a direction. But to her surprise, the tunnel was a straight shot, with no paths or curves she could see.

An indeterminable amount of time passed, marked

only by the burn in her thighs and the steady increase in their breathing. Both of them, fit as they were, were growing tired from the walk.

Just as she was about to ask how long these tunnels were, the darkness solidified ahead of them. The glow of Alaric's eyes soon illuminated a white marble wall with a ladder leading far overhead.

"Finally," he muttered, glancing back at her. "I don't know where this tunnel comes out, but I know the city like the back of my hand. So trust me—you'll get lost if you don't stick close to me."

"I'll be right behind you."

Alaric nodded and started climbing the ladder, his movements steady despite the fatigue settling into their muscles. After slinging the pickaxe over her shoulder, Reema followed, her eyes fixed on the glow of his as they ascended the seemingly endless rungs. The tunnel below them faded into shadow, the cool air growing warmer as they climbed.

At last, they reached a small landing, barely wide and tall enough for them both to fit. The landing faced what looked like a secret doorway, with a small wheel that could be turned to open it.

Alaric glanced at her, keeping his hand on her to steady them both. He pressed his ear to the doorway, listening intently before carefully turning the wheel. A sliver of light spilled through, revealing a grand bedroom with a four-poster bed made of dark wood. He climbed out and extended a hand to help her.

She took it, her breath catching as she stepped onto polished marble floors. The smooth surface reflected light from an intricately designed chandelier hanging from the vaulted ceiling. The walls were adorned with tapestries of the city and desert, vibrant colors woven with such skill they seemed almost alive. The four-poster bed was covered in silk of a quality she had never dreamed possible. The smell of exotic spices, mingled with the faint scent of flowers from the palace gardens, wafted through the air. It was nearly overwhelming, after being stuck in the dust of the tunnel below.

"My father's rooms," Alaric muttered, inspecting the edge of the doorway.

Reema ripped her hands away from the silk sheets with a disgusted grunt.

"This was one of the first places I checked for a tunnel, but..." The secret doorway clicked shut, perfectly blending back into the wall. "This is incredible."

He ran his hand over the wall again, a quiet curse escaping him.

"What is it?" she asked.

"I can't figure out how to open it again."

Voices echoed outside, and he scrambled toward her. He took her hand and drew her to the side. Beads of sweat ran down both their foreheads. When the voices passed, she looked at him.

"How're we getting out of here?" she asked.

"We'll figure it out. Worst case, you swing that pickaxe again and open another way down."

She nodded.

He gestured for her to follow, and they cautiously moved out of his father's rooms into the hall. Columns of red sandstone, carved with intricate swirling patterns, supported the high ceilings, creating an air of grandeur and elegance. She couldn't help but stare wide-eyed at everything they passed. She'd never seen anything so opulent.

They stuck to the shadows, sneaking through the palace. Every footstep seemed amplified in the silence, and Reema held her breath, acutely aware of the danger they were in. For a moment, it felt like they were back in the mines, where a single sound could mean death.

Voices drifted from a corridor ahead, and Alaric halted, pressing a finger to his lips. They ducked into an alcove, hearts pounding as a group of guards passed, their heavy boots echoing on the marble floor. When the footsteps faded, Alaric motioned for them to move.

Reema's nerves were stretched taut, every instinct screaming caution. They turned a corner, and the hallway split in multiple directions. Alaric hesitated, scanning each path, his brows furrowed in concentration. He started down one of them.

Reema was about to follow when a door behind her creaked open. More voices filled the space, and panic flared through her as she slid behind a column. When the voices faded, she stepped out.

Alaric was gone.

Her eyes flicked down the passages, trying to remember which one he'd taken. But damn the deep, they all looked the same. She pressed herself against the wall, steadying her breath, straining to hear any sound that might guide her to him.

Her mind raced. She couldn't afford to be discovered. She had to find him. Taking a deep breath, she moved, hoping to catch a glimpse of him around the next corner. The hallways twisted and turned endlessly, until at long last she reached the end of the hallway and paused, peering into a room on her right. It was dimly lit, a single torch casting eerie shadows on the walls. The room was far less opulent than the slave master's, but still meant for someone of high standing. She stepped inside, hoping to catch her breath and gather her thoughts. But no sooner had she entered than the door creaked open behind her.

Spinning around, she saw a palace guard enter, wearing polished steel armor trimmed with gold. Beneath the armor, a quilted tunic of deep blue was visible, and a jeweled, curved sword hung at his side. His eyes narrowed as they locked onto her. His gaze traveled over her, catching on the marble and sand-dusted tunic she wore. Suspicion flashed across his face.

"What's a slave doing here?" he demanded, his voice a low growl. His eyes widened when he saw the pickaxe slung over her shoulder. "You're a mine slave."

Her mind raced, weighing her options in the split second before the guard reached for his sword. From a quick glance, the only way out was behind him. She wasn't getting past him without a fight.

In one swift motion, she reached for the pickaxe on her shoulder. But the guard moved faster. His curved sword slashed through the air, nicking her shoulder and cutting the pickaxe free. It clattered to the floor as she staggered back, clutching her shoulder with a grimace.

The guard rushed her, his eyes dark and grim. She dove at his legs, knocking him off his feet. In a wild scramble, she climbed on top of him, smashing his sword hand against the floor. She kicked the sword away, but she was too slow to dodge his heavy fist swinging toward her.

Lights exploded in her vision as she fell back. The guard's face loomed above her, twisted in ugly anger. He wrapped his hands around her throat and squeezed.

Reema gasped for air as she fought his grip.

Her eyes darted around, searching for something—*anything* she could use as a weapon. But there was nothing.

With a growl, she reached up and slid the guard's helmet out of place, obscuring his vision. Instinctively, he reached up with one hand to fix it.

By the time he realized his mistake, it was too late.

She broke his grip and snapped a punch up at him. While she might not have his strength, her knuckles had been sharpened by years of fighting in the mines. She hit hard enough to cut his lip, driving him off her.

She scrambled to the side, reaching for the pickaxe.

He reached for his sword.

This time, she was faster.

She swung the pickaxe at him with a soundless scream, magic thrumming through her body, the image of his broken form fixed in her mind. The steel pick cleaved through him like butter.

He drew a sharp breath, his eyes jolting wide in pain. But he was dead before he could scream. The top half of his body, hewn from shoulder to waist, slid away while the bottom half stayed on its knees. It landed with a heavy thud. A massive pool of blood spread, staining the marble with a darkness that could never be cleaned.

Reema lay back, panting, covered in sweat.

Just then, the door creaked open. Her eyes darted to it in fear. But instead of a guard, Alaric stood in the doorway. He breathed a sigh of relief at the sight of her, then his worried gaze shifted to the dead guard. His mouth parted.

"Shit."

She had to agree—now she wasn't just a slave who shouldn't be in the palace, but a blood-covered one.

"Are you okay?" he whispered, shutting the door and rushing forward to help her to her feet. His eyes found the wound along her shoulder. Blood dribbled out, staining her top.

"I'm fine," she breathed. "It's just a cut. Bastard got lucky."

His brows furrowed, but he nodded. "Take your clothes off."

"What?"

He hurried to the nearby bed and tore the sheets off, tossing them over the guard's body. In moments, the sheets were soaked with blood. Somehow, the sight was even grimmer than before.

"I said take your clothes off," he repeated, ripping open the wardrobe and pulling out silken outfits. His voice was thick with frustration, like he was angry at himself for how close Reema had come to dying. "It was a mistake to go around the palace dressed as slaves in the first place."

Reema glanced once more at the closed door before

stripping off her top and bottoms. For some reason, she felt awkward in her nakedness. Maybe it was because it wasn't night, and in the torchlight, he could see how thin she was, and every imperfection. She wasn't sure she'd ever felt more vulnerable than this.

But any worry she had about how he'd perceive her nakedness was gone as she watched him strip down, removing the sturdy linen clothing of the miners. Her eyes traced the contours of his chest, trailing down until a flush of heat rose within her. She should look away, but couldn't. Instead, all she could think of was how that body had moved over her, how his lips grazed her and lit her aflame.

Alaric reached for blue trousers, the fabric shimmering in the dim torchlight, and slipped them on. He pulled out a blue top embroidered with gold thread in intricate patterns along the collar and cuffs. As he pulled it on, she couldn't help but think how the deep blue color complemented his glowing brown eyes. He would have looked regal, if not for his unruly beard and wild, tousled hair—not to mention the slightly oversized clothing.

Realizing she was staring, Reema met his eyes. The corner of his lips lifted in a knowing smirk, his gaze growing intense as it roamed over her naked form. Despite the danger and the blood-soaked room, a spark of something undeniable passed between them.

With a slow, deliberate movement, Alaric reached into the wardrobe and pulled out a dress. He tossed it to her, the rich fabric unfolding in midair before landing in her hands.

"Here," he said, his voice low, laced with something that made her heart race. "Put this on."

She looked down at it. The dress was made of luxurious silk, a deep red that contrasted sharply with what he wore. It was beautiful, but there was just one problem.

"Are you serious?" she asked.

"What?"

"I've never worn a dress."

"So?"

"Why can't I wear something like what you've got?"

"Because this is for *men*. If you think slave clothing is suspicious, what do you think will happen when people see a Commonborn wearing this?"

Her face twisted as she looked down at the dress. She didn't want to wear it, but if the Ifrit had to wear a sundamned dress, it might as well be red. And red would hide any blood from her wound.

She quickly slipped it over her head, the cool fabric sliding against her skin. Though snug against her body, she couldn't deny it at least had a good range of movement.

Alaric stepped closer, adjusting the dress at her shoulders with a gentle touch before fixing the strands of her hair. "We need to be careful," he murmured, his eyes never leaving hers. "Keep your eyes down, don't say anything. We don't want to draw attention to ourselves —people *will* notice how filthy we are."

She looked up at him, worry creeping in. In a place where clean skin mattered, she felt out of her element.

He smiled. "Don't worry. We'll get through this."

"What about the pickaxe?" she asked, her eyes going to where it lay.

His smile vanished as he glanced around the room, searching for something to keep it in. His brows shot up.

He went back to the wardrobe and pulled out a Bloodlined traveler's sack, made from what looked like the finest leather. He looped the pickaxe against the back and slung the bag over his shoulder.

"Let's just hope nobody asks any questions."

He crossed the room and, grabbing her hand, led them back into the terror of the palace.

CHAPTER
SIX

They walked through the hallways, heads bowed toward one another as if engaged in a hushed, important conversation. Reema's heart pounded, every footstep echoing ominously in her ears.

"What if someone recognizes you?" Reema whispered.

Another couple emerged in the hallway ahead, and it took everything she had not to look up and meet them with an intimidating stare. In the mines, it was instinct to never look away from potential enemies. But doing that here would be the death of them.

Alaric shushed her gently, drawing her into a conversation to maintain their disguise.

"Did you like what you saw?" he asked, adjusting the bag slung over his shoulder with a casual grace that belied the tension in the air.

"What?" she asked, momentarily thrown by the question.

The corner of his mouth twitched into a smirk. "I caught you staring, my love."

"My *love*?" she scoffed, but a small smile tugged at her lips despite the gravity of their situation. She felt light at the word spilling from his lips.

They continued their charade, bantering as they moved smoothly through the palace corridors. Other Bloodlineds attempted to greet them, but as Reema and Alaric ignored them, she heard their soft, grunts at the disrespect.

Finally, they reached the library doors, tall and imposing, made of polished mahogany and inlaid with gold. She couldn't imagine the cost of such a large piece of wood—wood wasn't exactly common in the desert. But her attention shifted as she realized the intricate carvings on the door depicted desert creatures, their surfaces gleaming in the dim hallway light.

When Alaric reached for the door, she saw the handles were fashioned from pure gold, shaped like desert cats' heads, their eyes set with pink quartz—the same kind that covered the walls of Hana's cave.

Alaric ushered her inside and shut the door firmly behind them. He bent down and twisted a mechanism at the base of the door, locking it to prevent anyone from entering.

Reema glanced around, unsure of what to expect. She was surprised to find a simple desk guarding a smaller pair of doors. An old Commonborn man sat at the desk, wearing a long white thobe embroidered with twisting lines, denoting his position as a librarian.

He glanced up from the parchment he'd been writing

on, his brow furrowing so deep it seemed to stretch to his ears. A long gray beard reached past his chest, and his skin, wrinkled like parchment, made it impossible to guess his age.

"Excuse me," he called in a weary, old voice. "Please do not do that."

When Alaric didn't listen, he stood, his chair scraping noisily against the marble floor. His back was firmer and straighter than she expected.

"I offer you one more warning. Heed it, or you will—"

Alaric straightened, flashing the librarian a wide smile.

The librarian's words faltered, caught off guard by Alaric's sudden warmth. Reema's gaze flicked between them, trying to understand their relationship, because Alaric's smile *was* genuine.

When the librarian didn't respond, Alaric laughed. "Oh, come now, Master Saif. Don't tell me you don't recognize me."

Master Saif's gaze narrowed as he tugged at the threads of memory. Then, all at once, like the sun bursting from behind dark clouds, his eyes widened.

"Alaric?"

The old man crossed the distance and swept Alaric into his arms, surprising Reema with a strength that shouldn't have been possible for someone so old—especially someone who spent their days in the library. Laughter spilled from both of them, making them seem like young boys at school as they squeezed each other and nearly jumped with excitement. Reema thought it impossible, but by the time they separated, their grins had grown even wider.

Master Saif grabbed Alaric's face, tugging at his unruly beard.

"Angel's heavens, look at *you*. What is this?"

"What, you don't like the new look?"

The master librarian gave an incredulous laugh and shook his head.

"Never did I think I'd see the day when Alaric Damaris let himself go."

Alaric poked the old man's stomach.

"That could be said for both of us."

Master Saif patted Alaric's shoulders, surprised at their solidness. He frowned at the scar striped across Alaric's eyeline, where the steel band had been heated and broken away.

"Indeed it could. How in the seven heavens are you still *alive*, my boy?"

Alaric's eyes flicked to Reema, his gaze turning intense. Master Saif followed his gaze, brow lifting slightly at the sight of Reema, as though just now realizing she was there.

"And who is this beautiful soul?"

Reema blinked and, despite herself, smiled at the compliment.

"I'm Reema, but they call me the Ifrit."

"Do they?" he glanced at Alaric.

"I have much to catch you up on, Master. But first, is the library clear? I don't need to state the obvious that I shouldn't be seen."

Master Saif let out a long, disappointed sigh.

"You should know how empty the library is, Alaric. It's like people have forgotten the wonders of books."

Alaric grunted. Master Saif motioned for them to follow, leading them past the desk and through a second set of doors. Reema's breath caught at the sight of the library. The room opened into a vast expanse, stretching farther than she could have imagined. Endless rows of towering shelves, filled with books of every shape and size, extended into the distance, their spines gleaming under the soft, golden light bathing the room.

For a moment, Reema stood rooted, overwhelmed by the sheer magnitude of it all. She had never seen so many books in her life. Before Alaric helped her to read, she wouldn't have cared about these dusty things. But now, she knew better. Each book was a portal to another world, a doorway to countless adventures. She was surprised to feel the weight of her guilt and worries lift from her shoulders. Her fingers itched to touch the spines, to pull books from the shelves and lose herself in their pages.

As she wandered toward the nearest aisle, she heard Master Saif behind her.

"Someone who loves books as much as you?" he muttered to Alaric, sounding surprised.

Alaric mumbled something back, but she didn't hear it, too absorbed in the world around her. Her eyes widened with wonder as she ran her hand along the books. She slowly read the titles, her mouth stumbling over the words as she mouthed them in elegant scripts. She felt a deep sense of awe and wanted nothing more than to pull a book from the shelves and open it. No wonder Alaric had fallen in love with reading, with all of *this* waiting for him.

As she walked the rows, she heard Alaric's soft voice as he spoke with Master Saif, catching him up on everything that had happened. She was too absorbed in her exploration to listen closely. She turned down another row, marveling at the variety of books—some bound in leather, others in cloth, their covers adorned with intricate designs and symbols. Some she could read, others seemed written in a different language.

She stopped in front of a particularly large book, its spine embossed with a gold leaf. She pulled it from the shelf, grunting at its heavy weight, and traced her fingers over the title, slowly reading it.

The Grand Comp ... en ... dium ...

She frowned. What in the sundamned hells was *that* word? She skipped it, recognizing only two words in the title: thousand, bugs.

She flipped the book open, and the smell of old paper and leather filled her nostrils. It was a strangely comforting, familiar scent that reminded her of reading in the mines with Alaric. A soft smile tugged at her lips as she flipped through the pages.

It didn't have the same simple language as *Beneath the Sands of Sorrows*, and with the size and complexity of the words, it was sundamned impossible to read. But the images kept her attention for a long moment, with bugs and different kinds of insects drawn on the pages. She could hardly believe someone had taken the time to document so much of these creatures' lives. And the *detail* with which they were illustrated, it was truly amazing.

Still, she slid it back onto the shelf with a grunt. To her, the book was everything she'd imagined books to be: a useless waste of time. She longed for tales of adventure, of characters facing the same life-and-death choices she did.

She moved deeper into the library, Alaric and Master Saif's voices fading into the background. A strange silence wrapped around her; it was different from the silence in the mines or the desert. This silence wasn't sinister, but it carried a force that compelled her to obey, as if she shouldn't dare disturb the slumber of the books.

Then her eyes caught a title that was all too familiar.

Beneath the Sands of Sorrow.

Before she knew it, she had slipped the book off the shelf and found a small alcove with a cushioned bench. She settled down and opened it, her heart fluttering rapidly. She thought this book was gone. She let herself get lost in the words, the world dissolving around her, transporting her back to the mines and the warmth of Alaric's voice as he recited the story to her.

Eventually, soft footsteps brought her back to the present. She looked up to see Master Saif standing at the end of the aisle, his expression a mixture of curiosity and amusement.

"Alaric used to sit in that very spot for hours reading that book." He slowly approached, studying her with a scrutinizing gaze. There was a great intelligence behind those gray eyes.

"He said it was his mother's favorite book."

"He told you that?"

"He did."

"Interesting."

She wondered what was so interesting about that, but before she could ask, Master Saif offered his hand. She stared at it, then up at the old man in confusion.

"I must offer you my thanks, it seems, for keeping him alive. I was sure that I had seen the last of him when his father and his guards dragged him from here."

Tentatively, she stood and shook his hand. His hands were soft, wrinkled. He smiled at her and gestured back toward through the aisles.

"I know the joys of getting lost in a book, but will you join us?"

Reema tucked the book under her arm and nodded. She followed Master Saif back to Alaric and joined them at a small round table near the front of the library. The warmth of a cushioned chair welcomed her, stealing a satisfied sigh from her lips. She felt that if given the chance, she could sit here for hours without feeling the slightest twinge of pain.

Alaric's eyes caught on the book under her arm.

"Beneath the Sands of Sorrow," he said, his glowing brown eyes crinkling with a smile. He turned toward the master librarian. "I was sure my father had purged the library of that book."

The old man snorted. "And when has your father ever stepped foot into this place?"

"Never."

"And just as well. Knowledge like this would be wasted on cruel men like Kaiden Damaris."

Reema's eyes lifted at how openly Master Saif spoke about Alaric's father. Alaric noticed her look.

"Master Saif here has always been quite forward with his opinions, haven't you?"

"I'm irreplaceable," he said, gesturing toward the countless rows of books. "There's not a man alive who could catalog these books the way I've done. Kill me, and all this knowledge is lost."

"What do you mean?" Reema asked.

"How do you find a particular needle in a stack of needles, my dear?" he asked.

Reema frowned, glancing at the rest of the library. Suddenly, she understood. She couldn't fathom trying to find *Beneath the Sands of Sorrows* amongst all the books. When she looked back, he wiggled his bushy eyebrows and pointed to his head.

"It all lives up here."

"You know where *every* book is?"

"Not just that," Alaric said, jumping in. "He's read them all too."

"You're lying," she scoffed in disbelief.

"Look at this long beard of mine," Master Saif said. "It's the result of all the wisdom I've soaked in from these wonderful tomes."

"You've even read that book about the bugs, the grand comp ..." she trailed off, struggling to form the words of the title.

"*The Grand Compendium of a Thousand Bugs: An Encyclopedic Exploration of Insects*, you mean?"

She blinked, slowly turning her gaze to Alaric, who

smirked at her. He spread his hands as if to prove his point.

Besides," Master Saif continued, "I can be as free with my opinions as I want. Your father's not even here to debate them."

Reema exchanged a glance with Alaric but found him frowning at Master Saif.

"What do you mean he's not here?"

Master Saif's smile faded, the humor in his gray eyes disappearing. "I thought you knew."

"Knew what?"

"He's marched on Zareen. He's spent months gathering the Bloodlined and all their relic weapons. I imagine he finally felt they had everything they needed to take down the Commonborn Queen."

Alaric's face stilled, cold rage evident in his eyes. Where Reema would have let loose an explosive shout or curse, he simply stayed silent, and somehow that was even more terrifying.

"I see," he said. "Then we do not have long. Master Saif, how much do you know about the Angel's past?"

Master Saif's face scrunched in confusion, his gaze meeting Reema's for a moment before turning back to Alaric. "The Angel? Probably more than any man alive, except for some of the Faithful. But you know what they're like. Why?"

"Have you ever heard of the Djinn?"

Master Saif waved his hand. "Sure, but he's a myth. A scary story parents tell their children at night."

"He is not."

The librarian froze. "What?"

"When we were in the mines, we found black marble, and behind it, the Djinn was imprisoned by magic."

"If this is one of your jokes, Alaric, then I must tell you, I do not find it funny."

"It's no joke," Reema said.

Master Saif's worried eyes flicked toward her as the truth began to settle on him. His long, bushy brows furrowed, and he suddenly seemed older than before.

"What did he look like?" he asked, leaping to his feet with an energy that seemed impossible for someone his age. His thobe fluttered as he rushed toward the endless rows of books, with Alaric and Reema on his heels.

"Like fire," she said. "He was made entirely of fire."

He threw a worried glance over his shoulder, mumbling to himself. He led them to the far back, where the air was thick with dust. It was clear no one had ventured this far into the library in a long time.

"Fire, fire, fire," he muttered, his hands going to his head as if ransacking his memories for mention of the Djinn. He suddenly turned down one of the aisles, practically running now.

Reema noticed the spines of the books were written in an ancient language she couldn't decipher. Judging by the interest in Alaric's eyes, she wasn't alone.

Master Saif stopped abruptly, pulling a thin book from the shelf. A plume of dust rose toward the vaulted ceiling as he opened it, running his finger along the lines, still muttering "fire" under his breath.

Then he froze, horror dawning on his face. It seemed to seep into his very bones, and the way it radiated off him sent a chill down Reema's spine.

"What is it?" Alaric asked.

"How did I forget this? How?" he asked himself, as if it were unthinkable he could forget any piece of knowledge the library held.

"Forget *what*?"

Master Saif lifted his gaze to Alaric. "There *was* mention of a Djinn. In this."

Master Saif's hands trembled as he turned the thin book toward them, the faded pages revealing a story told through vivid illustrations. The images seemed out of place, whimsical in style. But the Djinn's fiery form was unmistakable, as was the aura of darkness rising from the pages.

"Is that a children's book?" Alaric asked in disbelief.

"It is." Master Saif turned the pages slowly, unable to bring himself to read the tale aloud. But he didn't need to; the illustrations were clear enough for them to grasp the gist of the story.

Reema and Alaric leaned in, scanning the drawings. A thriving world, filled with people and greenery as far as the eye could see, with a monstrous figure of fire and shadow looming overhead. The Djinn was captured mid-roar, his eyes like burning coals, striking terror into the people below. He was a force of chaos, a being of pure malice that ravaged the world.

Her breath hitched as Master Saif turned the page. The Djinn's destruction was vividly detailed: cities reduced to ashes, desert sands set aflame, faraway mountains crumbling under his wrath. Her stomach churned at the sight of people fleeing, their faces twisted in horror and despair, but there was nowhere for them to run.

A seething, relentless rage burned within her, not at the Djinn, but at herself. Her chest tightened with every passing page. She clenched her fists until her knuckles turned white as guilt rose bitterly in her throat. All she could think about was the memory of freeing the Djinn, replaying like a haunting echo.

What had she done?

For all the evil the slave master had done, nothing compared to the damage she had caused. Her vision narrowed as she fought to keep the rage from overwhelming her. She wanted to scream, to lash out, to punish herself.

Then the tone of the illustrations shifted. Amid the chaos and despair, a radiant figure appeared. The Angel, wings outstretched, haloed in light, descended from the seven heavens.

He cast his light upon the world, healing it as the fleeing people returned home, relief and smiles on their faces. The Djinn rose into the sky, ready to battle the Angel, but he was no match.

The Angel blasted him into the earth, where he was meant to never return.

Reema felt her stomach drop.

"You need to find the Angel," Master Saif said, a nervous bead of sweat trailing down through the wrinkles of his forehead.

"Master," Alaric said.

"I have seen one old text, written by an outcast, theorize that the Angel didn't return to the heavens but instead went west, toward the mountains beyond the desert."

"Master."

"If the Djinn remains, then it's possible that the Angel does too. You could find out. I wouldn't be able to make the trip, but the two of you, you're—"

"*Master Saif,*" Alaric said, his voice cutting through the librarian's like a scalpel.

The librarian stared at them. "What is it?"

"The Angel is dead."

He shook his head, "No, no, that is mere speculation. A nasty rumour spread by the uneducated—"

"The Djinn confirmed it himself," Alaric said, touching the scarred burn mark across his eye line. "He was the one who removed my father's band, because he wanted one of the Angel's bloodline to witness what he was going to do."

The master librarian looked from Alaric to Reema, as if he was hoping that this was all one cruel trick. But Reema's face told him the truth. He squeezed his eyes shut, his mouth turning downward as he slowly closed the book and returned it to the shelf.

Then he turned to the pair of them and gave them a sad smile, "Then you must cherish what little time you have left on this earth."

Reema leaned against the bookshelf, black dots swimming in her vision as the weight of her guilt drowned her.

"There must be something else," Alaric said, denial lacing his voice. "A weapon, something that can kill the Djinn."

The master librarian shook his head, "If there is, then I do not know of it."

"Or you *forgot*!" Alaric spat.

Master Saif gave Alaric a long, pitying look. "Despite this book, I am not in the habit of forgetting things."

Alaric grabbed Reema's hand, pulling her close. His grip was tighter than she'd ever felt.

Guilt upon guilt. She felt numb, beyond feeling.

"And I am not in the habit of giving up. Neither of us are."

He turned, pulling Reema along behind him, leaving the old librarian behind. Master Saif's weary voice called after them, but it only quickened Alaric's pace. She was forced into a jog as his long strides devoured the floor. He grabbed the bag with the pickaxe attached. She had no idea what he planned, but what did it matter? The world was lost. The city he loved was lost. And soon, he would be lost to her too.

CHAPTER
SEVEN

The journey back through the palace was a blur. Her thoughts assaulted her like the winds of a sandstorm, relentless and breaking. Reema tried to keep them at bay, but how could she, after what they had discovered? There was no weapon to stop the Djinn, and the only being that possibly could was dead.

When they reached the room with the secret tunnel, Alaric went to the wall and began running his fingers over the area they'd emerged from. While he worked, she looked around the room. Before, when she realized the slave master had slept here, an eternal rage had begged her to destroy everything. But standing here now, she couldn't help but think: What was the point? The Djinn would destroy it all soon enough anyway. Her rage sputtered out, its embers dying, leaving only defeat and numbness.

A growl drew her attention to Alaric, where he continued to struggle with the secret entrance to the tunnel. She frowned, retrieved the pickaxe from where he had set the pack down, and went to the wall.

With a single tap of the pickaxe's head against the stone, the palace walls shook. She could hear the shocked voices of others out in the hallway. Alaric put his arm across her chest and they backed away as the wall crumbled, revealing the entrance.

"You didn't need to do that. I nearly had it," he said.

She didn't say anything as she stepped onto the landing with the ladder that would take them down into the tunnel. It was difficult to climb down the ladder in the red dress, but she made it work.

When she touched down at the bottom, she waited for Alaric. He dropped from the ladder with a snarl, his glowing brown eyes unusually dark as he took her hand and started off. They walked in silence. The air was thick with tension. He was angry now at the Djinn, but soon enough, he'd realize she was the one who doomed his city and everyone in it.

She dipped her head in dismay. The apology caught in her throat like dry cotton, impossible to force out. There was nothing she could say that would make things better, but still, she felt the urge to say *something*.

Just as she opened her mouth, he spoke, his voice low and heavy.

"I was wrong."

His words caught her by surprise. "What?"

"I thought that Master Saif would have an answer. I was wrong. We're going to have to figure things out for ourselves."

She frowned as they walked on, the silence draping

over them like a heavy shroud. Then, she asked, "What if there is no way to stop the Djinn?"

Alaric came to an abrupt halt and she bumped into his back. He turned his intense gaze on her. "Do you believe that?"

She couldn't bring herself to answer.

His lip curled. Out of frustration, disgust, she didn't know. But whatever it was, it made her wilt and look away.

"There is a way. I know there is."

He took her hand with a steadying grip, drawing her attention back to him.

"Do you think that people would have said it was possible for the Angel to die?"

The thought was laughable—she never would have believed it, except for the way the Djinn had laughed at them. There was a certain arrogance and joy in his laughter, the truth ringing through her like a bell.

"No," she answered.

"Then have faith. If the Angel can die at the hands of us miserable mortals, then the Djinn can too."

She stared into his eyes, searching for some kind of doubt. But to her surprise, there was none. He fully believed what he was saying. She drew a deep, shaky breath, letting him calm her, then nodded.

"Okay."

With a firm nod, he placed her hand on his shoulder again and led the way through the dusty tunnel. The tunnel stretched on endlessly, pulling Reema and her thoughts into a quiet numbness. But eventually, they reached the end, where another ladder waited for them.

Alaric began to climb first, his gaze fixed overhead. Reema followed, gripping the rungs tightly as she climbed. The hem of her red dress caught on a splintered edge of the ladder. She cursed under her breath as she yanked it free, the hem tearing with a harsh rip. She climbed faster, trying to ignore the guilt and dread that gnawed away at her insides.

When they reached the top, Alaric pushed against the hatch. It resisted, the steel straining against his efforts. He gritted his teeth, muscles tensing as he put his weight into it. Finally, with a groan, the hatch gave way, and a wave of sand rained down over them. Reema shielded her eyes, coughing as the fine grains fell past them to settle on the tunnel floor.

They emerged into the open air, the bright light of day momentarily blinding. Reema blinked, her eyes adjusting to the brilliance. The smell of camel shit, hay, and spices from the inner city created a stomach-turning mix that made her eyes water. As she covered her nose and her vision cleared, she found herself standing at the centre of a dusty courtyard, surrounded by old camel stables.

Her eyes wandered, taking in her surroundings. In the distance, the spire of Sandspire rose, its white marble surface gleaming in the sunlight. It almost looked majestic against the backdrop of the blue sky and the red sandstone buildings around it. She'd known that it was huge from when she'd seen it in the desert, but standing here in the shadow of the spire, it stole her breath away. She could not fathom how many lives were lost in the mining of it, let alone the building of it.

Just then, the sound of clopping hooves echoed through the courtyard. Reema's gaze snapped to the side, where a grizzled Commonborn with a weathered face came around the corner, holding the reins to an old camel. He was leaning toward it, like he was talking to the beast. Reema and Alaric's sudden appearance startled him to a halt.

"Can I help you?" he called out, his voice unsure. Next to him, the camel shifted, able to sense the man's nervousness.

Alaric approached, his back straight like any Bloodlined. The Commonborn eyed them warily, his free hand shifting to his side. If Reema had to bet, she'd guess that he had a small dagger hidden away. It was likely more utilitarian than a weapon, meant for stable work, but in a moment of danger, it would suffice.

Despite the threat, Alaric continued to stalk toward him.

"We'll need your camel," he said, his tone brooking no argument. "Now."

The Commonborn's gaze narrowed. "This camel isn't for sale."

Reema knew this kind of dangerous standoff wasn't something Alaric was used to. After all, he was Bloodlined, likely accustomed to Commonborns obeying his commands without question.

She, however, was the Ifrit, ganglord over the most vicious of slaves. She stepped forward, opening her mouth to demand the man hand over the camel.

But Alaric's arm blocked her.

His expression darkened, and Reema noticed his eyes

—hard, filled with a ruthlessness that reminded her of his father. He stepped closer to the man, his presence imposing.

"It was not a request," he said coldly.

The Commonborn hesitated, realizing too late that he was defying a Bloodlined. Intimidated by the unspoken threat in Alaric's words, he took a single step back.

"The camel's how I make my living."

"Look at me," Alaric said, his eyes flashing dangerously. "Do you know who I am?"

The man swallowed, his gaze flicking from Alaric to Reema, like she could help him somehow. But she was busy studying Alaric, a frown forming. He didn't sound or look like himself at all.

"I am Lord Alaric Damaris."

The man's knees wobbled.

A grim smile crept across Alaric's face. "Yes, you recognize the name, don't you?"

The man spoke with a trembling voice. "You're Lord Kaiden Damaris's son?"

"I am," he answered, his tone like ice.

The man nodded as his eyes darted around, searching for an escape or perhaps a sympathetic face.

Reema's frown deepened, her mind racing, but she remained silent. This wasn't the Alaric she knew. The man before her was nothing like the compassionate, kind-hearted soul she had come to trust.

Alaric stepped closer, his voice dropping to a menacing whisper. "You have two choices: hand over the camel and walk away, or I shall take it, and leave you *wishing* you could walk away."

The man swallowed hard. The pungent stench of urine reached Reema. With shaking hands, he extended the reins to Alaric. "The camel's yours."

Alaric snatched the reins with a cold smirk, "Smart choice."

He mounted the camel swiftly, turning to Reema and extending a hand.

Reema hesitated, her eyes searching his face for any trace of the man she knew. All she saw was a mask of ruthless determination. Wordlessly, she took his hand and climbed up behind him. The Commonborn man stepped aside, his eyes downcast and his shoulder drooping. It was clear how much the camel meant to him.

Alaric snapped the reins, leaving the stunned and shaken Commonborn behind. Try as she might, she couldn't shake the image of Alaric's hard eyes, the cold threat in his voice, or how he treated the poor man like he was worth less than the sand beneath his feet.

Reema wrapped her arms around his waist, hoping to feel some tension in his body—anything to prove he wasn't as in his element as he appeared. But to her dismay, he felt calm. The realisation unsettled her, her thoughts swirling with worry.

Alaric rode them through the stables, through the emptied streets along the outskirts of Sandspire, and out into the desert.

CHAPTER
EIGHT

Despite the concern and worry swirling in her mind, Reema couldn't deny how much easier it was to cross the desert atop the camel. The beast had seemed old at first, but its long strides and quick pace devoured the desert faster than they could have ever dreamed on foot. That was fortunate, because they soon realized they had made a near-fatal mistake.

They had little water or food; only that which had been left on the stolen camel.

Reema buried her face against Alaric's sweat-soaked back, trying to shield herself from the cruel sun and ignore the dryness of her skin, mouth, and the twist in her stomach. Her red dress, blazing under the relentless sun, offered little protection. The fabric seemed to amplify the heat, her arms baking, skin prickling under the merciless glare. She was used to hunger, but she'd never felt it under the full weight of the sun.

Her breathing was ragged, but despite the pain in her throat, she asked, "Do you see them yet?"

Alaric shook his head, slumped over in exhaustion of his own. At least Reema could relax against him, hide in his shadow for what little good that did. He had to stay alert, in case they came across any slavers or anybody else. This far out in the desert, it wasn't like they had guards they could call for. Their survival was their own responsibility.

She cursed the day that she thought it was a good idea to separate from the army of miners, with all their food and water. But they couldn't be much further ahead. They only had a day's lead. Two at most. With the camel, they should be finding them soon.

Just as despair began to tighten its grip, she spotted something in the distance. It was a speck amongst the golden sea of sand, dancing like a mirage.

"There," she croaked, pointing a trembling finger ahead. "Do you see it?"

Alaric squinted, his eyes following her direction. "What do you see?"

"You can't see it? It's right *there*."

He held a hand over his eyes, shading them so that he could see better. He cursed, "Hells, I miss my glasses."

The mention of glasses caught her off guard. Stunned, she leaned to the side to get a better look at him, and he turned to meet her eyes.

"Glasses?" she asked, wincing at the throbbing pain in her throat. She shouldn't be speaking, but she had to know.

"I'm near sighted."

She blinked, suddenly trying to picture him with glasses. And somehow, it seemed *right*. A strange sound bubbled out of her, growing into full belly laughter that scratched her throat and brought tears to her eyes.

"You find that funny?" he asked, his eyes twitching with irritation, though the corner of his mouth lifted at the sound of her laughter.

He suddenly seemed more like himself again, gazing out over the sands, his expression softened and the ruthless edge gone. She carried hope that perhaps it was all just a momentary lapse. After all, it wasn't like she was exactly herself either. The stress and worry of the Djinn's threat weighed on them both, not just her.

Suddenly, her laughter turned into a series of violent coughs. Her hands flew to her throat as it constricted painfully, making her regret asking about his glasses.

"Wait," Alaric said, his gaze shifting back to where she pointed. "I think I see it now."

He snapped the reins, and the camel quickened its pace. As they approached, the shape became clearer—a body lying motionless in the sand. Reema's heart pounded. They dismounted as the camel grumbled and knelt. Alaric knelt beside the body, turning it over gently.

"It's one of the miners," he said, his voice rough. Despite the gruesome discovery, a spark of hope lit his eyes. "We must be close."

Reema nodded, her throat too parched for words. The sight of the miner, though tragic, meant they were on the right path. Her gang, their food and water— everything they needed—was within reach.

She gathered her strength and steeled herself, determined to push forward. She mounted the camel again, this time extending a hand to Alaric.

"Come on," she said.

"Leading a camel is different from riding one," he said.

"It can't be that hard."

His brow lifted, that sundamned smirk returning. He shrugged and took her hand, sliding in behind her. His hand instinctively wrapped around her waist, settling on her stomach. A sudden tension surrounded them, as if they both remembered the last time their bodies had been so close to one another. And try as she might, she could not tear her mind away from the fact that the warmth of his hand against her felt *good*.

She snapped the reins like Alaric had, emboldened by the fact that they had a lifeline now, hope that they would find the miners before the starvation or dying thirst took them.

They resumed their ride, the camel moving steadily across the golden sea of sand. Her confidence was tested sooner than expected. The camel began to veer off course, and try as she might, the sundamned beast wouldn't listen to her.

She cursed it beneath her breath as she realized that Alaric was chuckling behind her. His hand lifted from her stomach, and she immediately missed its warmth.

His hands gently covered hers on the reins. He pulled her closer, his chin resting on her shoulder. She felt his breath on her ear and the warmth of his body pressing even closer.

"Like this," he murmured, his voice strained as he struggled to get the words out. He guided her hands, showing her the subtle movements needed to take control of the camel and lead it properly.

She smelled him—a mix of sweat and the scent of old book pages. The closeness made her burn, both from guilt and from an undeniable desire. She tried to focus on his instructions, but the feel of him pressed against her made it difficult. Eventually, once she got the hang of leading the camel, his hands returned to her waist.

They continued to cross the desert, finding the next body a mere hour later. She glanced back over her shoulder at Alaric with a frown. It wasn't the only other body they found. Soon, more came, the bodies scorched and burnt from the sun and the heated sand.

Worry crept through her, and she wondered if she had underestimated the journey across the desert with the miner army at her back. None of them would be used to the insufferable heat. And for most of them, their sturdy linen tunics were torn and tattered, exposing their bare skin against the harsh threat of the sun. That alone, forgetting any other dangers of the desert like sand-storms or wandering raiders, was enough to make her think maybe it'd been a mistake.

Her worry deepened as the trail of bodies lengthened.

CHAPTER
NINE

Two days later, Reema and Alaric stared at the three miners sprawled in the sand, their chests caved in by the sharp puncture of pickaxes. Blood seeped into the sand, crimson so vibrant it seemed to spill from the reds of the sunset sky overhead. The silence was heavy. Reema's worry deepened into dread—she knew what this meant.

It was the miners' first attempt at mutiny. There could be no other explanation for the killings—an unmistakable display of force to rein the others in.

She drew a deep, shaky breath. They needed to get back to the miners. It was one thing to be led by a former gang lord; another to be led by the Ifrit herself. They wouldn't have dared try anything with her there to keep them in check.

Gripping the reins tighter, she snapped them, urging the camel forward. She didn't say anything, and neither did Alaric. They knew they needed to hurry, both too exhausted to waste energy speaking.

The sun slipped toward the horizon, setting the sky

ablaze with dark, blood-red hues. That alone might not have been enough to worry her, but the moon was tinted red too. Reema wasn't one for superstitions, but she couldn't deny the terror creeping through her, raising the hairs on the back of her neck.

The camel grunted as she urged it faster. They rode through the sunset and into a strangely starless night, until finally, they found the miners.

She heard them before she saw them—angry shouts echoing across the desert. She glanced over her shoulder, meeting Alaric's eyes to make sure she wasn't imagining it.

His expression was as tense and worried as hers, a pinch in his forehead and his brows furrowed.

She urged the camel faster, climbing a massive sand dune where the dark sky softened by the glow of miners' torches. When they crested it, the miners appeared.

They circled two fighters, shouting and jeering, their ugly faces illuminated by waving torches. From the throng of bodies surrounding the fighters, it was impossible to see who they were, but Reema had a sneaking suspicion.

She cursed under her breath, snapped the reins, and dug her heels in, driving the camel into a full sprint. Alaric's grip on her tightened. The sand kicked up behind them as they sped toward the miners. The wind howled in her ears, and her heart pounded in her chest like the beat of a heavy drum.

A sharp scream rent the air, followed by a guttural, frustrated growl that sounded all too familiar. Reema's nerves spiked as she neared the crowd of miners.

The ones at the back were the first to notice her arrival, their eyes scanning her and Alaric's fine red and blue silk outfits. They parted for her, surprised, but she could see the anger sparking within.

She knew what they thought: they had crossed the cursed desert on foot, wearing tattered slave garb, while Reema and Alaric seemed to have gone to a party in the finest clothes they'd ever seen, returning on a sundamned camel.

She lifted her chin, shedding the guilt and worry, revealing the mask of the Ifrit. She did not need to explain herself. She was gang lord over them all, free to do as she pleased.

The crowd of miners parted like desert sands, surprised to see the camel towering over them. But when two refused to move, their faces twisted with betrayal and violence, Reema dismounted.

She dropped onto the sand with a heavy thud, shadows flickering across her face from the torches ahead. She raised her dark gaze.

The first man *sneered*, slowly withdrawing his shiv.

"And the boss comes running back in her little red dress," he muttered, barely audible beneath the cacophony of shouting miners. He turned toward the other, about to say something when Reema shot forward.

She was exhausted, her legs like weighted blocks of marble. Every muscle ached from the long camel ride, and she was so thirsty she could smell the water in the nearby jugs. But none of that mattered.

Before the man could blink, she grabbed his shiv and

buried it in his neck. Blood gushed over her, painting her face red to match her dress.

He let out a gurgled scream, clutching his throat as he stumbled back into the men in the inner circle. They spun toward him, curses on their lips and eyes flashing with anger, only to fall back, shocked at the sight of the dying man.

He hit the sand, hands scrambling for purchase against the grains around him as though there was something in reach that could save him.

Reema turned to the other man who had defied her, drenched in blood so hot it seemed to steam off her in the cold desert night.

The second man's eyes narrowed, his lips pulling back to reveal rotting teeth. He growled as his grip tightened on a steel blade that he must have found back at the guards' barracks.

"You aren't going to catch me by surprise, Ifrit," he spat. "I'm going to gut you for the fleeing coward you are."

Alaric's face darkened at the threat, and he began to dismount. But with a subtle shake of her head, he stopped.

The man rushed toward her, swinging with a wild, desperate arc. She let the rage consume her, her mind flashing back to the helplessness she'd felt at the hands of the slavers, Kaiden Damaris, and now, the Djinn. She let out a frustrated scream that silenced the nearby miners as they realized the Ifrit had returned.

She didn't move with the deadly grace or speed she'd

shown earlier, but with a violent intensity that sent waves of fear through the man.

She ducked under his swing and tackled him to the sand. Before he could recover, she seized his wrist and twisted it. A crack echoed through the night, followed by his terrified scream.

With him beneath her, she drove her elbow into his throat, silencing him and leaving him gasping for breath. His face morphed into that of her enemies, and the seed of hatred buried in her heart sprouted into blind violence. Her vision turned red as she hammered her fists into his face.

When she ran out of breath, she paused, staring down at him. He was unrecognizable, his skull fractured, his face pulp. He lay still, except for the quiet, choking gasp escaping his broken lips.

She rose, breathing heavily, the adrenaline still coursing through her veins. The heat of his blood on her hands and face radiated off her, mingling with the sweat and grime of the desert. Her red dress clung to her like a second skin, now drenched in crimson. She turned to the crowd of miners, her eyes blazing with fury.

The miners stared back, fear and awe mixed in their expressions. Reema stepped forward, snatching a torch from a nearby watcher. The flames flickered, casting eerie shadows on her blood-smeared face. She forced her way through the throng. The crowd parted, first reluctantly, then with speed as they saw the Ifrit back in their midst. Murmurs grew louder as she pushed her way to the center of the circle.

The light of the torch revealed Renfri and Asif

standing across from two other miners, including a wiry man with a scar running down his cheek. Reema couldn't recall his name, but he seemed familiar. Then it clicked. He had been Renfri's Second, before she joined forces with Reema. They must be challenging Renfri and Asif for control of the miners.

All four were still poised to attack, despite the blood soaking their clothes. But the sight of Reema brought them to an abrupt halt, the shock evident in their eyes.

For a moment, Reema watched, assessing the situation. She could see how exhausted Renfri and Asif were, the weariness in their eyes. She had never seen Asif so tired from a single fight, but she suspected they'd been struggling for a while to maintain control of the harsh desert trek.

Reema's voice rang out, cutting through the voices of the miners who hadn't yet realized what happened. "Enough!"

Renfri and Asif lowered their blades, breathing heavily. She thought she saw a whisper of relief in Renfri's gaze, but it could have been a trick of the light.

Reema stepped further into the circle, the torch held high. The flames cast an ominous glow over her, highlighting the blood drenching her and the dress. The wiry, scarred man and his partner exchanged glances.

"Lower your weapons," she said. Her voice was quiet, cracked from thirst, but it still carried a note of danger that struck fear into the miners. She saw it in their eyes as they flicked between her and the surrounding miners, searching for a sign they weren't alone.

But they were alone. The Ifrit had returned, and after

her brutal murder of the two defying her, none of the others would dare lift a finger.

The partner tossed his weapon to the side, his shoulders slumping in defeat. He dropped to his knees. A small cloud of sand rose into the air.

But the scarred man stood his ground, bristling with rage at his partner's submission.

Reema's gaze narrowed. She slowly, quietly went to Renfri.

"Hand me your shiv," Reema said to Renfri.

Renfri passed it to her, hilt first, and before anyone could blink, she spun and threw the shiv. It hissed through the air, burying itself in the scarred man's stomach with a sickening, wet thud.

A guttural groan escaped his lips, mingling with the faint gurgle of blood seeping from the wound. He fell to his knees, bending over with his hands to the wound.

"Hells," another miner whispered.

Reema turned to the gathered miners, her voice rising above the whispers. "Are there any other challengers?"

The crowd shifted uneasily, their eyes reflecting a mix of fear and disappointment. Not a soul stepped forward.

She clenched her fists and pursed her lips. "I'll ask one more time. Do any of you fools want to fight me?"

Silence.

She scanned the crowd, searching for anyone who dared to meet her eyes. None did. She took a deep breath as the adrenaline ebbed away.

"Then grab your shit and start walking. We do not

rest," she said to the miners. She looked back at the two defeated men. "As for you two ... Asif, Renfri, strip them of their clothes and take their supplies."

The scarred man lifted his head from where he lay. "You *bitch*. You're taking our clothes?"

Reema crouched over him and stared into his eyes. "I will, not because I want the sun to have you, but so you'll remember, when you're burning alive, that you were stupid enough to think you could take control from the Ifrit."

"But you were gone!" the second man protested to the side, his eyes wide with fear and horror. He pointed at Renfri and Asif. "We were trying to take control from them."

"Don't you get it? *They* represent *me*."

Reema stood and began to walk away, ignoring the man's incoherent sobs. Asif flashed a grin at her as he stalked toward the man. Renfri, uncharacteristically stoic, kept her expression guarded.

The crowd watched as they stripped the two men, silencing them with heavy fists.

"Did you not hear me?" Reema called again, her voice cutting through the silence like a razor. "Start *walking*!"

The miners exchanged glances, the tension palpable in the air. Slowly, one by one, they obeyed.

Reema lowered the torch, its flames casting long shadows across the sand. She glanced at Alaric, who had stayed back, expecting to see him shocked by the brutal display of how she seized control. To her surprise and worry, his intense gaze was impossible to read.

"Damn the deep, I'm glad to see you," Asif breathed,

drawing her attention away from Alaric as Asif pulled her into a rare display of affection. His long, scruffy beard scratched against her shoulder. He smelled of body odor and sweat, but Reema embraced him anyway.

"Came just in time to save your ass," she smirked.

He grumbled, but didn't deny it. He offered her the second man's linen. "Red looks good on you, but you might want this."

She nodded, taking it from him and pushing Alaric from her mind. The miners would have trouble respecting her so long as she wore a dress. She could change when she felt like they'd gone far enough for the miners to regret cheering for Asif and Renfri's death.

But even more important than the clothing was the water skin he passed her. Over her shoulder, she saw Renfri hand one to Alaric, who walked beside the camel.

Reema lifted the water skin to her lips and drank, doing her best not to drink too much, despite how much her body craved it. She knew from experience that drinking too much too quickly could make you too sick to walk. And out here in the desert, that was as good as a death sentence.

They trailed after the miners toward Zareen, Reema sipping from the water skin and listening to the screams of the two naked men they'd left behind. The scarred one would probably die before morning. As for the second? Who knew how long someone could last naked in the desert, and Reema doubted anyone had ever been foolish enough to try.

When they were far enough that the screams faded,

leaving only soft murmurs and the shuffling sounds of miners walking, Reema leaned toward Asif.

"What was that about?" she asked in a low voice, to avoid drawing attention.

"Things have been hard since you left. The heat, this sundamned desert, it's getting to them."

She nodded, scanning the miners for any sign of dissent as they walked. Judging by their sluggish steps and the burns on their necks and arms, it wouldn't be long before more of them collapsed into the golden sands.

"They're starting to forget why we even came to the surface," Asif continued. "I've even heard them say they want to go back to the mines."

Reema understood the feeling. Life wasn't wonderful in the mines, with the constant danger of collapse. But at least underground, they never had to worry about the Angel-damned sun.

Funny how so many longed to see the surface again, only to forget how cruel it could be. But Reema hadn't made that mistake. She knew what she was getting into by leaving the mines.

"Can't do that. We have to stop the Djinn," she said.

"You don't have to tell *me*. You don't even have to tell them that. Just seeing your pretty face will help them remember."

She looked at him out of the corner of her eye, catching his subtle warning: leave them again, and it might all fall to shit.

"I hear you."

He nodded, pleased that she understood.

"Where are Omar and Ra'ad?" she asked. Normally, they'd have shown up by now with a wise joke, but they hadn't. She wasn't worried, though; she hadn't seen them in the trail of bodies they followed to find the miners.

"We have a small group of scouts about a half day ahead. I didn't trust them not to piss off and leave us blind in the desert, so ... I *convinced* Renfri to assign them to lead the scouts. They're supposed to find us by morning."

Reema nodded, choosing to ignore how he emphasized the need to convince Renfri rather than simply ordering it himself. It was likely a sore spot for him, but he knew making Renfri her Second was necessary.

"And Renfri?" Reema asked.

He turned toward her, suddenly tense. "What about her?"

Reema eyed him. "How's she doing?"

He relaxed. "She's fine."

They continued walking, the throng of miners offering a comforting warmth against the crisp night air.

After a few minutes, Asif spoke. "She's good. Got a head for strategy, for getting the miners in line."

Reema raised a brow. "Are you complimenting her?"

He snarled. "No. Just saying your choice of her as Second wasn't a bad one."

Asif cleared his throat, running his hands through his beard. He glanced around conspiratorially before continuing. "Did you find what we needed?"

"A way to kill the Djinn?" she asked, nearly stumbling over a dip in the sand.

He nodded.

Reema chewed her lip, guilt gnawing at her again. She knew she could trust Asif with the truth, that they'd have to figure out some way to stop the Djinn. But she also knew Asif would see through her, see her doubt and regret. He would see her growing weak. She couldn't have that.

"We did," she lied, her tone making it clear he shouldn't ask more questions.

If he was surprised by her tone, he didn't show it. Instead, he nodded and glanced over his shoulder as Alaric approached from behind.

"We'll talk more later," he said, before slowing down to shout at the miners who were lagging behind.

"How is he?" Alaric asked as he joined her, the massive camel walking alongside him.

"A little battered from the fight, but you know he can take a few punches."

Alaric chuckled, thinking back to when he had gotten into a fight with Asif himself. "That, I do know. But I meant, how *is* he?"

Reema considered him, surprised that he was truly asking after Asif. "You care about him, don't you?"

Alaric shrugged, lifting his gaze to study the stars as they walked. "I am part of the gang, right? That means he is family."

A slow grin passed across Reema's face. "That makes us family too?"

He met her eyes. "You and I, we're not family. We're something else."

Reema's heart skipped a beat at his words. She took a

deep breath, steadying herself. "I told Asif we found a way to kill the Djinn," she said quietly, glancing at Alaric to gauge his reaction.

Alaric nodded, understanding the need for the lie. "We'll figure it out," he promised.

They walked in silence for a while, the only sound the soft padding of their feet on the sand and the occasional grunt from the camel. Reema's gaze drifted to Alaric repeatedly, surprised by the longing she felt. She realized they couldn't continue what they had started out in the desert, not with the miners here. She had to be strong, couldn't show even a moment of weakness or vulnerability, or she too would lose control.

Still, she wished she could reach out and hold his hand, feel the warmth of his skin against hers. She wondered when she would have that chance again.

Renfri appeared, emerging between two thin miners. Reema caught Alaric's attention and nodded.

"I need to speak to Renfri."

Alaric nodded, tugging on the camel's reins and walking ahead. With a heavy sigh, Reema approached Renfri.

"Close call, wasn't it?" she asked.

"I had it under control," Renfri said, her voice stiff and sharp.

"No, you didn't."

After a long moment of silence, Renfri drew a hissed breath between clenched teeth. "I didn't."

Reema nodded, not twisting the knife any further.

But Renfri was the one to continue. "I did everything I could to keep the miners in line. I tried to incentivize them at first, gave them extra lentils and water to keep going, because Angel knows this desert is crueler to them than I could ever be. But when that didn't work, I tried to put fear into them."

Her fingers curled into fists.

"It didn't work, and do you know why?" She looked at Reema, her dark eyes full of frustration. "Because the *Ifrit* is their gang lord. Not me."

She spat to the side.

"You're too harsh on yourself," Reema said.

"It was a mistake making me your Second. I never even had a chance to run this gang when you left."

"It wasn't a mistake making you my Second."

"And what in the deep makes you say that?"

"Asif."

She stumbled, nearly falling flat on her face in the sand. She scowled as she straightened. "What did that ugly bastard have to say?"

"He said enough for me to keep trusting you. I know you won't let me down again."

Renfri eyed her, then looked ahead, saying nothing as they continued to walk next to one another. The night was cool, the stars were bright, and for a short while, they lost themselves in the monotonous action of putting one foot in front of the other.

Reema's thoughts and eyes drifted back toward Alaric, where he walked with the camel at his side. There was something especially beautiful about him at night. She didn't know if it was because his eyes seemed to glow a little brighter or if it was the way the moonlight seemed to follow him. How could such a tortured man have such a gentle soul? Reema nestled a quiet thought, thinking there couldn't be another soul like him.

"You lay with him, didn't you?" Renfri asked.

Reema stiffened, realizing Renfri had caught her staring. "What are you talking about?"

"Oh, come on. Don't bother lying to me. I can tell by the way you're looking at him."

Reema felt a rush of heat to her cheeks, anger and embarrassment warring within her. "This isn't the time, Renfri."

Renfri's expression sobered, though the glint in her eyes remained. "Maybe not, but it's true, isn't it? Remember what I said?"

"I do," she said in a curt tone.

"So you're going to cut him loose then?"

Reema took a deep breath, trying to regain her composure. Her delay in answering was answer enough.

"You're catching feelings for him," Renfri said, her smile fading into a deep-set frown.

"I know what I'm doing."

"I don't think you do." Renfri leaned in. "I know what others say about me—that I seduce and control men, and kill them when I grow tired of them."

Reema glanced toward her, eyes narrowing. "What are you getting at, Renfri?"

"I'm going to tell you a story, so listen closely. A long time ago, before I was a gang lord, I had a friend named Duraid. He was strong, more cunning than me, and you know I don't say that lightly. He understood me in a way no one else did. He knew what I wanted, and before you ever took the southern mines for yourself, he helped me take over the central pit."

Another miner drifted toward them, lost in thought. Renfri scowled and kicked him aside. The look on Renfri's face sent him scampering away.

Once no one was close enough to hear, Renfri leaned in and continued.

"I named Duraid as my Second. We became close—closer than I ever allowed myself to be with anyone."

Reema listened, her curiosity piqued by the rare vulnerability in Renfri's voice.

"We spent every moment we could together. Angel knows the sex was great, but it was more than just that. For a short while, it felt like all the world was right, like it didn't matter that we'd been sentenced to become a pair of sundamned slaves."

Then the shadows gathered in her eyes as they hardened, and her voice took on a bitter edge.

"But the other men in my gang saw it. They saw how I favored him, and they used it against me. They took him hostage, told me to do as they said or they'd cut his throat."

Reema's breath caught in her throat. "What did you do?"

Renfri's gaze met hers, and the pain there was raw and real. "I cut Duraid's throat for them. It was the only way to set myself free. To show them that I couldn't be controlled, that no one could use my heart against me."

Reema could hardly believe what she was hearing. The thought of slitting Alaric's throat, his hot blood gushing out, was impossible to imagine. How could Renfri have done that?

Renfri's eyes gleamed with a bitter intensity as she continued. "I don't kill the men I seduce because I grow tired of them. I do it because I grow attached, because love is dangerous. It'll make you weak, make you vulnerable, and in this world, vulnerability gets you killed. That's why every time I put a blade to a man's neck, they're surprised—like they never saw it coming."

Reema felt a chill run down her spine. She could see the truth in Renfri's words, the pain etched into every line of her face. Renfri turned to her, noticing the shock in Reema's face.

Her voice softened, almost tender. "Listen, Reema. I can see what's happening between you and Alaric. I know that look, that longing. Let me take care of him for you. Let me keep your heart safe for you."

Reema's eyes widened in horror. "No, Renfri. No."

Renfri's expression darkened, her patience wearing thin. "You're a fool if you think you can have both love and power. One will destroy the other. If you won't let me do it, then you need to handle it yourself."

Her heart pounded as she was rendered speechless, emotions warring on her face.

Renfri's anger flared, her eyes flashing with frustration. "Handle it, *Ifrit*. Before it's too late."

Then she was gone, disappearing into the throng of miners.

As the night wore on, Reema walked in silence, her thoughts tangled in fear and desire. She glanced at Alaric, his silhouette outlined by the flickering torchlight. Freeing the Djinn had been the first dose of poison that would doom them both. He had never told her he loved her, and despite how desperately she craved those words, she couldn't help but wonder ... with the Djinn free to wreak havoc, how long was it before he regretted knowing her?

She shook her head and looked away, the truth a bitter, sour taste. There could be nothing between them until she undid it *all*. And until then, it was better to do as Renfri said.

Kill her own heart.

CHAPTER
TEN

The next day, the sun beat down on Reema. She wore sturdy miner linen tunics again, but this time with strips of the red dress protecting her exposed skin. Even so, the sun's heat made life miserable.

She scanned the desert as she walked, conscious of how worried Asif was getting. Omar, Ra'ad, and the scouts were supposed to return by morning, but so far, nothing.

Then, she noticed two specks in the far distance. At first, she thought it was a mirage, but it didn't waver. Instead, it slowly made its way toward them. Soon, it became clear that it was two men, and there was something familiar about them, about the way they walked.

She nudged Asif, drawing his attention. He narrowed his gaze, and soon, a curse spilled from his lips.

"That's Omar and Ra'ad."

Reema grinned, excited to see them after what felt like so long. But her grin faltered at the concern on Asif's face.

"What is it?" she asked.

"Where are the other five scouts?"

A cold fear filled her, prickling her skin with worry. She and Asif started toward them, the sands slipping and sliding down after them. The miners watched them go but didn't deviate from their path, not with Renfri's voice cutting through the silence, demanding they keep pace.

As Reema and Asif crossed the distance, she noticed how rough a shape they were in, with their cracked lips, scorched skin, and slumped shoulders.

"Omar, Ra'ad!" Asif called, a note of relief in his voice. She understood his relief—whatever tragedy they had faced, at least they had returned.

Omar raised a hand, faltering in his steps. Ra'ad grabbed Omar's arm, and together, they crossed the rest of the distance.

Omar tried to smile, his voice like grating rocks. "The great Ifrit's still alive."

Reema waited for Ra'ad to add his comment, but instead he only grunted, clasping her hand. Omar drew her in for a stiff hug. Her arms came away tinged with blood, and she gasped, realizing he was injured.

Asif rushed forward, but Omar batted him away.

"I'm fine," Omar said. "It's just a flesh wound."

Reema's gaze narrowed. "Show us."

Omar hesitated, his eyes catching on Reema's. He didn't want to, but he also wasn't one to disobey his gang lord. With a reluctant sigh, he gingerly lifted the edge of his shirt.

Ra'ad looked away, and that's when she knew it would be bad.

Reema's heart pounded as her breath caught at the sight of Omar's wound, a deep cut running across his ribcage. It was an angry, infected red.

A curse slipped from Asif's lips. "What in the sundamned hells happened?"

"We came across some slavers."

Her hatred for the slavers ignited, a familiar desire for vengeance burning hotter than the desert sun.

Asif's eyes flared with the same fury, his hands clenched into fists. Ra'ad stood silent and tense, struggling to keep his emotions in check. His jaw was clenched, eyes glistening with barely suppressed rage and worry.

"Slavers," Asif spat, the word dripping with venom. "Where are they now?"

Before Omar could respond, Reema interjected, "The wound looks infected. Let's get them back first, get them treated with anything we've got. Then we'll get the bastards that did this to them."

Omar shook his head, a tired but defiant grin spreading over his cracked lips. "We already got our revenge."

Reema's gaze flicked between Omar and Ra'ad, her eyes narrowing. "What do you mean?"

Omar chuckled, though it was more a pained rasp. "They caught us off guard. Butchered the others that came with us. But we turned the tables on them, didn't we, Ra'ad?"

"Took down every last one of them," Ra'ad said slowly, softly, his eyes downcast.

Omar's grin widened, despite the pain it clearly

caused him. Unsteady on his feet, his eyes drifted past Reema's shoulder. "We got our revenge, didn't we?"

He fell forward.

Ra'ad caught him before he hit the sand. His gaze was tormented, his face twisted in concern and grief as he held his brother.

"Your rage is ours, and ours is yours," Omar whispered, his hand resting limp in the sand. His eyes began to flutter shut.

A sudden dread and fear gripped Reema, constricting her chest.

Asif moved swiftly, taking Omar from Ra'ad and lifting him with desperate strength. Without a word, he began running back toward the army, Omar's limp body bouncing slightly with each hurried step.

Reema and Ra'ad sprinted after him, their feet slipping and sliding in the sand. The hot desert air burned in her lungs, but she pushed through the pain, her mind focused solely on Omar.

As a member of her gang, he was family, a brother to not just Ra'ad, but to Reema and Asif. The idea of losing him made her stumble. Ra'ad helped her with a terrifying strength that belied his fear, and they raced faster toward the army.

As they neared the army, Renfri's voice cut through the noise, "Asif?"

But Asif didn't answer. His eyes scanned the crowd for one person. When he spotted him, he shouldered the miners aside.

"Yaqoub!"

A tall man with a weathered face and sharp eyes,

carrying a heavy pack, looked up. He saw Asif carrying Omar and immediately understood the gravity of the situation.

He knelt and set his pack on the ground as Asif shouted for the miners to clear a space.

Asif laid Omar down gently, his face etched with worry. Yaqoub was already there, his hands moving with a practiced efficiency that surprised Reema. He must have learned this before the mines; this kind of confidence and speed wasn't something miners picked up in the deep.

He tore away the remnants of Omar's shirt, revealing the angry, infected wound.

"Water and some sundamned clean cloths," Yaqoub barked at Asif, like he was just another miner.

But Reema watched as Asif listened, darting off into the crowd like Omar's life depended on it. And maybe it did. That thought terrified Reema.

Ra'ad knelt next to Omar, clutching his hand as Yaqoub opened his pack and pulled out herbs he'd taken from the guards' barracks.

Reema's knees hit the hot sand, ignoring the burn of them. Her hands trembled as she brushed the hair from Omar's forehead.

Omar's eyes opened just as Alaric appeared over her shoulder, glowing eyes peering down at Omar with sadness and worry.

"The Angel's coming for me," Omar whispered, his voice faint.

"No, he's not," Ra'ad growled, his face a mask of anguish. "You're going to be okay. Tell him, boss!"

Omar's head rolled toward Reema, and he gave her a weak smile. "Don't worry, Ifrit. I'll put in a good word for you."

Reema's throat tightened, and she fought back the tears threatening to spill. "Just hang on, Omar. You're going to be fine."

Asif returned and handed everything to Yaqoub. The healer's hands moved swiftly, cleaning the wound, water and blood mixing in the golden sand beneath.

Reema ground her teeth, her eyes on the blood-stained sand, struggling to contain her emotions. She wished she could bring the slavers back to life just so *she* could be the one to kill them.

The air was thick with tension as the miners continued to pass by, forced to keep marching by Renfri's shouts. Yaqoub mixed a poultice of crushed herbs, applying it to the wound with a gentle touch. But even with that gentle touch, Omar cried out feverishly.

Reema leaned in, her voice deadly and low. "If he dies, you die. Do you understand?"

Yaqoub paused, his eyes lifting to meet hers. His voice was calm and steady. "Ifrit, you keep distracting me and *you* could be the reason he dies."

She swallowed, her heart still pounding. Alaric rested his hand on her shoulder.

"Come on," he said gently, but firmly.

She paused. Yaqoub waited.

"Please, Reema," Ra'ad said.

Reema nodded, her lips pursed as she stood. Heart still pounding, she turned and followed Alaric.

Grief and fear stormed inside her, making it hard to

breathe. She waited nearby, just close enough for them to call her. The miners continued to pass by her, none daring to meet her eyes for fear she would lash out. She wanted to. She wanted to break something, someone.

And the only person in reach was Alaric.

He reached for her in some pathetic attempt to comfort her, and instead, she shoved him back as hard as she could.

A look of surprise crossed his face.

Again, she drove her hands into his chest, driving him back with a growl born from that awful place of helplessness.

"Get away from me," she seethed, the edges of her vision pulsing. "Leave me alone!"

Alaric's brows furrowed, but he simply nodded and retreated into the passing crowd.

Alone, she watched from a distance as Yaqoub worked. A few moments later, Asif joined her, a scowl clear on his face. He didn't notice Reema's own anger.

"He told me to piss off too. Apparently, me standing over him makes it impossible to work."

"You do make a daunting figure, standing over him like a shadow," Renfri said as she appeared. "What's happening?"

"The scouts ran into the slavers."

She drew a hissed breath, no doubt feeling the same rage that Reema felt at the mention of them. It was clear there was some history between Renfri and the slavers too.

"And?" Renfri asked.

"The slavers are dead. But Omar's injured."

Renfri was smart enough not to say anything.

Heart still pounding, Reema said, "Stop the miners. We're not moving Omar until that bastard Yaqoub says it's safe."

"Miners won't like hearing the special treatment."

"I don't care."

"They'll ask why we're stopping for him, but none of the others. It'll cause issues."

"Then we'll handle them," Reema snapped. "Let them start something, and I'll show you how red these sands can get."

Renfri exchanged a glance with Asif. After a long, tense moment, she nodded and backed away. A few minutes later, the miners came to a complete halt, grumbling and setting up what little shade they could to protect them from the sun.

Reema and Asif stood next to each other, the tension still lingering in the tightness of their breaths. Neither spoke, afraid that words might break the spell keeping Omar tethered to this earth.

But then, after what seemed like an eternity, Yaqoub rose from where he had been working. He quickly instructed several miners to build a makeshift stretcher, using the sticks of broken pickaxes and linen from fallen miners who would never rise again.

Sighing heavily, with shadowed eyes, he approached Reema and Asif.

"I applied some herbs that should help draw out the infection," he said, his voice calm and steady. But his eyes spoke the truth of the worry he felt. "He needs rest."

Reema stared at Omar's limp form, and at Ra'ad still next to him.

"You'll keep an eye on him if things get worse?" Asif asked quietly.

"Yes."

"Good."

Dismissed, Yaqoub left them alone.

"While we're stopped, get a group of miners out there to keep scouting. I want to know if there are any more slavers out there," Reema said.

Asif nodded and left to do as she said.

Reema waited for Ra'ad, the rage in her chest dying to embers, replaced by helpless frustration. When he finished, he stood and pulled her aside, away from the resting miners.

It was strange, seeing him standing while his twin brother lay on the verge of death. She tried to imagine a world where there was no Omar and only Ra'ad, but she couldn't. Who would finish his sentences?

Ra'ad's face was grim, his eyes glittering with tears as he met her gaze.

"He's going to be okay," Reema said, her voice firm and strong, despite the worry and weakness she felt inside. She had to be the one that held him steady now. She was the gang lord. "I promise you."

Turned away from the miners, Ra'ad shook his head and buried his face in his hands. She stepped closer, her voice dipping low and solemn.

"He *will* be okay," she reiterated, feeling more conviction than ever. Omar was strong, just as strong as her, Asif, Javid, and the rest of her gang. Her gang was made from the best, the ones whose rage wouldn't let them die easily.

But when Ra'ad lifted his eyes to hers, they were filled with such tormented grief that her conviction died in her chest, and a creeping dread danced down her spine.

"There was something I didn't tell you," Ra'ad whispered, his voice broken.

"What is it?"

His breaths were tight, his eyes shifting into a blackness so deep that it was eerily familiar, and despair etched itself into every line of his face as he spoke. "When I put my blade to the last slaver's neck, the one who cut Omar, he laughed at me. Do you know why?"

She shook her head slowly.

"He'd poisoned his dagger."

Ra'ad's words hit like a blow, stealing her breath and making her vision swim. The world narrowed to the torment in his eyes, pulling her into a spiral of dread. Her heart pounded in her chest, and the dread pressed down on her, suffocating her.

Ra'ad's haunted, hollow eyes met hers. "My twin brother isn't infected. He's poisoned, and ..."

He couldn't finish, his voice breaking. Reema felt a cold sweat trickle down her spine, because she knew what he was going to say.

Omar was dying.

CHAPTER
ELEVEN

Reema stalked through the miners, her heart pounding like a relentless drum. Each step felt heavy, burdened by what Ra'ad told her. She shoved aside those in her way, ignoring the startled, annoyed glances they shot her. She had one focus, one goal.

Asif.

She found him barking orders to the new group of miners he assembled on her orders to scout ahead. He saw her approaching, his eyes widening in surprise at the intensity in her gaze.

"What is it?" he asked.

Reema saw the others craning forward, curious to hear what had her wound so tight.

"Piss off, miners, unless you want me to peel your ears from your heads."

Their faces paled, and they immediately dispersed.

Asif frowned as she grabbed his arm and pulled him away.

"Asif," she said, her voice low and urgent. "Ra'ad said he thought he saw a village nearby. We have to go."

"Why?"

She glanced toward Ra'ad, who had laid down beside his brother in an attempt to rest—rest that she doubted he would find.

"Omar isn't infected."

Color drained from his face. "He's poisoned?"

"The slaver's dagger, apparently. I know Yaqoub said he needs rest, but he's going to die if we don't do something about it."

His jaw clenched, anger flashing in his eyes. "Sundamned bastards..."

"I don't think he'll make it to Zareen. If it were the mines, he might last longer, but out here in the desert?"

He shook his head, agreeing. "Did Ra'ad say what kind of poison it was?"

"No. But *think*, what kind of poison would a slaver have access to out here?"

He grimaced, running his hand over his skull, fingers brushing against stubble. "Snakes, maybe?"

"Could be a gold-scaled viper, who knows. But the closest desert village might have some antidote that could save him, or at least keep him alive long enough until we reach Zareen."

Asif looked at her, gears turning in his mind. Then he nodded. "I'll go with the scouts, see what I find there."

"I can't just stand by and watch Omar die. I'm going with you."

"No way in the seven hells, you will," a voice snapped.

Reema and Asif spun to see Renfri stomping through the sand toward them. Her face flushed with fury. "I'm guessing you two have some idea to save your friend, but if you leave, the rest of this army will *crumble*."

"So *let* it," Reema seethed. "Let it crumble if it means Omar lives."

Renfri's voice softened, her fury cooling, but she still stood firm. "You came to the surface, promising to do everything you could to stop the Djinn. This army of miners trusted their lives to you. You can't piss off anytime you like. You're their gang lord."

Reema clenched and unclenched her hands, frustration radiating from her in waves. Renfri had a point. As much as she hated to think it, she shouldn't be leaving the miners.

"What's going on?"

Alaric approached, drawing their attention. Renfri rolled her eyes, and Asif grumbled about this turning into an Angel-damned party.

"You're going somewhere?" Alaric asked.

"A local village to find an antidote for Omar," Asif said, drawing Alaric's attention. "He's poisoned."

Alaric glanced at Reema. "I'll go with you."

"Damn the deep, do *none* of you care about these miners?" Renfri asked. "It'll be bad enough when they see that you're gone, Reema, but it'll be worse when they see you've *both* gone. *Again*."

Reema ground her teeth, feeling trapped. Her eyes passed from Renfri's to Asif's and then, finally, to Alaric's. She gazed into the glow of his brown eyes.

"Unless they think she's still here," Alaric said softly.

"What?" Renfri asked.

"You could pretend to be Reema."

"I thought when that steel band came off you'd be able to see. But it's clear you're still sundamned blind. I don't look anything like her."

"Not up close, no. But at a distance? Maybe."

"You're not making any sense."

"What I'm saying is," Alaric glanced toward Reema, "while they're resting here until Omar gets better, you and I can spend our time on a nearby dune. Close enough for them to see, but far enough they can't tell who. I'll bring the camel, make it more convincing."

Reema froze, Renfri's words suddenly playing in her mind. *Let me take care of him for you.* They would be alone, and all she could think of was how it would be the perfect time for Renfri to make good on her threat.

"That's a terrible idea," Asif said flatly.

"Actually, it might work," Renfri said with a shake of her head. "If you and the other scouts slip away at sunset, you'll have a night's worth of time to get what you need. But you *have* to be back by morning. Any longer, and things go wrong."

The thought of Alaric spending a night with Renfri on an isolated dune left a bad taste in Reema's mouth. Not because she was jealous—she wasn't—but because she remembered Renfri's promise to handle things if she did not. And what better opportunity was there to put an end to Alaric than with Reema gone?

Tension settled into her muscles, bringing an ache that made her want to draw her shiv and slit her Second's throat. But doing something like that would splinter her army, and Angel knows she would need them in the days to come.

She studied Renfri carefully. Asif vouched for her, said she had a good head on her shoulders. And Renfri, for as cruel as Reema had always known her to be, had surprised her by being vulnerable. What if this was simply her giving Reema a chance to save someone close to her?

"Reema?" Alaric asked, his brows furrowed in concern.

She met his gaze, and in the glow of those brown eyes, remembered her promise to herself. She had to kill her own heart, sever the ties between them until she deserved him, until she'd fixed everything she'd done. Otherwise, the world—and he—would fall to ruin beneath the weight of her distraction.

"Fine," she said, trying to keep her voice neutral. But it came out far too cold. "I'll go with the miners, and we'll be back by morning, whatever happens."

She looked away from Alaric before she could see his expression.

"Asif, go with her," Renfri said. "Keep her safe, cause if she does something stupid, then..." She shook her head. "Can you just do that? For my own Angel-damned sanity?"

"I will," Asif said with a serious nod.

Renfri clapped her hands with a sudden grin, the sharp sound echoing across the chasm formed between Reema and Alaric. "Then I'll see you at first light." Her smile disappeared as fast as it came. "Don't mess things up."

She spun on her heel and walked away. Reema and Alaric stared at each other.

"I'll get the scouts ready, let them know what's going on," Asif muttered before taking his leave.

"Reema, I—" Alaric started.

She turned away. She didn't have time to do this with Alaric. Omar's life depended on her finding an antidote. She made her way to Ra'ad, hoping he could share more details about the village. He'd want to come, but with how fast they'd have to move, and how exhausted he had to be, there was no chance she could allow that. Besides, if Omar *did* pass away while they were gone ... she couldn't stomach the idea of Ra'ad not being here for him.

Reema could feel Alaric's eyes on her, following her, waiting for her to look back. But she didn't.

CHAPTER
TWELVE

Waiting for the sun to finally touch the horizon was torture. But when it did, it painted the sky with brush-strokes of purples, reds, and oranges. Omar muttered something about it being beautiful, how the Angel had gifted him this sight one last time, as if he knew he wouldn't live to see another sunset.

But damn the deep, Reema wouldn't let that happen.

The scouts waited at the edge of the miners' army, prepared and grim-faced. They knew their true mission and the consequences if they let slip that Reema was stepping away. Their expressions showed they thought it best she stayed with the miners, but they had no say in it, and they knew it.

Reema found her way to Renfri and began to pass over the strips of red fabric from the dress that had kept her skin covered. She doubted that even at a middling range, the miners would get them confused. But she hoped that with some distance and the distinct red markers, the miners wouldn't feel the need to look too close.

As Renfri tied the strips over her bare skin, her gaze met Reema's. "Love or power. Did you decide what you want, Ifrit?"

"I did."

"And?"

Reema's expression hardened.

Renfri's smile was taunting. "Good. Be safe out there."

Reema nodded, returning to where Asif waited with the other miners. As she walked away, it took all her strength not to look at Alaric's silhouette on the distant sand dune, camel at his side, the glow of his brown eyes lost in the distance.

But she couldn't help herself. When her eyes landed on him, she felt a pang in her heart at the sight of him watching the horizon, knowing that things wouldn't be the same when she returned. For her, this was more than leaving him to save Omar. It was cutting the thread between them, freeing him so she could focus on what truly mattered—the Djinn.

Asif stood with his hands on his hips, a worried expression on his face. Behind him, the miners were straightening the ties on their sandals and adjusting their weapons.

"You ready?" he asked.

"Let's go."

Asif motioned for the miners, and carefully, discreetly, they surrounded Reema, obscuring her from view. They started off toward the empty expanse of the desert, the moon and stars shining brilliantly overhead, and the cold desert air blowing gently past them.

With Omar's life on the line, Reema pushed her way through the scouts to the front, setting the pace as sand kicked up behind her.

The endless expanse offered her peace from the turmoil of her thoughts, and she seized it with both hands. She pushed herself harder, the cool night air whipping past, carrying the sting of sand and the smell of rising dust. Her feet pounded up and over the sand dunes, each step a rhythmic beat that matched her racing heart.

Her muscles burned as she lost herself in the steady rhythm of the run. The desert stretched out before her, a sea of shadows and moonlight. The sight was breathtaking, and try as she might, she couldn't help but be reminded of the night she lay with Alaric.

Tears burned behind her eyes. She gritted her teeth and pushed herself faster, ignoring the miners' curses behind her. Asif ran at her side, his clenched jaw and steely gaze focused forward, as though he were fighting his own demons.

She checked the stars, following the direction Ra'ad had given. His directions were simple: keep the North Star to the west.

Soon, the world around her blurred into motion. Time stretched and bent, minutes blending into hours. Reema's body ached, rebelling as she had never run this far, but she pushed through the pain, driven by the fear of Omar's death.

Finally, after what felt like an eternity, she saw it—a

small cluster of buildings rising from the sand. Her gaze narrowed, searching for some flicker of light, but there was nothing. It was dark.

Reema slowed her pace, her breaths coming in ragged gasps. She stumbled, her legs trembling from exertion. She glanced over her shoulder, seeing the others catching their breath, hands on their heads to open their lungs. Everyone had managed to keep up. That was good.

"Keep quiet," she said, in case it wasn't obvious. They might not be in the mines anymore, but out here, in the endless, empty desert, sound had a way of carrying too.

As they approached the village, Reema felt something strangely familiar about the place. She tried to place it, pulling at the depths of her memory.

"Do you hear that?" Asif breathed next to her, his voice soft enough for only her to hear.

She frowned and craned her head, listening for a distinctive sound. But she heard nothing. She shook her head.

"Exactly."

She exchanged a glance with him and quietly drew the shiv from her waist. The others drew their weapons —pickaxes slung over their shoulders, small blades taken from the barracks by the Hole, and their marble shivs from the mines. She searched their faces for any nervousness, but to her surprise, their gazes were sturdy, hardened. She suspected Asif had handpicked them for that very reason.

As they grew closer to the village, the familiar sensation intensified until it made it difficult to breathe. A

long-forgotten memory surfaced—her and Hana as children, running through a small street, their laughter
echoing in her mind.

She slowed, goosebumps rising along her arms as the
hairs on the back of her neck stood up.

"What is it?" Asif asked.

As memory after memory assaulted her, the sounds
of the past pulling her deeper into fear and hope, she
scanned the buildings, searching for the one thing that
could distinguish the village.

Then she saw it.

The well at the edge of the village, exactly where she
remembered it. Her heart sputtered, and her stomach
dropped. Her eyes caught on the small block of sandstone next to the well, a long-forgotten memory rising to
the surface of a time when she'd tripped over it as a child
and fell into the well. She could remember how her
screams echoed off the walls, how she had plunged into
the water, her only hope against drowning being the
small bucket tied to the surface. Her mother had come
running, calling her name in pure fear. And when her
father had pulled her back to the surface, he yelled at her.
She had been hurt back then, confused why he'd yell at
her after she nearly died. But she understood now—he'd
been so afraid to lose her. That was why he and her
mother held her so tight it hurt.

Her mouth parted as her gaze shifted slowly to where
she knew her home was, where her parents might still
be. All of a sudden, the hard shell of the Ifrit cracked, and
the frightened girl who had been kidnapped by the
slavers returned.

"Baba," she whispered, her voice cracked. It was the first time she'd called for her father since the day Hana was murdered.

She shot forward, blasting past the miners and racing toward the village of Mirash. Asif called after her, but his voice was drowned out by the roar of blood in her ears. She whispered for her father again, and her mother, an unbidden smile coming to her lips. She could imagine their arms wrapping around her, holding her tight after so many years. She could imagine the scent of tobacco on her father, from when he smoked. She could imagine her mother's kisses on her brow. She could imagine how they'd cry when they heard about Hana's murder.

But just then, the wind shifted.

All thoughts of her parents vanished with the sudden stench of smoke and ash wafting over her.

A sense of doom settled over her as the realization sank in. Grief, worry, and fear surged through her, hitting like a physical blow. It was as if the universe itself conspired to tear her apart, piece by piece. She could barely breathe, her lungs constricting under the weight of fear.

Asif called for her, his voice booming through the damning silence, but she ignored him as she raced through Mirash. The golden sands were burnt black, the sandstone walls ruined beneath crumbling roofs.

Her mind filled with images of the people who once lived here. The blacksmith who always smiled at her and Hana, the baker who gave them sweet rolls when they sang for her, the old teacher who taught them Sundara's history. All of them were gone, their homes destroyed and turned to ruins.

She slowed as she approached her childhood home, the sight of it stopping her dead in her tracks. Here, the strong walls and roof that had sheltered her from the cruel sun were gone, reduced to ash. Her eyes passed over the sand, scorched by something so hot it had turned to shards of glass.

Her pounding heart stilled. She longed to go inside, to find proof her parents had escaped, but she hesitated. The fear of what she might find rooted her to the spot.

The soft crunch of Asif's footsteps over the sand reached her ears, and a moment later, she felt his hand on her shoulder. She looked at him over her shoulder, seeing his eyes filled with a deep sadness, reflecting the grief that threatened to consume her.

"We should go," he said, his voice soft.

She looked back toward her destroyed home.

"Reema," he said again, more insistent.

But she pulled away. She crossed the shards of glass, not caring how they cut her, because she had to know.

Her heart ached with every step, the weight of memories pressing down on her. She could almost hear the laughter that once filled these walls, echoes of happier times. Grief overwhelmed her, a tidal wave of sorrow threatening to drown her.

She reached the ruins and began to push aside the rubble. The smell of smoke wormed into her lungs, making it hard to breathe. She struggled to see through the gloom. With a grunt, she reached for a fallen block of sandstone. She drew her hand back with a hiss—it was still hot.

Frustrated, she wrapped her hands in her tunic and set them against the wall. The veins in her neck strained as she lifted it, pushing it aside.

Then she froze.

The sight before her was more gruesome than any nightmare she'd ever had. Her parents' bodies lay next to one another, twisted into grotesque shapes, charred black. Their mouths were stretched in silent screams, their skulls locked in eternal agony. The air was thick with the acrid stench of burnt flesh, clinging to her skin and filling her lungs.

She stumbled back, staring at the blackened corpses, unable to tear her eyes away from the remains of her mother and father. This was all that was left of the parents who had held her, loved her, protected her.

A strangled sob escaped her. This was her doing. By releasing the Djinn, she'd brought this upon them. The realization was a dagger in her heart, twisting with every breath.

Asif came from behind, having followed her through the glass-sharded sand. He saw what she saw and grabbed her, despite her protests, carrying her away. But it didn't matter how far he took her, because the sight of her parents in agonizing pain as they held each other in their final moments would stay with her until the end of her days.

She didn't remember much after that, except that Asif took her into the desert, and she screamed until she had no voice left. The scouts returned later, empty-handed despite having searched every building still standing in Mirash.

As they made their way back to the miner army, crossing the empty desert, Reema noticed the darkness had snuffed out the stars and the moon. The cold air seeped into her bones, trying to snuff out any remaining warmth. But it would find none.

Like her parents, she was nothing but ash and memories.

CHAPTER
THIRTEEN

Reema, Asif, and the rest of the scout miners returned before sunrise. The darkness began to soften, preparing for the first rays of sunlight to kiss the sky. She could already tell the dawn would be breathtaking. But it didn't matter. The somber mood draped over her made her blind to it.

All she could see was torment: the corpses of her parents and, soon, the grief-stricken face of Ra'ad when she told him the news.

Omar would die.

One glance to her side told her Asif was thinking the same, his eyes downcast, his steps slow and heavy. He seemed to age with every moment, older than she had ever seen him. She imagined he would tell her the same.

Sensing the darkness, the miners parted as she made her way through the crowd. Confusion flickered on their faces, glances cast toward the sand dune where Alaric and Renfri were.

At last, she saw Ra'ad. He was sleeping near Omar,

his face worried but peaceful, wearing an expression of hope she knew he would never feel again. She paused, the crunch of sand beneath her feet fading into silence. A heavy silence rushed in.

"Let me tell him," Asif said, standing next to her, staring at Ra'ad.

"No. I'm the gang lord. I should be the one to do it."

He let out a heavy breath but nodded, knowing she was right.

Movement caught her eye—Alaric, Renfri, and the camel descending the far dune, making their way toward them. She quickly looked away and, in an effort to put him out of her mind, moved toward Ra'ad, the cold air seizing her heart.

She reached him, kneeling by his side, and gently touched his shoulder. He jolted awake, eyes wide, hands scrambling in the sand as he freed himself from the nightmares that plagued him.

Realizing where he was, he looked up at her, hope filling his eyes and a deep smile spreading across his lips. The Ifrit had never let him or his brother down. He was part of her *family*, a member of her gang. He knew she would ravage the earth to save those close to her.

But when she said nothing, her eyes filled with dark truth, she saw the belief in her shatter. At first, he was confused, as if it was unthinkable she could return without an antidote. But then the truth settled in.

"No ..." he whispered, his cracked lips parting. He shook his head, tears welling in his eyes. He grabbed fistfuls of his hair, pulling as if he could wake himself from this nightmare.

"We'll make them all pay," Reema said, not knowing what else to say, her promise of revenge feeling empty. Omar was still alive, for now.

Ra'ad stood, and Reema rose to meet him, only to be shoved down. He stood over her, his eyes blazing with rage, the silence around them thick and suffocating. He opened his mouth as if to speak, but what was there to say?

She stood again, and again he shoved her down. It wasn't enough. She saw it in his eyes—the desire to hurt her so she could feel his pain.

And Angel knows she wanted that punishment. She wanted something greater than the pain in her chest—punishment for failing to save Omar, for releasing the Djinn and condemning her parents to a tortured death; a death the world would soon know.

She rose again.

This time, Ra'ad's eyes flashed, tears spilling down his cheeks. He drew his fist back, only for Asif to step in and stop him.

"Not like this," Asif muttered. "He is our brother too."

Ra'ad struggled against Asif for a moment, but he had always been smaller and weaker. With a single, ravaging scream, he let the world hear the grief sinking into his heart. He turned into Asif, and Asif held him as a brother would.

Reema stared at them, her chin trembling and her hands shaking.

Renfri appeared, her skin more flushed than usual, concern evident in her eyes. Noticing the crowd of miners quietly staring at Reema, Asif, and Ra'ad, she shouted, "Find something to do, or I'll take your clothes and leave you to burn in this Angel-damned desert!"

The miners quickly found other places to be, shuffling through the sand, soft murmurs running through them like an undercurrent. Renfri sensed this moment wasn't for her and quietly left.

"Reema."

When Reema turned to meet Alaric's gaze, she found the glow of his warm, brown eyes soaking her in, and despite herself, all she wanted was for him to draw her close, like he had in the darkness of the mines. Instead, she felt herself plunge into a black void of hopelessness and despair. It had been so long since she felt helpless, and damn the deep if there wasn't a feeling she hated more.

"What do you want?" she snapped, her helplessness manifesting as fury. If only she had left him in the mines, she wouldn't have learned there was something beyond rage and hatred. She could have stayed ignorant, safe from this unrelenting sorrow. She stalked toward him, fists clenched. "What in the sundamned hells do you *want?*"

Alaric stood his ground, his eyes filled with compassion, which only fueled her anger. Why did he have to be so good to her, after everything she'd done? Didn't he see? She deserved worse. Couldn't he go away? Couldn't he just—

The sound of a loud crack rang through the air, and suddenly, Alaric was on his back. Her knuckles stung as she realized she had punched him. Her heart dropped a little further.

Alaric lifted his head toward her, a fresh red welt already visible across his jawline. He rubbed it in surprise. But before either of them could say anything, a voice interrupted them.

"Ifrit."

Omar's voice made her freeze. She looked back over her shoulder, seeing Ra'ad kneeling over his brother, his face a mask of despair. Omar was staring at her, the corner of his lips lifted in a gentle smile. His eyes were lucid, and somehow that scared her more than anything.

She rushed toward him, kneeling next to Ra'ad. Asif and Alaric's shadows loomed over her shoulder.

"Omar," she said, taking his hand and trying to find a smile in herself, but it was too hard.

He pressed his other hand against hers, his skin clammy and cold despite the rising heat.

"Your rage is ours, and ours is yours. Remember?" he asked.

She nodded. "Your brother and I will get the revenge you deserve on the slavers and the uncle who sold you to them. Don't worry."

Omar shook his head, wincing as a sharp jolt of pain traversed his body. His hand shot to his ribs, holding it there until the pain passed. He drew a deep, shaky breath, and this time more gently, shook his head.

"I have something to tell you," he whispered.

"Omar," Ra'ad said, choking with emotion. A heavy tear slipped from his eye, falling to splash onto his brother's shoulder.

"It's a lie," Omar said.

"What?" Reema asked, her brow furrowed in confusion. "What's a lie?"

"All of it," Omar chuckled in a weak voice. "Isn't that right, brother?"

Ra'ad bowed his head. "It's true."

"What're you saying?" she asked.

Omar fell into a fit of deep coughs, drawing worried looks from each of them. When his coughs subsided, Omar motioned for Ra'ad to explain.

"We don't have an uncle," Ra'ad said softly. "We never came across slavers before the mines. We were just orphans, thrown into the mines for petty theft."

"*Theft?*" Asif breathed in shock behind her. That was far too light a crime to be thrown into the marble mines of Sandspire.

"It was either that or—" Ra'ad began.

"The gallows," Omar finished.

They all looked back at him. Reema knew she was going to miss him, but to hear him finishing Ra'ad's sentence ... it hurt.

"We just wanted to be part of your gang," Omar said. He suddenly broke into a coughing fit, then whispered, "Led by the fearsome Ifrit, that was all we wanted."

Reema stared at them, her mind spinning. The absurdity of it, the sheer unexpectedness of their confession, began breaking through her grief and anger. A bubbling sound rose in her throat, and before she could stop herself, she burst out into laughter. It was a raw, unrestrained sound, echoing through the desert night. Soon, she heard Asif's laughter mix with hers.

Ra'ad watched her, a faint, sad smile tugging at the

corners of his lips. He glanced at Omar, who managed a weak grin despite his pain. The sight of his brother attempting to smile in his final moments made Ra'ad's voice break as he spoke.

"It was never about revenge for us, boss," Omar said, his face growing paler with each struggling breath. "We just wanted to belong."

Reema's laughter slowly faded. She wiped the tears from her eyes and gave Omar a rare smile. She couldn't help but notice how shallow his breaths had become.

"You sundamned idiots," she whispered. Her gaze passed from Ra'ad to Omar as she took his hand. "You will always belong."

Omar's eyes sparkled with a faint light, his grip on her hand tightening slightly. "Thank you, Ifrit," he whispered, his voice barely audible. "Thank you for everything."

Reema leaned in, pressing her forehead gently against his. "Rest now, Omar. I'll take care of your brother."

Omar smiled at her, before looking to his brother. His eyes slowly began to flutter, his face relaxing. He turned to his brother. "I guess I'll ... see you ..."

His eyes fell shut, and his words hung on empty air. His last rattling breath passed through stilled lips, like all the wind had gone out of the world.

Ra'ad let out a strained noise, like a wounded animal. He bent over his brother as his heart shattered with grief. Through gasping sobs, she heard him whisper the rest of his brother's sentence one last time.

"... in the seventh hell."

Reema's heart seized as she stared, waiting for him to open his eyes and for them to announce that it was all a trick just to see how emotional they could make her. But it wasn't.

When she stood, her knees quivered, as if they might buckle under the weight of her emotions. Her face was dry of tears, like she was empty of them. But next to her, Asif's eyes were as wet as she had ever seen them. Even Alaric, who had known Omar for only a brief time, seemed somber.

"Asif, gather the pickaxes," she said.

He nodded and left.

"Would you like for me to fetch the relic from the camel?" Alaric asked, no longer resting in the sand. The angry welt on his face caught her eye, but she felt no guilt. She was too numb for that.

"No. Omar deserves a grave made from nothing less than my own hands."

He nodded, and a moment later, Asif returned with a handful of pickaxes. He handed the first one to her. It felt heavier than ever. She thought she should be threatened by the grief, knowing how it wanted to consume her. But to her surprise, she felt empty, as if she were getting used to it. She blinked slowly, releasing a heavy breath.

Ra'ad, Alaric, and Asif stood beside her, holding their pickaxes, waiting for her to swing. As gang lord, only she could grant Omar this one, final honor before he crossed into the afterlife.

Reema walked until it felt right, then looked back at the three remaining men of her gang and the army around them. With a great, guttural roar, she lifted the pickaxe and swung it deep into the sand.

Grains of sand flew around her as she worked, grunting with each swing, the edges of her vision pulsing with darkness. She saw Omar's smiling face, heard her mother humming, smelled her father smoking nearby. Swing after swing, she dug, not realizing until later how quickly Ra'ad, Alaric, and Asif joined her.

They worked alone as the other miners gathered round, forming a solemn circle as they watched. She could tell it meant something to them, using a pickaxe to dig a grave out here in the cruel desert.

It was customary for the members of a gang to be responsible for burying their own. For as long as she could remember, it had been that way in the mines. But that day, the other miners helped.

At first, it was just a couple who stepped in with their pickaxes, but soon, it seemed like half the army was working together to mine a hole through the dune, determined to find a patch of earth suitable enough to hold Omar's body. When they found it at last, with the sun high in the sky casting long shadows over the desert sands, they stopped.

Ra'ad carried Omar's body down the mountain of sand, his feet sliding through the grains. But he didn't falter or trip—not with his brother in his arms. When he reached the bottom, he laid Omar gently into the ground, with the army of miners surrounding them. Ra'ad's hands shook as he placed a simple, carefully chosen rock at his brother's head.

Reema's heart ached for him. Ra'ad was no longer a

twin; he was a soul torn in half, left to navigate a world that would forever feel incomplete. Asif, his strong facade cracking, let his tears run down into his beard.

Alaric stood nearby. He was strangely hard to read again, his face stoic and his body tense. And despite all that she felt, Reema let herself lean into his comfort, if only for a moment. She felt his hand rest gently on her shoulder.

When Ra'ad stood, he took a handful of sand and slowly let it fall, watching as the grains covered Omar's body in a final, silent farewell. The desert winds seemed to sing a mournful dirge, carrying his grief to the heavens. Asif went next, pouring sand over him, and then Reema. She could feel every grain leaving her hand. Renfri followed, respectfully leading the other miners as, one by one, they buried Omar with handfuls of sand, until the dune returned, with a twin buried at its heart.

By the time the sun touched the highest point in the sky, they were on the move again, heading toward Zareen. The miners did not talk, a strange somber mood passing over them, as if each was remembering their own losses.

That long day, the sun didn't seem so harsh. Perhaps it knew they had already suffered enough and offered a brief respite from its cruelty.

But Reema would have rather burned.

CHAPTER
FOURTEEN

It was night. A black sky ruled overhead, devoid of the moon and stars. Reema could hear the soft rumbles of snoring miners from where she sat at the bottom of the dune. But she knew that not everyone slept.

Though days had passed, Ra'ad was still awake, his soul yearning for its other half, numb and empty. She had seen him looking over his shoulder, as though he could discern which of the sand dunes in the desert sea his brother lay under. As hard as it was to accept, she knew there was no comfort she could offer him. He had to go through this on his own. He had to accept that he was the last of his blood on this earth.

Just like Reema.

She drew her knees up to her chest, ignoring the teeth of the night chill as she tried not to think about how she, too, had looked over her shoulder. She had always accepted the possibility that, after so many years in the mines, her parents might be gone. That was the way of life. People lived and died. There was no reason to think her parents would be any different. But she had never thought she would be the reason they died. Especially so ... painfully.

That knowledge was a poison, slowly coursing through her veins, twisting her heart with dark thoughts and waves of pain. It was difficult to breathe. It felt like she was back underground, in the dark western tunnels with Alaric, where the earth pressed down, trying to crush them.

Sand crunched nearby.

A shadow with glowing eyes settled beside her in the sand. She waited for him to say something, but just like back in the rose quartz cave, he was content to sit quietly next to her.

She glanced at him out of the corner of her eye. Somewhere along the way, his boyish handsomeness had turned rugged, almost roguish. He bore the wounds of others: the dagger cut on his palm from back in the mines, the scars on his chest from a cruel father, and the parallel scars where the steel band had been burned off by the Djinn. Here was a man who knew difficulty, who had every reason for his heart to be blackened by hatred. Yet she saw the purity of his soul shining through his eyes.

"My father would have liked you," she said, looking away.

"Is that so?"

It took her a long moment to answer. "He would have thought you a bit soft, but with you, that's to be expected."

"Naturally. I do my best to live up to expectations."

The corner of her mouth nearly quirked. Nearly.

"Tell me about him," he said.

She drew a deep breath. "From what I remember... my father was a kind and caring man, someone who never gave beggars his back. But you'd never know it by looking at his knuckles."

"His knuckles?"

"He was a fighter."

Alaric's brow rose, and he chuckled. "How fitting."

She grunted, her heart slowly beginning to thaw. "Some days, when he'd made it back from Zareen or Sandspire, he'd be battered and bruised, more blue and black than anything else. But I don't think he ever lost a fight."

"Why's that?"

"Because I don't think he ever came home without a smile on his face."

"Did you ever consider that maybe it had nothing to do with winning or losing?" He eyed her. His unspoken words hung in the air, settling somewhere in the back of her mind. *Maybe it had something to do with you.*

Reema didn't comment, instead saying, "My mother used to complain about him getting hurt all the time, but I think she secretly liked that he was capable. Not that she couldn't handle herself. She was a fighter too, just in her own way."

"Of course. Did she work? Out in Mirash?"

"She did. She ..." her brow furrowed as she struggled to remember what her mother had actually done. Her mother had always been home, yet Reema was sure she had been a working woman.

"Don't remember," she said. Then, more softly, she added, "It's been a long time."

Reema's gaze drifted away as the warm memories of her parents faded like the last embers of a dying fire. She hadn't meant to bring up her mother, hadn't meant to expose the hollow spaces where those memories should have been. But the silence between them, filled with only the soft whispers of the desert wind, forced her to confront it. The more she tried to recall her mother's face or voice, the more those memories slipped away, like sand through her fingers.

She shook her head, trying to rid herself of the emptiness that thought brought. But another memory surged forward, unbidden—her parents holding each other, their corpses burnt black. Guilt clawed at her heart, and she instinctively wrapped her arms around herself, as if trying to hold it all in.

Alaric's voice broke through her thoughts, his tone as gentle as it had been before. "It's not your fault. None of it is."

She froze, her eyes narrowing as they met his. So he had heard about what happened in Mirash then. He knew what she was feeling, the pain, the guilt. But he was wrong. This time, it *was* her fault. She had swung the relic pickaxe, setting the Djinn free with ill intentions. If she had never done that, her parents would still be alive.

She'd forced herself to accept that. Now, it was all she could do to hope that she might someday fix things. Even if she did, the world would still come to know that it was Reema of Mirash who set the devil free. Hells, she would likely find herself at the gallows once it was all said and done. Her fingers drifted to her throat, wondering what the rope would feel like against her neck. Would she feel the strands of the frayed rope scratching as she swung?

"I mean it," he said, this time more insistently.

"I know you do. But your words don't change how I feel, Alaric."

"Then what will?"

She released a heavy breath and finally met his eyes. "I don't know."

The silence lingered between them. The muscles in his jaw flexed as the compassion in his eyes shifted to frustration, born from helplessness. When he did speak, his voice was hardened.

"My father and the Djinn have one thing in common. They like to break you, and make you think it's your own fault." He paused, as though a painful memory flashed through his mind. "This guilt, it's shackling you down. And the Reema I met the day I was thrown into the mines, the infamous *Ifrit*, would have broken those shackles a long time ago. She'd be hell-bent on getting the revenge that's deserved."

Reema remained silent, her fingers still lingering against the tender skin of her neck. A moment ago, she'd been imagining the rough scrape of the rope, wondering how it'd feel to finally experience release, even if it was through death. Slowly, her fingers fell away in shame. Alaric was right.

"Maybe that Reema was just a fool," she muttered.

He stood and brushed the sand off. "Isn't it better to be a fool than *weak?*"

Reema flinched, but before she could say anything

back, he was gone. She stared after his retreating silhou-ette, her brow furrowing as she tried to process that Alaric Damaris had called her weak.

She couldn't remember the last time anyone dared to call her weak. The Ifrit of the mines had been feared, a force of nature that demanded respect. But Alaric's words struck a nerve she hadn't known was so raw.

As she sat there, lost in thought, she barely registered the sight of Asif making his way down the dune toward her. His voice reached her ears as he passed Alaric. But Alaric didn't slow, didn't even acknowledge him. He walked right past Asif like he wasn't even there.

Asif paused, confused, watching Alaric crest the dune and disappear from view. His gaze then shifted to Reema. He made the rest of the way down the dune.

"What was that about?" Asif asked, brows raised. "Don't think I've seen him like that before."

She blinked, looking past him like she could still see Alaric. "He called me weak."

"*Him?* He called you weak?"

She nodded.

He shook his head in disbelief before leaning back to stare up at the endless sky. With a heavy sigh, she pushed Alaric from her mind and lay back on the sand beside Asif. They stayed like that for a while, both lost in the numbness of themselves. The silence between them was thick, but companionable, like together they drifted amidst the sea of their thoughts.

Hesitant to break the silence, she asked, "Asif?"

"Yeah?"

"I've been... different. Haven't I?"

"You've been through a lot. We all have."

She grunted.

"Things change so fast," he said, his voice rough with exhaustion and sorrow.

Looking away from the black sky, she saw him with his hand stroking his beard, his eyes fallen to the dark sands beside them.

"Remember when it was the six of us?" he asked. "We might not have had as many miners in our gang, but damn the deep if all of them back there didn't fear us. You could never have convinced me back then that we'd be taking in a Bloodlined, let alone the son of the bastard who put us all in there. Or that any of us would die like we did."

Reema remained silent, staring into the black expanse above. After a long silence, she spoke. "I don't think any of us could've seen it coming."

Asif glanced at her, his eyes reflecting the deep ache in her chest. He understood what she meant. *It* didn't just include everything that had happened to her gang, but what happened to her parents too.

Sundamned hells, it really did feel like forever since the simpler days of mining marble.

"You, me, Ra'ad ... just the three of us now. Four, if you count him. We've lost too much."

She felt a lump in her throat, and all she could do was nod. She felt the truth of that statement down to the core of her soul. Fate had not been kind to them. Not for many, many years.

Asif reached for something tucked away in his waist-band, his shuffling drawing her attention. Her mouth parted in surprise as he pulled out something familiar. It was a pipe, made from hand-shaped clay. And inside, it was stuffed with tobacco. A whisper of a memory surfaced: her father standing outside their home, pipe in his mouth, smoke rolling from his nostrils and lips as he worked. Her mother would tell him how bad it was for him, and he'd just wink at Reema in response.

"One of the scouts found this in the village, outside the blacksmith's," Asif said. "It's been a long time since I smoked."

"You used to smoke?"

He stroked his beard, his lips pulling back naturally as he stuck the pipe in his mouth with the ease of a man who'd done it a thousand times. "I used to enjoy the taste of tobacco on late nights."

He lifted a rock, struck it against another, and drove sparks into the pipe's opening. It took a moment, but soon the sweet smell of tobacco rose into the desert air. He drew from it, closing his eyes with a soft smile before exhaling.

Reema watched the smoke drift through the air before disappearing into nothingness. She drew a deep breath, and somehow, the smell of it comforted her. Suddenly, she remembered more than just her father. She could remember how he smelled.

Asif offered her the pipe, "A smoke for our fallen brothers?"

She took it, fit it to her mouth. "To our fallen brothers."

A moment later, she was coughing, her lungs tight and her eyes watering. Despite the grief twisting blades into both of them, Asif's laughter rang through the air. He took the pipe back from her and continued to smoke, a humored smile playing at his lips.

"Smoking's not for everyone," he commented before releasing another wave of smoke.

She quietly agreed and lay back, her mind turning elsewhere. Recognizing it, his smile disappeared.

"Do you want to talk about it?"

She looked at him, her eyes narrowing. "Talk about what?"

His brow lifted. She knew what he meant. Mirash.

"No."

He nodded, knowing her well enough not to force the conversation. "And Alaric?"

She wasn't the only one who'd changed. Lately, Alaric had a look in his eyes she didn't recognize. She looked back at the black, empty sky. "I'm not worried about Alaric."

"Aren't you?"

She didn't answer.

"We've known each other for a long time, Reema," he said, pulling the pipe from his mouth. He seemed to be cleaning off the ash from its end. "I know you've fallen for the glowing-eyed fool."

A sudden bitterness filled her mouth. "The feelings I have … they'll go away. I've got to focus on the Djinn. He's all that matters now."

He chuckled, fitting the pipe back to his mouth. "The feelings don't go that easily though, do they?"

"And you would know?" she asked in an accusatory tone.

She thought he would play the part of a fool, act like he didn't know what she was talking about. But to her surprise, his gaze dropped, and he frowned.

"I *would* know."

"Renfri."

His gaze snapped toward her, questioning how long she'd known. But truth was, she hadn't known until this moment. He saw that in her eyes, and with a disgruntled grunt, he looked away.

"You're to blame for this, you know," he said.

"Me?"

"Well, you and that Bloodlined bastard both."

"What do you mean?"

"The way the two of you look at each other, it makes me miss old things." He paused. "Old people."

His wife had died in childbirth, leaving him with a daughter. Sometimes, she forgot that.

"And you want *Renfri* to look at you that way?"

He pulled the pipe from his mouth, running his tongue over his lips as if tasting the tobacco. He ran a hand over his head, fingers brushing against the stubble. She realized he looked stressed, a strange sight because, while he didn't always have control, he had never seemed so … stuck.

"I might," he admitted quietly, as if the words were a burden lifted from his shoulders. "When you and Alaric left me with her, I kept an eye on her, and eventually, I thought... she's alright."

Reema's eyes softened as she watched him.

"But I know I'm not the first one to think that," he

said bitterly. "There's a graveyard full of men who thought that and tried to act on it."

She bit her lip, trying to imagine Asif with Renfri. It felt strange at first, but as the seconds passed, she realized they fit well together.

"Life's short," she said, the words spilling from her lips before she could stop them.

A deep frown etched lines in his face. "It is, and I shouldn't let her make it any shorter."

"That's not what I meant. I meant that as long as you're careful, you should at least ... consider it."

He blinked, the pipe hanging slack from his lips. His brows furrowed. "Consider it?" He stuck his finger in his ear, like he was trying to clear them. "Did I hear you right? The Ifrit wants me to consider being with *Renfri*, the gang lord who is renowned for seducing men before killing them?"

"You heard right."

His eyes narrowed. "And what do you know that I don't?"

"I know that you deserve a bit of happiness, after all the shit that's happened to us."

"Killing Kaiden Damaris will make me happy."

"Something beyond revenge," she said, hardly believing the words were coming out of her mouth. "I also know that the only reason those men lay dead is because she was afraid of falling for them."

He stared at her for a long moment, unblinking, barely breathing. Then, in a voice so soft it was nearly carried away by the desert breeze, he whispered, "So I'd have to make her fall fast, before she knows it."

Reema pushed herself to her feet, rested her hand on his shoulder. "Good luck, *old man*."

She started back up the dune, but his voice brought her to a halt.

"And you?"

She looked back over her shoulder at him, seeing the smoke rise up from his silhouette. "What about me?"

"Don't you deserve a bit of happiness? Beyond revenge?"

She stared at him for a long moment, the silence heavy with unspoken words. As he glanced over his shoulder to see if she was still there, she shook her head slightly and said, "Get some sleep soon. We've got some long days ahead."

With that, she turned and continued up the dune, leaving Asif to smoke the last of his pipe.

CHAPTER
FIFTEEN

The travel across the desert was beginning to take its toll. Their supplies were dwindling, forcing tighter rations. If that were all, the miner army might have handled it. But the cruel sun grew hotter with each passing day, wearing down even the toughest of them. By Reema's orders, Asif and Renfri had kept the army in line with harsh threats, punishing any who dared to think about rebellion or stealing the remaining rations. Reema could hardly blame the miners for thinking of it, though. Desperation had grown over the past week. One by one, they were dropping to the sand, breathing their last as the sun scorched their corpses.

The army had once numbered nearly a hundred and fifty miners. Now, they were just under a hundred. Those were heavy losses, and they hadn't even faced the Djinn yet—a fact every miner was keenly aware of.

Reema stood on the peak of a dune, staring out across the sea of the Sundara desert. The sun was falling, painting the sky an ominous blood red. The shadows stretched around her like quiet monsters, waiting to attack the moment her exhaustion-laden eyes finally shut. They'd bring with them the tormented screams of her parents, forever captured in dying flames and crumbling ash.

Night after night, Reema withstood the assault, washing away her guilt with the desire for revenge. Alaric hadn't approached her again, knowing she needed to work through this on her own. But he had been right. There was a time and place for weakness, and now was not it—not with her leading an army of miners who depended on her.

Sand crunched behind her. She turned to see Renfri approaching, lips curled into a satisfied smile.

"What is it?" Reema asked, her tone sharper and crueler than she intended.

If Renfri noticed, she didn't show it. She stood beside Reema, staring out at the horizon. "I've been asked to pass along a message."

"It's about Alaric, isn't it?"

Renfri nodded.

"And why isn't he bringing his message to me himself?" Reema asked, feeling a twinge of disappointment.

"He was headed your way, but I thought it best he keep his space from you."

A muscle flexed in Reema's jaw as she struggled to contain her anger. She turned on her Second. "Let's make one thing clear, Renfri. You don't keep anyone in my gang from seeing me unless you've got a death wish. Got it?"

"Not much of your gang is left," Renfri rolled her eyes, instantly boiling Reema's blood. But before she could do anything, Renfri continued. "I'm proud of you. I told you love or power, and it seems from how distant the two of you have been this past week that you made the right choice. But love is a damned fickle thing, and it has a way of going back and forth. So yes, I kept him from seeing you."

Reema frowned, realizing Renfri misunderstood the situation. Grunting, she looked back to the horizon.

"I thought you'd kill him that night on the dune."

"The night you went to Mirash."

Reema remained quiet.

"I can be cruel, but as a Bloodlined, Alaric has his place in this army. Just as you do, my Ifrit."

A beat passed.

"You do know why the miners follow you and not me, right?"

Reema glanced toward her.

"It was because they—we—all knew that you'd do anything it took to get back at the enemy, no matter what it took."

"And if I'm the enemy?" Reema asked in a rare moment of vulnerability.

Renfri scoffed. "If that were true, I'd have strung you up in the mines myself. The enemy's out there," she said, stabbing toward the horizon. "And damn the deep, you better remember that. I'd hate to find out I crossed the desert following a sundamned fool."

Asif had told her that her choice in Renfri as her Second wasn't a bad one, and she could see what he meant. There were more similarities between them than she thought.

"I hear you," Reema said, the last remaining tides of guilt and grief pulling back. They still lingered there, on the edge of her consciousness, but so long as that was where they remained, she could do her job: figure out a way to get rid of the Angel-damned Djinn. "What's the message?"

"We're close. He said something about the stars, I don't know. But we're two days out, it sounded like."

Reema closed her eyes, and a cool sensation brushed through her mind. Relief, because finally, they were coming to the end of things. She tried to focus on that relief and not the creeping worry that they still hadn't found a way to defeat the Djinn. If she let that show now, Renfri might catch on, and if she *did* … bad things would happen.

When she opened her eyes, they were drawn to the darkening horizon where Alaric was just a silhouette against the distant dunes. She hadn't known Alaric had an eye for the stars, but it didn't surprise her. It was probably something he picked up from a book.

She felt a sudden ache in her chest, longing for the days when she'd sneak away to read with him.

Renfri followed her gaze but said nothing. She turned to go, but before Reema could stop herself, she called after her.

"Would you take a message to Asif for me?" Reema asked.

Renfri's eyes flashed, and for an instant, the corner of her lips turned up. The expression lasted but a moment before it was gone. "What's the message?"

"Asif, huh?" Reema asked, making it clear she had noticed.

"He's good company, that's it. Don't make it into something that it's not."

"Sure." Reema paused. She glanced back at the setting sun, letting the last traces of warmth seep into her bones. "Renfri?"

"What?"

"You hurt him, I'll kill you. I hope you know that."

A pause.

"As I said, he's good company. Nothing more."

The silence stretched between them.

Renfri cleared her throat. "The message?"

"Tell him to help spread the word through the army. Let them know how close we are to Zareen. Nothing to keep the bastards in line like a light at the end of the tunnel."

Renfri nodded and turned to go. But before she left, she looked back over her shoulder and said, "For what it's worth, the Bloodlined does care about you. Maybe after everything's done, he'll be there for you."

Reema opened her mouth to respond, but by the time she found the words, her Second was already gone. She turned her attention back to the horizon, the sun finally below the horizon. The moon was bright tonight, and so were the stars.

A memory surfaced, of a time long ago, when her father sat her down in his lap and told her how the moon came to be in the sky. She touched a finger to her cheek, tracing the scar left by the Djinn's tear. Rage built inside her once more, its flames hotter than ever before. Behind her, a wave of cheers split the night.

The end was coming.

CHAPTER
SIXTEEN

Reema's army marched through the sands, Alaric's news spreading like wildfire among the miners. A newfound energy quickened their pace and put grins on their faces as they wielded their pickaxes, shivs, and stolen blades, eager to shed the enemy's blood. But Reema knew the miners hadn't faced the Djinn. It was easy to be brave against something unknown. She knew that when they laid eyes on the Djinn and saw his power, their readiness for war would waver. And when it did, she needed an answer.

On the final day before reaching Zareen, she reluctantly sought out Alaric, her face stoic and unreadable, as if nothing had happened between them.

"Alaric, we're nearly there. We need to talk," she said, fighting to keep herself composed. She couldn't afford to be open and vulnerable with him, not now. Anything less than her full focus to right her wrongs could mean Sundara's destruction.

Hearing her voice, Alaric smiled, as if the ruthlessness in his eyes when he'd called her weak was now just a distant memory. And when he turned those deep brown eyes on her, her heart ached.

"Do you miss reading with me?" he asked.

"Alaric," she said, struggling to keep her voice flat.

"Do you?"

With a frustrated sigh, she asked, "Why are you asking me that?"

"Humor me. Do you miss it?"

"Yes. I do."

He nodded, as if he already knew. "I taught you letters, words, showed you how they made worlds. But you taught me something too."

"Yes, how to survive the mines, I know."

"There's more to that than you realize. You taught me to accept that certain things were out of my control, and that the best thing I could do was adapt."

She frowned. "And what's your point?"

"My point is this. Close your eyes, Reema. What do you see?"

"I'm not closing my eyes," she said, her voice firm. She knew what nightmares lurked in the darkness, and she wasn't about to let them haunt her days too.

She thought he was going to push her, to demand it, but to her surprise, he simply nodded. "Okay."

He closed his eyes, squeezing them shut. Reema looked more fully at him, taking him in, realizing how much she missed being able to stare at him without him knowing. But the corner of his eyes crinkled and the corner of his mouth lifted. She wondered if he had always known.

"You know what I see when I close my eyes?" Alaric asked, his voice soft but intense.

Reema crossed her arms, impatience simmering beneath her calm exterior. "What do you see, Alaric?"

"Nothing," he said simply. "And that's the point. I see nothing, because I know what's out there is beyond my control. So, I prepare for nothing. I anticipate it. I make the move that matters because I expect the unexpected."

She frowned, trying to understand his meaning. "And how does that help us with what's coming? With your father, or the queen, or the Angel-damned Djinn?"

Alaric opened his eyes, meeting her gaze with a steady calm. "My father is a fan of making others submit to him. He could find a way past Zareen's walls and take the city by force, but he won't want to. He'll surround the city, force the queen to step out from behind the walls, and surrender under his threat to crush it beneath his heels. Then he'll punish her."

"How do you—" she stopped, remembering the whip scars across his chest. If there was anyone who knew the extent of his father's cruelty better than her, it was him.

"I know him. He is … predictable. That doesn't make him less dangerous, but it means we can beat him if we stay flexible and adapt to whatever comes our way. For now, our only goal is to meet the Queen. We'll worry about the Djinn after that."

"And how're we supposed to do that if the city's surrounded?"

He smirked, saying nothing more than, "Leave that to me."

Reema's miner army crept closer to Zareen, the soft rumble of Kaiden Damaris's encampment reaching their ears like the distant growl of a beast. The air was thick with the scent of smoke and sweat. Reema held up a hand, signaling for the miners to halt.

Charged energy rippled through the miners as they exchanged determined glances and snarls, their weapons shifting in their hands. They were itching to attack, but it wasn't time yet.

"Good luck," Renfri muttered as she passed Reema, issuing sharp orders to the miners to stay silent unless they wanted to feel the edge of her shiv in their guts. She knew how vital it was for them to stay hidden, out of sight of the encampment, to avoid giving themselves away.

Reema looked over the restless miners, searching for any sign of dissent, but judging by the way they listened to Renfri, she didn't think there would be any problems while she was gone.

Alaric approached, adjusting the cloth covering his face, hiding his features except for the glow of his brown eyes. "Ready?"

She nodded, before Asif and Ra'ad appeared.

"We're coming with you," Asif said.

Ra'ad glowered beside him, his face shadowed by rage and his eyes red from lack of sleep.

She met Alaric's eyes. It wasn't a good idea.

"You should stay—"

"You owe me," Ra'ad spat.

She opened her mouth to protest, hardly thinking that she owed him. But the look on Ra'ad's face told her he was *trying* to forgive her, and himself. This was his bridge across the dark chasm that threatened to swallow him whole.

"Okay," she said to both of them. If Ra'ad was coming, she needed Asif there to keep him in control.

Asif looked from Reema to Alaric and back. "So what's the plan?"

Even with Alaric's face obscured by the cloth, she could sense the sundamned smirk behind it. He turned and mounted the camel with practiced ease, his posture transforming into that of a commanding figure.

A moment later, he tossed down a rope tied to the back of the camel.

"Tie yourselves up, slaves."

Asif's eyes flashed with anger as he glanced at Reema.

She shrugged at him. "You said you wanted to come."

He grumbled and began to tie his wrists together with the rope, before passing it back to Ra'ad. Ra'ad tied himself in behind, leaving room for Reema at the front. She looked up into Alaric's eyes as she tied herself in.

Alaric's voice softened, "Just stay close and follow my lead. Remember, just like you, I have a part to play. Don't take what I have to say to heart."

"Damn the deep, are you going to talk all day, Bloodlined?" Asif shouted from behind Reema, the sudden vehemence in his voice startling her. "You dung-eyed, ugly piece of shit!"

They all looked at Asif.

He grinned, shrugged, and said, "I think I'm going to enjoy this."

Alaric's eyes hardened and narrowed. "Silence, slave!"

He yanked the rope hard, making them all stumble forward. Asif's grin wiped away, replaced by a deep scowl.

"You asshole."

Alaric said nothing as he flicked the reins. The camel grumbled and started toward the encampment. There was a different air about Alaric now, like he'd given in to that strange, unreadable mask of his.

The sun began to dip toward the horizon. In a couple of hours, the red sky would fade, replaced by darkness to cover their attempt to sneak into the city.

Alaric led the way, the camel's slow, steady gait carrying him forward with an air of authority. The rest of them trudged behind, their heads bowed, appearing every bit the defeated prisoners they were meant to be.

The murmur of the slave master's army grew louder, a cacophony of voices and clinking armor. It was only when they crested the fourth dune ahead that she saw them.

The sight of the army stole her breath away. It was a sea of opulence: rich, vibrant tents stretched as far as she could see, their colors vivid against the sandy backdrop. Bloodlined strolled between the tents, dressed in tunics and thobes embroidered with gold and silver, outfits she could never dream of affording. Relics granted by the Angel were incredibly rare, but she spotted a few: gleaming swords, daggers, and water skins that never seemed to empty. What stood out most were their cocky smiles, lifted chins, and the ease with which they moved, as if it was a certainty that the Commonborn Queen would surrender.

Behind her, Asif murmured, "It's more beautiful than I remember."

She'd nearly forgotten that Asif had come from Zareen, all those years ago. She followed his gaze to the city beyond, protected by its towering sandstone walls, and her mouth parted. She stared in awe at the great palace, its golden dome shining brilliantly against the falling sun, and its thousand spires piercing the crimson sky, shadowed only by the Angel's throne itself, resting atop the red, flat-topped mountain beside the city. It loomed over them, crafted from an ethereal black stone that seemed to swallow both light and shadow.

She couldn't tear her eyes from the Angel's throne, where the Angel had once ruled the desert for a thousand years before ascending—

No, that wasn't true. He was dead now.

She tore her eyes away from the mountain as they began to descend the dune, the murmurs of the camp growing louder, the rich scent of spiced food mingling with the acrid smell of sweat and leather.

She watched in disbelief as they approached. With how relaxed everyone seemed, you'd never guess they were at war. Some Bloodlined were even *dancing*, as if they were at a sundamned ball.

Alaric led them confidently toward the encampment entrance, unfazed by the pair of guards in shining silver armor. They gripped their weapons, their faces hard as Alaric approached.

"Hold," the lead guard barked, his voice harsh and unyielding.

But Alaric did not. Instead, he continued to ride, his voice dripping with condescension as he spoke. "Out of my way, *dog*."

The guard blinked, his gaze shooting to meet Alaric's. He noticed the brown glow and exchanged a glance with the other guard.

"Sir, would you please reveal yourself? We are under strict orders to—"

"And let the sand blow in my face? I think not. You should know who I am."

Reema craned her neck to get a better look at the second guard, only to feel the harsh yank of the rope.

"Keep your head down, slave!"

Reema instinctively looked up, her lip curling in fury. But to her surprise, she was met with the bottom of Alaric's leather sandals. She stumbled back, Asif catching her. She reeled with shock that Alaric had actually kicked her.

"Look at me one more time, and I will send your ass back to the mines."

She bristled but kept her head bowed, struggling to contain herself.

"If you cannot already tell, I have had a difficult journey," Alaric said, turning his attention back to the guard.

"Yes, my lord, but—"

"I am sure that Lord Damaris is waiting for me, as he has personally requested that I bring the relic that is key to breaking open the city walls." Alaric patted the bag attached to the camel that held the pickaxe. He gave a grim smile. "Should it come to that, that is."

"Personally?" the first guard asked, a note of skepticism in his voice.

The other guard cleared his throat, clearly not wanting to get themselves into trouble. "Apologies for disturbing you, my lord. You may pass."

"But why would he need a relic, after—"

"Quiet!" the second guard snapped.

Alaric huffed, shook his head, and flicked the camel reins again. Reema stumbled along after them as they passed the guards. Her gaze darted around, taking in the scene.

The Commonborn hurried past them, their eyes downcast, their bodies bent under the weight of their burdens. She could see the fear in their eyes, the way they flinched at the slightest hint of attention from the Bloodlined. As they moved through the camp, weaving between the erected tents and burning campfires, she studied the other Commonborns, intrigued to see them as more than just guards and slaves. These were skilled men, shaping iron, mending clothes, and cooking pots whose smell made Reema's mouth water. When she locked eyes with them, they met her gaze with pity. It made her blood boil, the rage simmering beneath the surface.

The deeper they moved into the camp, the more elaborate the tents became. Alaric kept a tight grip on the rope, leading them with an iron will. The tension in the air made it hard to breathe. She knew if any of these men, Bloodlined or Commonborn, found out who they were, there would be no escape. They'd be as good as dead.

She glanced over her shoulder at Asif, seeing his face tight. He gave her a quiet nod, letting her know that he felt it too. Her gaze flicked past him to Ra'ad, whose gaze scanned the crowd with an intensity that alarmed her.

She instinctively slowed to speak with him, only to feel the harsh tug of the rope.

"Keep up!" Alaric snapped.

Reema growled, making a mental note to drag him through the sand when this was all over.

"Ra'ad." Asif's whisper was sharp, urgent.

She looked back over her shoulder. Asif was pulling on the rope, trying to get Ra'ad to focus on him. But Ra'ad ignored Asif, the intensity in his eyes replaced by a visceral hatred that drew her gaze to a tight cluster of tents, taller and grander than the rest.

A sharp *snip* reached Reema's ears, and the rope went slack. She and Asif cursed as Ra'ad slipped into the crowd with his shiv in hand.

Alaric pulled the rope again, his eyes flashing back with a look she didn't recognize. But it instantly disappeared as he realized Ra'ad was gone. He scanned the area before his gaze landed on the distant cluster of tents.

"Reema?" he asked, hoping she would say Ra'ad headed in a different direction.

"Free us from the rope," she demanded.

"Now!" Asif seethed, drawing a curious glance from a passing Commonborn.

Alaric stared the Commonborn down until the man decided minding his own business was good for his health. Once the man was gone, Alaric dismounted the camel and grabbed the rope, leading them and the camel toward the cluster of tents. His pace was fast enough that they stumbled to keep up.

"Why are you keeping us tied?" Reema asked in a quiet voice, just loud enough for him to hear. "Let us go."

"I cannot. You and Asif are wearing the linen of miner slaves. If I let you free, questions will be asked." He glanced up at the horizon, spotting how far the sun had fallen. He cursed. "All Ra'ad had to do was *wait*."

As they approached the cluster of tents, the crowd thickened, filled with more Bloodlined than anywhere else she'd seen. Alaric gestured sharply toward a narrow alley between two large tents. The shadows lengthened as the sun dipped, offering them a semblance of cover.

"Stay here," he said. "I will find him."

She opened her mouth to protest, but Asif's voice cut her off.

"Fine."

Before she could stop Alaric, he was gone.

"What did you do that for?" she began, but stopped when she realized Asif had grabbed the end of the rope and was trying to untie it.

"I'm not wasting time arguing with the Bloodlined fool. Our brother needs us." His hands worked fast, unknotting the end, increasing the slack they had. He'd have them free inside of another minute.

Reema kept watch for any wandering Commonborn or Bloodlined. Fortunately, none noticed. The ropes slid from her hands, and she massaged the blood back into them. A moment later, she and Asif headed in the direction Ra'ad had gone.

Her heart pounded as she struggled to remain stoic. Whatever she and Asif did, they couldn't let their emotions show—the panic and the worry. It was bad enough that they were dressed as mine slaves.

She lifted her chin, acting as if she and Asif were walking under the orders of some Bloodlined. To her relief, the men and women passing them seemed to buy it. But their gazes grew more skeptical as they neared the heart of the encampment, where a cluster of tents waited.

Asif nudged her, drawing her attention to a Bloodlined picking up his things from the ground, his face flushed with anger as curses spilled from his mouth. As they grew closer, his gaze stabbed into them with the sharpness of a dagger.

"You!"

Reema's face paled. She exchanged glances with Asif.

"Me?" she asked, touching her finger to her chest.

"Yes, you. Who's your master?" he spat to the side, his glowing purple eyes blazing with rage.

Names passed through her mind as she struggled to come up with something.

"We've just been brought from the mines for Kaiden Damaris," Asif said. "We're here to do his bidding."

The Bloodlined's eyes flicked down over their clothing, seemingly noticing the sturdy linen for the first time. He scowled, but his tone softened.

"I'll pass word to Kaiden later then of how ... disrespectful his new slaves are." He shook his head. "Unthinkable how your friend bumped into me and ran off."

Asif shot Reema a look, his face twisting in feigned outrage. "*Again*, we'll be punished because of him."

Reema pursed her lips. "Tell us which direction he went, and we'll straighten him out."

The Bloodlined appraised them before a slow smile spread across his face. He pointed a dismissive hand toward the heart of the encampment. "He went that way, toward the main tents. Give him a good lesson, and I may forget about telling Kaiden at all."

"Oh, we plan to," Asif replied.

As they moved away, the Bloodlined's gaze lingered on them for a moment before he turned back to his own matters.

Once out of earshot, Asif cursed and whispered, "He's going to try to kill the slave master."

"I know," Reema said, struggling to swallow past the rising lump in her throat. If Ra'ad tried to assassinate Kaiden *here*, they were as good as dead, along with all the miners hidden a few dunes away. If that happened, then there would be nobody left to stop the Djinn.

They wove through the encampment, slipping between tents. Reema's heart pounded harder with each step as she scanned the surroundings, searching for any sign of him.

Suddenly, she froze. Her eyes locked onto the man at the center of the forming crowd outside the largest tent she'd seen. It was like a nightmare had sprung from her mind, stepping into reality with a cold shock that traveled down her spine.

Kaiden Damaris looked exactly the same as she remembered.

Dressed in a shining black thobe, he towered over the other Bloodlined, his long black hair slicked back, and his beard meticulously shaped along a sharp jawline and high cheekbones. He wore the same dark smirk as the day he'd murdered her sister. But she couldn't tear her eyes away from the brilliant glow of his ice-blue eyes. Cruelty lived in them, born from the deepest depths of the seventh hell.

She hesitated, her desire to find Ra'ad wavering as rage surged within her. The night air was cool, yet her skin burned. Why was she trying to stop Ra'ad from killing him? Damn the deep, why was she trying to *save* the slave master from a fate he deserved?

A flicker of movement tore her gaze from him. Ra'ad crouched in the shadow of a nearby tent, his eyes locked on Kaiden, shiv clutched tightly in his hand. His face was a mix of anger and desperation.

Emotions warring within her, she waited for Alaric to appear, to stop Ra'ad so she didn't have to. She *wanted* to let him take the revenge he deserved, that they all deserved. But the longer she waited for Alaric, and the longer he didn't come, she found herself inching forward. It made her sick, knowing she was going to stop Ra'ad from killing the man who had ruined all their lives. She couldn't even look his way, afraid she'd be convinced to let Ra'ad finish the bastard.

The murmurs of the encampment grew louder as

Kaiden approached, surrounded by his closest guards and Bloodlined. The anticipation hung heavy in the air. Reema quickened her pace, her resolve to stop Ra'ad hardening. She would get her chance to take revenge on Kaiden Damaris, but only when she knew the world wouldn't pay for it. With a single look over her shoulder, she saw Asif following, the same expression on his face. He, too, seemed to struggle with letting Kaiden live, but like her, he'd decided he'd rather survive in the end.

Just as they neared where Ra'ad hid, the flap to the tent next to them opened, and two Bloodlined men emerged. Reema and Alaric stopped, too slow to hide as the Bloodlined ran their gazes over them, their smiles souring at the sight of their outfits.

"What are two slaves doing here?" one asked, his voice loud enough to make Reema wince.

She glanced past them and locked eyes with Ra'ad. At first, she saw relief, his features softening as he thought his gang lord had come to help him take revenge. But when he saw her expression, the relief burned away, replaced by a hardness that made her pale.

"Ra'ad!" a familiar voice whispered, just loud enough for her to hear.

But it was too late. Ra'ad shot forward. Chaos erupted.

Reema's heart pounded as Ra'ad sprinted ahead, his eyes blazing with fury. The world seemed to slow, each second stretching into eternity as chaos erupted around them. Bloodlined men shouted, their voices rising in alarm. The hiss of drawn steel filled the air, but Ra'ad was already too far ahead.

Asif's heavy breathing matched hers as they raced to catch up, their footsteps pounding the hard-packed sand. Reema's mind raced, desperation clawing at her insides. She had to stop him. She had to—

Ra'ad reached Kaiden Damaris, a blur of raw rage. The guards barely had time to react before Ra'ad was on the slave master, his shiv aimed for Kaiden's heart.

"No!" Reema's scream tore from her throat, but it was too late.

The shiv sank into Kaiden's chest with a sickening thud. Blood sprayed across Reema's face, warm and sticky. Kaiden's eyes widened in shock, his mouth opening in a silent scream as he staggered back, clutching the blade in his chest.

Time seemed to freeze as Kaiden Damaris fell to his knees, his lifeblood staining the sand dark crimson. Reema stumbled to a stop, and like everyone around her, they watched the light fade from Kaiden's eyes.

It was shocking to see someone so powerful and cruel reduced to a dying figure. She waited for him to stand and laugh in their faces before sentencing them back to the mines. But instead, blood bubbled from his lips, and he collapsed to the sand.

The silence was broken only by Ra'ad's ragged breathing as he stood over him. For a moment, he seemed lost in the sight of the man who had caused them so much pain, now lying dead at his feet.

Reema should have felt a dark thrill at her lifelong dream realized, but instead, she felt only a deep *wrongness*.

The guards finally reacted, tackling Reema and Asif

to the ground, the roars of their fury blending with the shouts as they beat Ra'ad to a pulp.

"Ra'ad!" Reema shouted, her voice breaking—whether from fear, grief, or the desert's dryness, she didn't know. "Get away from him!"

By the time the guards bound Reema and Asif and pulled them to their knees, they had already broken Ra'ad. He lay in the sand, a rattle escaping through his lips. His eyes were swollen and glassy as he met Reema's gaze.

Despite everything, the corner of his lip curled into a dark grin. He whispered something, his words lost beneath the murmurs and curses around them. But she knew what he said.

"We did it, boss."

Her chin trembled as her heart twisted with pain and grief. She wanted to go to him, to hold him in his final moments. But the guards held her tight. Try as she might, there was no budging. Ra'ad would die without comfort.

Gasps rippled through the air.

Reema looked up from Ra'ad to the shadow looming behind him. She went numb.

Kaiden's eyes narrowed as he took in Ra'ad's beaten form before they flicked to Reema and Asif.

A cruel smile crept across his face.

CHAPTER
SEVENTEEN

"Well, well," Kaiden said, his cold voice echoing her nightmares. "What do we have here?"

Reema squeezed her eyes shut, shaking her head as if she could wake from this dark dream. But when she opened them again, the same impossible sight greeted her. Kaiden was alive.

His chin, beard, and thobe were soaked in blood. The shiv was still buried in his chest, directly where his blackened heart should have been. He should be on his way to the seven hells, but instead, he stood straight, as if he had never been stabbed.

He took a deep breath of satisfaction before walking forward. The sand crunched under each slow step. He stepped over Ra'ad. Reema's heart twisted as she saw realization strike Ra'ad, the gleam of satisfaction replaced by one of grief.

Weakly, he clutched at Kaiden's sandals, but the guards behind him drove their boots into him.

Kaiden's shadow blotted out the sun as he stood over Reema.

"Three slaves, from my very own mines."

He lifted her chin with a long finger so she'd stare into his cold, blue eyes.

"You are a long way from home."

She bared her teeth, a scream of rage stuck in her throat.

He frowned, surprised by the visceral hatred she displayed toward him.

"Do I know you?" he asked.

She vibrated with the intensity of her anger. This man and her rage for him were *all* she had ever known. She'd spent countless hours imagining the day she'd bring him to ruin. She'd spent every night in the clutches of her nightmares. And yet, he—the man who had ruined her whole life—did not even recognize her.

She surged toward him, only to be pulled violently back by the guards holding her and Asif captive. Reema's eyes burned with tears as she struggled. If only she could reach the shiv buried in his chest, maybe she could twist it, finish the job.

He followed her gaze to his chest. She watched in horror as he calmly gripped the shiv's handle and drew it out, the sickening *slick* cutting through the silence. He looked at it for a moment, as if admiring the weapon's craft, then shrugged and tossed it aside.

He folded his hands behind his back and turned away, only to come to an abrupt halt. He cocked his head, like he was listening to something else. Then he turned back, his voice layered with something else.

"Reema of Mirash."

She blinked, drawn aback by the sudden sense of recognition. Her breath hitched, and a cold sweat broke across her skin. This wasn't just Kaiden Damaris. This was something else, something far more sinister. The realization struck her like a blow to the chest. Somehow, Kaiden had been possessed by the Djinn.

It explained his unnatural resilience, his immunity to death itself. It was both the Djinn and the slave master speaking now, their voices blending into a single, terrifying entity.

"*This* is the great Ifrit beneath the earth," he said to the men around them. "You would not know it, but she held your fates in her hands, and she chose to let you live."

Dozens of eyes settled on her, studying her as if she were more than a simple slave. For Kaiden to know someone's name, they had to be special.

Kaiden crouched before her, his cold blue eyes boring into hers with an intensity that sent chills down her spine. She tried to look away, but his grip tightened on her chin, forcing her to meet his gaze. As she stared into his eyes, something shifted—a flicker of dark energy that consumed the blue, replacing it with a depthless black.

"Daughter to a burned mother, daughter to a burned father, would you like to hear their screams?"

Reema growled, loosing a scream of rage and grief that took her back to the mines. She knew if he wished, he could summon the flames, and she would hear their screams as if she were right there, watching it happen.

Kaiden stood, his thin lips stretched into a pleased grin. He gestured toward her. "See? This is the enemy."

He pointed toward a glowering Asif. "This is the enemy."

Finally, he walked to Ra'ad, standing over him. His voice dipped lower. "This is the enemy."

Despite their unease at Kaiden's sudden change, the Bloodlined nodded. After all, he was the Bloodlined lord who led them all to justice. He was the one who promised to depose the Commonborn Queen who dared to steal the throne. He was the one they would follow through the dark and back, too blind to see the ruin of the world until it was too late.

Kaiden returned to her, his voice a low, rumbling growl, layered with a darkness that wasn't his own. "I told you that I was immortal, that I was the infernal, the fire that burns without end. Do you see it now? Do you understand what you are up against?"

She gritted her teeth, refusing to give in to the terror clawing at her insides. But still, she couldn't help but wonder how they would stop this man, this *monster*.

"Let them go." A voice shattered the spell over them, drawing their attention to the man walking through the crowd. They parted before him, furrowed brows and frowns appearing at the sight of his glowing brown eyes. When Alaric stepped into the clearing, he removed the cloth from his face, revealing the burn scar left by the heated steel band.

The Bloodlined gasped when they saw who he was.

Kaiden's voice faltered as he stared at Alaric, shock

etched on his features. The crowd held its breath, the tension thick enough to cut with a knife.

"Alaric," Kaiden whispered. The Djinn lost its grip as he searched his son's face, trying to understand what he was seeing. "You're still—"

"Alive." Alaric cut him off, his eyes flicking toward Reema's. There was a quick flash of relief, but it lasted only an instant before they darkened.

His gaze shifted back to Kaiden's, the glow of his eyes was more black than brown. They blazed with a ruthlessness that mirrored Kaiden's. The resemblance between father and son was suddenly undeniable as they stared at one another.

Alaric lifted his chin, staring down his nose at the man across from him. "Not what you expected, was it, father?"

Kaiden's initial shock gave way to a slow, creeping smile. "So, you survived. What did you do, son? Beg this one to keep you alive?" He gestured toward Reema.

Alaric's response surprised Reema. A low, guttural laugh escaped him. "You still think I'm weak."

Kaiden's smile vanished. "I do. Your mother's blood tainted you, ruined you for the man you could have been."

"Don't speak about my mother!" Alaric shouted, his voice echoing across the stunned silence. He stalked across the sands, guards and Bloodlined alike falling back as if he, like his father, wielded powerful magic. "You cannot speak to me of weakness anymore."

"You think surviving the mines makes you strong?"

"I wasn't speaking about me." Alaric stopped behind Reema and Asif. "I was speaking about *you*."

"Me?"

"You once told me you would never submit to another soul. And yet, here you are, playing at the Djinn's whims." Alaric spat to the side. "If I could purge your weakness from my blood, I would."

The Bloodlined shifted uneasily, exchanging glances. Reema realized they didn't know about the Djinn, but they weren't fools. They had seen Kaiden rise from the dead, and no relic was that powerful. A small crack formed in Kaiden's formidable armor. Judging by the snarl on his face, he knew it. The blue glow burned brighter, the Djinn's flames swirling deeper within them as it took control of Kaiden again.

Reema's heart pounded as she waited for him to give the order for the guards to slaughter them. But to her surprise, he did not.

Instead, Kaiden simply smiled.

He clapped his hands, the sound striking the silence like a hammer on steel. "Very good, Alaric Damaris. I will grant your request. I will let your Commonborn friends go."

Reema breathed a sigh of relief as the guards released her and Asif. They rose to their feet, and she moved toward Ra'ad, a faint hope rising that there was still time to save him. The Commonborn Queen must have resources to keep him alive.

But that hope was short-lived.

Kaiden pressed his heel against Ra'ad's chest, forcing

another cough from him, blood streaming from the corner of his mouth. "But not this one."

"You bastard," Reema seethed. "Let him go."

He ignored her, his focus locked on Alaric. "Now that you have come, my plan can go forward. Carry a message to the Queen. Tell her to come forth and surrender, or I shall set the city aflame."

His dark grin made it clear he didn't expect the Queen to surrender.

Reema lunged forward, but Alaric caught her arm in a vice-like grip. She struggled against him, but there was no breaking free. His gaze flicked down to Ra'ad, who was barely clinging to consciousness. The ruthlessness in Alaric's eyes faded, replaced by pity.

The guards stepped between them and Ra'ad, their swords raised to snuff out any hope she had of fighting past them. She looked to Asif, seeing the same devastation on his face as she felt.

"We're going to fucking kill you," Asif said in a low voice.

Kaiden grinned and shifted his foot onto Ra'ad's throat. They were helpless, forced to watch as the light slowly disappeared from his eyes. Ra'ad's head rolled toward Reema, a single unspoken word on his lips.

Please.

Reema let out a shaky breath, tears burning behind her eyes. She clenched her fists, wishing she could kill Kaiden. But there was nothing. With the Djinn's power, he was immortal.

Alaric tugged gently on Reema's arm. "Come on, Reema."

Please.

Reema wrenched her arm free from Alaric's grip, desperation surging through her as she lunged forward. Her fingers found the shiv buried in the hardened sand, the sharpened marble cool against her skin. The world slowed around her, the shouts and the pounding of her heart fading into a muted background.

Without a second thought, she hurled the shiv. It cut through the air, a deadly whisper slicing through the tension. For a heartbeat, everything was still. Then the shiv embedded itself in Ra'ad's chest with a sickening thud. Blood spurted from the wound as his body convulsed violently once, twice, then fell still.

The guards shouted in surprise, closing the gap between Reema and Kaiden, wary of another weapon. The Bloodlined surged forward, confusion and fury driving them. But Kaiden's booming laughter stopped them in their tracks. The dark sound echoed through the air, silencing them all once again.

Reema stood frozen, her gaze locked on Ra'ad's lifeless body. His eyes, once so full of life, now stared blankly.

Kaiden's laughter echoed in her ears as Alaric wrapped his arms around her, pulling her away from Ra'ad's body. She resisted for a moment, her legs refusing to move, but with another tug, he guided her toward the city.

Asif followed in silence, his face a mask of grief and rage.

Another member of their family, of their beloved gang, was lost.

CHAPTER
EIGHTEEN

The sad multitude of stars shone overhead, blotted out only by the shadow of the Angel's empty throne atop the red, flat-topped mountain.

The bag holding the relic pickaxe was tied over Reema's shoulder, its weight dull against the one in her chest. It was all they could take from the camel before crossing the distance between the encampment and the outer walls of Zareen.

As they passed through the unguarded gate of the Glass District, she glanced down at the sands, where the moonlight danced across the micro shards of embedded glass. She wondered if grabbing a fistful of it would drive away the numbness creeping through her body. But she doubted it.

How did everything get to this point?

She had never been a fool. She always knew her gang wouldn't last. After all, men were mortal, and death was a fate that no man, woman, or child could escape in the mines of Sandspire. But for her gang to be shattered like this—by betrayal, murder, and ruin?

A single tear slipped from the corner of her eye, following the same path as the scar she'd gained when the Djinn boiled her tear the day she'd released him. She quickly wiped it away, hating how it mocked her. No matter what she did, the damage she caused only seemed to grow worse.

Ahead, Alaric walked with his head slightly bowed, his back stiff, and his fists clenched. He hadn't spoken since they left the encampment. None of them had, each lost in the darkness of their own thoughts. But somehow, his seemed deeper.

"Where is everyone?" Asif asked, his voice soft.

Reema frowned, lifting her gaze to study her surroundings more closely. The streets were quiet, save for the sound of rats skittering from shadow to shadow. Empty doorways led to buildings with roofs that looked near collapsing, and several sandstone walls had been burnt black. But the damage couldn't have been recent. Reema had a strong nose for smoke, and she smelled none. It seemed like everyone had simply ... left.

"You think they fled?" Reema asked. It's what she would have done, faced with the danger of being caught between the hopeless city and the cruel hand of Lord Kaiden Damaris. The desert would have given her a better chance of survival than this place.

"No. The Glass District might be cruel, but it was home for them," Alaric said. "They wouldn't have left so easily. Queen Nisha probably pulled them back into the city."

"And you think she can control them?" Asif asked.

Control them? Reema's frown deepened. What was the Queen trying to stop them from doing?

"If anyone could, it'd be her," Alaric answered.

"These are hard times, Bloodlined."

"I know."

"Then you'll know that the Market and Peak District residents are going to want someone to blame."

Alaric didn't respond.

"You put a lot of trust in her. Keeping Zareen intact while a Bloodlined army with relics waits at their door? You think she can do that, *and* stop the Djinn?"

Alaric paused, his harsh gaze locking with Asif's. "Why don't you say what's really on your mind."

Asif stepped up to him, face to face, his lips pulling back over bared teeth.

"I think you're a fool," Asif growled.

"Asif—" Reema started.

"No. This bastard"—he jabbed his finger into Alaric's chest—"has made fools of us too." He looked at Reema, his eyes red. "He sold us a fucking dream, Reema. Every step of the way, someone's died—Omar when we crossed the desert, *Ra'ad* when he tried to sneak us through the slave master's Angel-damned camp. And what happens when we meet this Commonborn Queen? What happens when we find out this place has gone to shit, and she doesn't have a way to kill the Djinn?"

She went cold, thinking about the book they'd found in the library, and how there had been only one solution to stopping the Djinn—the Angel. With the Angel dead, was there really any hope for them?

There must have been something in her eyes, a creeping doubt Asif recognized, because with a throat-tearing roar, he shoved Alaric to the ground.

The glass-sharded sand sliced at Alaric's skin, blood seeping out to stain the ground. He lay still for a moment, but his expression remained impassive. Slowly, he rose, brushing glass shards from his clothes with deliberate, measured movements. When he looked up, his eyes were cold, his face a mask of stoicism.

"You're right," Alaric said, his voice devoid of emotion. He touched his fingers to the scar striping across his face. "The steel band is gone, but I'm still as blind as I've ever been. Every step I've led us down has been a gamble, and Omar and Ra'ad paid the price." His gaze shifted to Reema, then back to Asif. "Doubt me if you want, but I *will* stop the Djinn from destroying this city, no matter the cost."

Asif breathed heavily, his chest heaving with the effort to contain his rage. He opened his mouth to speak, but before he could, an arrow thudded into the ground between them, quivering in the sand.

From the steeped shadows of the arched doorways, guards emerged, arrows fitted to bows. One of them, a woman with a long scar down her cheek and a buzz cut, stepped forward, her sharp gaze assessing each of them. It halted on Alaric, noticing his glowing brown eyes.

"You'll stop *who* from destroying the city?" she asked, her voice cutting through the tension like a blade. "Cause from my ears, that didn't sound like the name of the man outside our gates."

Alaric stepped forward, unfazed as the archers' aim

followed him. He approached the lead guard, his chin lifted without an ounce of fear.

"That's a conversation that I'll have with the Queen."

The guard chuckled. "All you Bloodlined think you're entitled to whatever you want." She raised her wrapped fist, studying it in the moonlight. "But there's only one thing you're entitled to."

Her fist shot into Alaric's jaw, sending him crashing into the sand. Reema took a single step forward, only to be halted by the dangerous creak of stretching bows.

"You made a mistake coming here, that's for sure." The guard crouched over Alaric. "You're a bit worse for wear, but we still recognize you, Lord Damaris."

Alaric wiped away the blood dripping from a split lip and stared up at her.

"Put him and the others in chains."

Another guard stepped toward Reema, and something in his eyes finally sparked her rage. The seven hells roared to life. Before anyone could react, she buried her fist in the guard's throat and ripped his sword from his belt. Asif moved in sync, wrestling a bow from the nearest guard's hands.

The bows creaked, but it was too late. She held the sword to her captive's neck, positioning his body between them, while Asif aimed an arrow at the lead guard.

"You're not putting us in chains," Reema snarled.

The lead guard's eyes shifted to Asif, lingering for a long moment, her brow furrowing in thought before flicking back to Reema. She studied Reema more closely, realizing she'd made a mistake in ignoring her.

"You're mine slaves."

"So you've got eyes. Let's see if you've got a brain too. Take us to the Queen, or I'll spill this man's blood all over the sand."

A long, tense moment stretched, the silence holding all of them hostage against the pounding of their own hearts. But then the lead guard nodded to her men.

"Lower your weapons."

The guards complied, though their eyes stayed watchful. The lead guard stepped closer, her expression softening slightly.

"Do you know who this Bloodlined is?"

"We know," Reema said. "Now take us to the sundamned Queen. I didn't come this far to be stopped by a pissant like you."

"Pissant? We're—"

"Insignificant. You're worth less than the marble dust beneath the earth. That's why you're out here, not in there." Reema jerked her head toward the inner walls of Zareen.

The lead guard's lip curled, and her fists clenched. "You won't get far with *him* at your side, unchained."

"So put him in chains then."

The guard narrowed her eyes but, after a long moment, finally motioned to the others. They clapped chains over Alaric's wrists, leaving Reema and Asif free.

"Now let my man go," the guard said. "I won't nego-tiate with a sword at his throat."

Reema narrowed her gaze, staring into the guard's eyes, tension building as she searched for any sign of deceit. But she found none. Abruptly, she released the man, and he let out an explosive sigh of relief.

The lead guard studied Reema. "What's your name, slave?"

"Reema. Yours?"

"Sedra."

A sudden *snap* echoed, and an arrow hissed through the air. They all jumped back as it thudded into the sand in front of Sedra. Reema swung her gaze toward Asif, who stared blankly at Sedra, his bow hanging loose in his hand. As one, the remaining guards trained their arrows on Asif, their bows creaking as their expressions darkened.

"Wait!" Reema shouted, her heart pounding in fear at the idea of another member of her gang being killed.

"Hold!" Sedra held up her fist, her face painted a furious red.

"That was an accident," Reema said quickly. "Wasn't it, Asif?"

He blinked, swallowed past a lump in his throat, and glanced at her. "Just an accident," he muttered.

"Not like mine slaves have much experience with bows," Reema added, turning to face Sedra again.

Sedra shook her head in disbelief at how close she'd come to dying at the hands of an untrained mine slave. A string of curses spilled from her lips as she yanked the arrow from the sand and pointed it at Reema.

"Drop the sundamned sword and we'll talk. Last thing we need is another *accident*."

Reema glared at Asif but did as Sedra said. She dropped the sword, wincing as it hit the sand. It felt wrong being in a situation like this without a weapon in hand. She still had her shiv in her waistband, but it wouldn't mean much in a fight, and the relic pickaxe was still wrapped in the bag, out of easy reach.

"What's in the bag?" Sedra asked.

Reema hesitated, trying to think of a quick lie. But when Sedra's face darkened and her grip tightened on the arrow, Reema knew that would be a mistake.

"It's a pickaxe. Just a keepsake from the mines."

"Hand it over."

With a snarl, she pulled the bag from her shoulder. It pained her to give up the relic so easily, but she had no choice. She tossed it to the guard, and it landed with a heavy thud in the glass-sharded sand, the fabric settling around the pickaxe, outlining its form. That was enough to convince Sedra Reema hadn't lied.

Sedra snatched up the bag and passed it to another guard. "We'll take you to the queen and pass along the message that Kaiden Damaris's son wants to meet with her," Sedra said. "But if she refuses an audience, I don't want any trouble from you. It'll be the palace dungeons or your blood on the streets. Understand?"

As much as Reema hated it, she didn't have much of a choice. She pursed her lips and nodded. "We've got a deal."

Sedra swirled her finger in the air, signaling for the guards to stand down and get moving. They circled Reema, Alaric, and Asif before starting toward the city at a quick pace. It seemed they, like Reema, didn't want to stay out here any longer than necessary.

They marched Reema, Alaric, and Asif toward the

inner gate of Zareen, past the destitute homes of the Glass District. The stars overhead had vanished, giving way to a deep, velvety black canvas that made the looming city walls appear more ominous than they had in the daylight. Reema kept her steps in time with the guards, scanning the path ahead, her mind churning with unease.

The closer they came to the inner gate, the sharper her senses became. She could hear it now—the low murmur of voices, the occasional clatter of armor, the soft but insistent hum of life pulsing through the heart of Zareen, even at this hour. It should have been quiet, with most of the city asleep, but instead, the air was thick with a tension that mirrored her own. She imagined it was difficult to sleep for these surface walkers, knowing that death was on their doorstep.

As they drew close enough for Reema to make out the details of the inner gate, her breath caught. The path was crowded with armored soldiers, weapons gleaming in the torchlight. Some held long spears, others swords, and archers stood on raised platforms, their eyes trained on the approaching group. As they neared, Reema felt the weight of countless eyes on her, like a thousand needles pricking her skin.

She leaned toward Asif, keeping her eyes on the guards ahead. "These guards look more capable than the ones at the mines, don't they?"

She was answered with silence. She frowned and glanced at him. He was staring intensely at Sedra, his brow furrowed in deep thought.

"Asif?"

"Quiet!" Sedra snapped.

Reema snarled. If this guard knew who she was, or the violent reputation she carried in the mines, maybe she wouldn't have snapped at her so easily.

Behind her, the chains around Alaric's wrists clinked with every step, grinding at Reema's nerves.

Sedra marched ahead, her posture stiff.

"Sedra," one of the guards called out, his voice carrying a note of authority. From the way the guard at the gate regarded her, Reema guessed Sedra wasn't highly thought of.

"Khalil," she replied curtly.

"What scabs did you pick up out there?"

"Guests for the Queen."

"Oh, hear that, men? Guests for the Queen, she says."

The other guards chuckled. Reema bristled, scowling as she realized these guards weren't much different from the ones she knew at the Hole. Her fingers itched to draw her shiv.

"Kaiden Damaris's son is among them," Sedra added. "He requested an audience with the Queen."

The chuckles stopped instantly, replaced by a heavy, tense silence. Khalil's eyes narrowed, flicking to Alaric as he studied him more closely. His lip curled, revealing teeth ruined by emberdust. "Requested an audience, huh?"

He motioned, and the guards stalked forward, their swords hissing as they unsheathed them. Before Reema could react, Sedra and her men stepped in to block the way. The gate guards paused, eyes shifting nervously to Khalil.

"Out of the way, Sedra," Khalil said, walking forward with an arrogant sway, his hand resting confidently on the hilt of his sword. "This is above your station."

"We were the ones to pick him up, so we'll be the ones to escort him to the Queen."

"That, Sedra, is where you're mistaken." His hand tensed on the hilt.

Alaric shoved past Sedra, his back straight despite the clink of his chains. He stared Khalil down, appearing more his father's son than Reema had ever seen.

"Move aside, or I'll make sure Queen Nisha hears your name, *Khalil.*"

"Is that so?" Khalil growled, stepping closer. The guards around Reema bristled, tension thick enough to snap at any moment. "Who's to say you'll ever make it to the Queen? There are more than a few souls who'd love to see Kaiden Damaris's son swinging from the gallows."

"You do that, and everyone in this city dies," Reema interjected, her voice like ice.

His eyes flicked to her, scanning her in a way that made Reema even angrier. Her knuckles cracked as her fists clenched. He grinned, realizing her anger.

"That's a heavy statement from a mine slave."

Alaric laughed then, shaking his head as the sound jarred them all. "Mine slave? She leads an army positioned behind my father's, with enough numbers to change the tide of this war."

Sedra's eyes widened as she reconsidered Reema.

"You're lying," Khalil spat.

"Then run me through with that blade, you mutt. Go ahead. See what happens to you and this city."

Before Khalil could draw his sword, Sedra stepped forward, raising her arms to ease the tension. "Let's not have this end in bloodshed. Not *yet*, anyway. Come with me, and we'll escort these three through. If the Queen says they're liars, I'll leave them with you to do whatever you want. Sound fair?"

Khalil's lips drew back over his teeth, the vile sight churning Reema's stomach. "I'm not to leave the gate."

"Then I'll bring them back to you."

"Swear it."

"I swear."

"If you don't, I'll see to it you're stationed in my squad. We could use a woman."

Reema struggled to keep her anger in check, knowing exactly what he meant by "use a woman." But to her surprise, it was Asif who lost control. He pushed forward, face murderous, as the guards moved to grab him. Everyone stared, surprised by his sudden outburst.

"Asif," Reema hissed.

Asif's eyes met hers, fury blazing in the darkness.

"You're going to get all of us killed."

He glanced at the others, then reluctantly relaxed.

Sedra shook her head and returned her attention to Khalil. "As I said, I swear it. You going to let us through now?"

With a final look at each of them, Khalil stepped aside. "Reza, go with them. Make sure they reach the palace without trouble."

One of the guards motioned for Sedra to follow him.

Sedra signaled her men to surround Reema, Alaric, and Asif, and together, they followed Reza through the darkened streets of the Market District beyond.

CHAPTER
NINETEEN

The Market District was like nothing Reema had ever seen. The glass-sharded sand gave way to the paved road, its stone smoothed by what Reema guessed were the steps of thousands each day.

Night still lingered, bringing an emptiness that allowed her to stare in wonder. This was where Beneath the Sands of Sorrow had unfolded. The characters were fictional, she knew, but this place was not. It was everything the book had described.

She saw the spots in the road where vendors set up their booths, and the entrances to dark alleyways where shadows occasionally passed. When she lifted her gaze, the glow of lamps lit the Peak District streets, and beyond that, the silhouette of the golden-domed palace towered over all of Zareen.

There was something truly magical about Zareen. Maybe it was the love and grief Faisal experienced in these streets—falling for Tasneem before finding her body on this very road, then meeting Amira and walking with her at night. Or perhaps it was knowing the Angel himself had once ruled here, and some remnant of his power lingered. It could have been the fact that her father used to travel here and fight, and now she was following in his footsteps. Whatever it was, there was so much history that she couldn't help but be drawn into the city and wonder what it would be like to live here with Alaric.

The warmth in her stilled, ice creeping over her. A part of her knew it would never happen, that dreaming of it was a fool's task. The only thing that waited for her, even if she succeeded in undoing all the damage she'd caused, were the gallows.

Reema felt eyes on her and, looking up, found Alaric watching her. Something in his gaze halted the creeping ice, stirring the coldest parts of her soul. Warmth returned.

The quiet was broken only by the clop of the guards' boots on stone and the clinking of Alaric's chains. He drew closer, his chains clinking loud enough for Sedra to glance back over her shoulder.

When Sedra looked ahead again, he leaned in. "Is it what you imagined?"

Reema drew a deep breath, picturing merchants shouting their wares, drawing Bloodlined and Common-born alike to their warm bread, spices, and rich thobes and abayas.

"More than I imagined," she answered.

The seriousness on his face softened, his lips lifting in a gentle smile.

"You should see this place in the day," he said.

"Shoulder to shoulder, people on all sides, your ears ringing." He paused, his smile widening. "Things disappearing from your pockets, street rats running off with your coin."

"They'd never get mine."

He chuckled, drawing a look from Reza. "You shouldn't underestimate these thieves, Reema. They could steal the clothes from your back and you wouldn't even know it."

"You sound like you enjoy it. People stealing from you."

He shrugged. "Whatever coin they stole never belonged to me. It belonged to my father. As long as they kept their hands off my pass to the palace library, I couldn't care less."

"A library pass?"

"Is that amusing?"

"Just surprising. I thought you'd have your own library."

"I do, but I've read all those books already."

She glanced at him, imagining how long it must have taken to read all the books in his library. Each passing moment brought a thousand unspoken wishes—how she craved to leave behind the grime and dust of the mines and belong to a world with him and all the books she could ever desire. A sharp pain stabbed her heart, and she looked away.

A sharp intake of breath drew her attention to Asif. He was staring ahead, and when she followed his gaze, she saw the Peak District rising before them.

Lamps hanging from polished street poles kept the

darkness at bay, illuminating the road ahead. Mansions towered on all sides, built from the same polished white marble that Reema and Asif had spent their lives mining. There wasn't a speck of sand dust on them, and she imagined that under the desert sun, these mansions shone like stars.

It shocked her out of her thoughts. How many miners had died in the tunnels for these? How many traders had fallen in the sand, never to rise, as they transported these blocks across a hundred miles of harsh desert? How many builders had labored, fearful of a whip at their back if even the smallest crack formed in the marble? How much blood had soaked the sand to lift the egos of men who thought their ancestors' blood meant anything?

A dark splotch formed in her mind, staining the beauty of Zareen. Beneath the surface of trade and stories of love and friendship in the streets and alleys, there was ugliness, there was evil.

The weight of history pressed down on her, memories of the mines clawing at her mind. The thought of stopping the Djinn, of saving this city, twisted bitterly inside her chest.

Even Alaric's smile had faded, now fully aware of the cruelty behind these hallowed mansions.

She locked eyes with Alaric.

As much as her soul ached, as much as the darkness threatened to swallow her and let her rage consume her again, something stronger rose between them. A clarity —a knowing—that destroying this city wouldn't bring her justice or peace. Letting the Djinn burn it all to the ground might feel like vengeance, but it wasn't the answer. Not anymore.

They neared the palace, its silhouette rising against the softening sky—dawn approaching. She scanned her surroundings in awe of the thousand spires piercing the sky around them. Her fear that the palace was also made of marble vanished when she realized it was built from the same red sandstone as the flat-topped mountain near the city.

It was a breathtaking marvel, its walls adorned with elaborate swirling designs that drew her in. The steps leading up to the palace were gilded, a set of massive doors overlooking them. She had never seen wood so dark, and even these doors were inlaid with gold, as though it were a resource the Queen never had to fear losing.

Reema stepped off the hardened path onto soft sand that glowed in the approaching dawn. She leaned closer as she walked, and her jaw dropped. The sand was sprinkled with specks of *gold*.

She rose, struggling to find something to say to Alaric. But for the first time in a long while, she was struck speechless.

The guards came to a halt around them as Sedra and Reza stepped forward. A pair of guards, dressed in fine armor that reflected the dim light, met them at the base of the steps. Unlike the rough-edged soldiers at the Market District gate, these men stood tall and silent, their faces hidden behind rich cloth. Their weapons gleamed, long spears held upright with an ease that told her they were well-practiced.

Reema strained to hear the quiet exchange, catching only Alaric's name and a quick, sharp glance from the palace guards in their direction. One of the palace guards turned and started up the steps, while Sedra went with the other.

The wait was agonizing as they stood for the palace guard to return. When he did, Reema saw Sedra grimace. She nodded, returning with the palace guards behind her. She rested a hand on the hilt of her sword.

"Alaric Damaris, the Queen of Sundara has denied your audience. By her order, you're to be locked in the palace dungeons."

Alaric's face went slack, his eyes confused as he tried to process the information.

"What?" Reema blinked.

One of the muscle-bound palace guards stepped past Sedra and grabbed hold of Alaric. Reema drew her shiv and lunged at them, but there were too many guards around her. They forced her down, shoving her face into the gold-specked sand. Cursing, Sedra stripped Reema of her weapon as Reema screamed and struggled.

"Search him too!" Sedra barked, pointing at Asif. The guards grabbed him, roughly searching him. Moments later, they came up with a marble shiv nearly identical to hers.

Reema demanded they release Alaric, but they didn't listen—not to her, and not to Asif, who was strangely more compliant than she. Instead, they were helpless, forced to watch as the guards marched Alaric away.

Alaric cast her one long, regretful look over his

shoulder before he was hustled out of sight, a dark figure retreating against the shadow of the horizon.

When he was gone, Reema and Asif were dragged back to their knees. Reema spat at Sedra's boots, earning a backhanded slap across her cheek. The impact left her head reeling, stars flashing across her vision.

Sedra knelt before her, her face serious. "For whatever reason, the Queen will receive you. Well, you and this old man." She threw a sideways glance at Asif. "Angel knows why, but if you keep this up, we'll have to let her know you're incapacitated. I know that's a big word, but do you understand?"

Reema snarled but stayed quiet, knowing that if she had any chance of freeing Alaric, she'd have to get through to the Queen.

"Good. Then get up, dust yourself off, and make yourself somewhat presentable. And as for these ..." Sedra lifted the marble shiv. "I'll keep them safe, along with your pickaxe."

Sedra's men released Reema and Asif. Reema brushed the gold-specked sand from her clothes, and Asif did the same, glowering at the guards around him. When they were clean enough, Sedra signaled the palace guard, and he led them up the gilded steps to the palace.

They passed through the massive doors, where they were met with grandeur that shamed whatever displays of wealth the Peak District attempted. Vaulted ceilings soared above, adorned with intricate mosaics of the sun rising over the desert, shimmering with gold and lapis lazuli. The walls were lined with towering marble pillars set with precious stones that caught the light, casting a kaleidoscope of colors across the polished floor.

But Reema had eyes for none of it, feeling only the searing hatred roiling through her. She followed in the footsteps of the palace guard, ignoring the stares of both Commonborn and Bloodlined, no doubt curious as to why a pair of mine slaves were in the palace.

She half-expected to hear music and laughter—an attempt by the Commonborn Queen and the Bloodlined to drown out the danger outside these hallowed palace walls. Instead, there was only a deep, damning silence.

The palace guard led them through a series of opulent chambers, each more lavish than the last. It felt as if they should be filled with laughter and wine. Without the warmth of people, the space felt strangely cold, despite the soft glow from the ornate chandeliers overhead.

At last, they reached the intricately designed doors of the grand ballroom. Two more guards stood sentinel on either side, and as they approached, the guards pushed the doors open.

Reema, Asif, Sedra, and a few of her guards passed through.

The ceiling was a masterpiece, a vast canvas painted with stars, making it seem as if the night sky had been brought indoors. But her eyes dropped to the crowded space below, where a war room had been established on the ballroom floor.

Long tables stretched across the room, each covered with documents and an array of weaponry. Flickering candlelight and the steady glow of lamps illuminated the space, casting long shadows that danced across the faces of those gathered.

The ballroom wasn't just filled with commanders of the Queen's guard and army but also with Bloodlined nobles and Commonborns. Reema couldn't help but notice how their natures seemed irrelevant as they bent over the tables together, huddled in harsh, muted conversations. Nobles, thieves, wealthy merchants, city builders, warriors—all freely mixed, their expressions marked with the tension of a people on the brink of ruin.

Amid the organized chaos, Reema's eyes were drawn to the grand dais at the back, where a throne stood.

The Commonborn Queen of Sundara was not what Reema had expected. Nisha didn't wear the elaborate gowns of royalty as Reema had imagined; instead, she wore a fitted outfit that clung to her like a second skin. She appeared more like the thieves in the room than the nobles, except for her outfit, crafted from rich, dark velvet adorned with intricate gold and crimson embroidery. A crown rested in her short, tangled black hair, her sharp features softened only by the intelligence gleaming in her kohl-lined eyes.

Reema's eyes shifted from Queen Nisha to the man beside her, who exuded quiet strength—Lord Sher Vasir, her Consort. He was tall, with a tousled mane of jet-black hair and golden eyes. He wore a green tunic that complemented his eyes, but to her surprise, fine scars were visible just above the neckline. Before she could study them further, something glowed menacingly, pulling her attention to the ring on his finger, set with a black diamond.

A relic? Something was wrong with it, making every nerve scream for her to back away.

His face was calm, but his eyes were sharp as they scanned the room, taking in every detail. He wore an air of power so comfortably that she wondered why he chose to be the Queen's Consort rather than King.

The Queen's gaze flicked up as the doors closed behind Reema, Asif, and Sedra. The room fell into a heavy silence as those assembled turned their attention to the newcomers. Reema felt the weight of a hundred stares, appraising, suspicious, or outright hostile. The air was thick with tension, a palpable unease hanging over the gathering like a storm cloud.

Queen Nisha leaned forward.

"Sedra."

Reema blinked in surprise, noting Sedra's soft smile. She knew the name of a lowly guard?

"These are the two who were with Alaric?" Queen Nisha asked.

"Yes, my Queen."

Nisha's eyes fell on Reema and Asif, scrutinizing them carefully. Then in a loud voice that echoed across the ballroom, she uttered, "Get out."

The Bloodlined and Commonborn filed out of the room in unison, without protest.

"You too, Sedra."

Sedra dipped her head in respect and pivoted, marching out of the ballroom after the Bloodlined and Commonborn. Reema watched her leave.

"Are you sure you want to be alone with us?" Reema asked in a dark tone, eyeing the Queen.

The corner of the Queen's lips inched upward, as if amused by the threat in Reema's words. She rose from her throne and descended the steps, the soft tap of her boots echoing through the ballroom.

"You think I'm afraid of you?"

The ballroom doors slammed shut.

Reema suddenly remembered that despite the Consort's intimidating presence, Alaric had said *she* was the one who killed the Angel. Reema tensed, studying the Queen more closely, struggling to understand how someone so mortal, so mundane, had killed the divine.

At first, there seemed nothing special about the Queen. But then Reema noticed the smoothness of her movements, the confidence she carried. Even with Kaiden Damaris's army surrounding her city, there were no shadows beneath her eyes. This was a woman who knew hardship, who had stared death in the face time and again.

Something in Reema's soul called out to the Queen, sensing they were more kin than strangers. No wonder Alaric thought so highly of her.

Her knuckles whitened. "He trusted you, and you threw him in a dungeon. That was a mistake."

The Queen's eyes flickered, an emotion flashing too quickly for Reema to catch. Recognition? Regret? Whatever it was, it vanished as quickly as it appeared, replaced by a hard, inscrutable mask. She stepped closer, and Reema felt the tension between them crackle.

"Was it?" she asked, her voice smooth as silk but edged with steel. "Alaric's been gone a long time, and he reappears just as his father's armies surround my city? Trust isn't something I can afford right now."

"He's no threat to you."

"He *is*. He's a threat to this city's foundation. I'm guessing you had trouble getting into the city, didn't you?"

Reema stiffened but stayed silent.

"Alaric isn't the kind of man who'd travel with idiots. So, you know who his father is—the man who threw you into the mines so you could slave away to deliver him his pretty rocks?"

Reema's jaw flexed as she ground her teeth.

Queen Nisha chuckled. "I bet you almost slashed Alaric's throat when you found out."

Reema held a steady stare, hiding her expression. She hadn't been angry, or at least not as angry as the Queen suggested. Instead, she'd felt more … disappointed.

"Hells. You weren't."

Reema's eyes narrowed, the heat of her anger rising like steam from a boiling pot. She struggled to understand how easily the Queen stole her truths. She bit her tongue, refusing to reveal how deep her feelings went.

"Don't tell me you've *fallen* for the man."

Her fury boiled over, and with her heart pounding, she stepped toward the Queen. The tension heightened instantly, and Reema saw a dark glow emanating from Sher Vasir's black diamond ring just over the Queen's shoulder. But she refused to show weakness.

"You say you don't trust him," Reema snarled, her voice low and dangerous. "But I think you're scared."

Nisha's smile widened, devoid of warmth. "Scared?"

she echoed, as if the idea amused her. "I've seen the worst this world offers. I don't fear men—I just understand the cost of trusting the wrong one."

To Reema's surprise, Nisha extended a hand.

"What's your name, mine slave?" the Queen asked.

Reema glanced at the hand hanging in the air, her eyes flicking up to meet the Queen's. Slowly, Nisha lowered it.

Though she didn't take the hand, Reema introduced herself. "Reema of—" Mirash was gone. Destroyed. She cleared her throat. "Just Reema."

"Just Reema. I'm Nisha."

The Queen turned and walked back toward the dais.

Asif remained silent, his eyes locked on Sher Vasir. The two men stood still, their gazes unwavering, engaged in a silent battle of wills. Sher Vasir's golden eyes were unyielding, and though his posture seemed relaxed, a coiled tension ran through him, like a predator waiting to strike. Asif didn't flinch, his stare just as hard and focused.

The Queen's voice cut through the tension. "Maybe if everything weren't in the shits, I'd give Kaiden's son a chance. But it is, and that makes him a danger to everything I'm doing to save this city."

She stopped on the first step, looking back over her shoulder at Reema. "You, on the other hand, are a survivor. You know what it means to suffer, to endure, to fight for what you believe in."

Reema clenched her fists, nails biting into her palms as she forced herself to breathe, to stay calm. She had to figure out a way to convince Nisha, because here, violence and threats wouldn't get her any further than the nearest grave.

The Queen mounted the steps and sank into her throne with a grace that even Reema envied.

"I get why you've stuck with Alaric. I even get why you've fallen for him. But you don't need him anymore. Swear fealty to me, and you'll have the chance to do more than just survive. I'll free you from the chains that have bound you your entire sundamned life. You can forget the pain, the past. I'll even give you a place in this city. I could use someone like you to help root out the men who infect it." Her hard gaze softened, just slightly. "You could make a difference."

For a long moment, Reema said nothing, her mind racing to process everything. Alaric had been convinced they could trust this Commonborn Queen, and she had trusted his judgment. Alaric had a good sense of people. But something must have changed since he'd last been in Zareen, because Nisha wasn't what he said she'd be.

Still, Reema had led the miners across the desert, losing over fifty men and two brothers in the process. And more would die if she didn't convince the Queen to help stop the Djinn.

A whispered thought crept through the shadows at the back of her mind. Maybe to undo the damage she'd caused and to save the world, she would have to lose Alaric too.

Then something inside her snapped, like a tightly wound cord breaking under too much pressure. The anger, fear, and doubt—all coalesced into a single, burning truth.

"No," Reema said, her voice low but strong. Asif's gaze swung toward her, but she remained firm. She lifted her chin and met the Queen's eyes.

Nisha arched an eyebrow, mildly surprised. "You'd throw away your only chance at freedom for him?"

Reema stepped forward, her heart pounding like a war drum.

"I never cared about freedom. And besides, he's the only reason you and anyone else in the desert is alive. Keep going this way, and you won't be for long."

The Queen's eyes hardened, her expression unreadable as she took in Reema's defiance. For a moment, the tension in the room was suffocating, and Reema could feel Sher Vasir's assessing her.

Then, unexpectedly, Nisha smiled—a genuine, warm smile that lit up her entire face.

"So, Alaric found himself a good one," she said softly, almost to herself. Her voice grew louder. "Someone with some real sundamned stones."

Reema blinked, her anger faltering. She exchanged a confused look with Asif. "What?"

Nisha stepped back, her posture relaxing, as if a great weight had lifted from her shoulders. "This was a test, Reema, and you've shown me exactly what I needed to see."

Reema's mind reeled, the Queen's sudden shift leaving her off balance. "A test? What about the dungeon?"

Sher Vasir shook his head, a grin breaking through his stony facade.

"What's so funny?"

"Alaric will be fine. We left him some books," Nisha said.

"I don't get it."

"I just wanted to see what kind of person you were—someone loyal, or a backstabbing rat who'd sell him out to save your own skin. Now I know you're not." She turned toward Asif. "Now, who's your friend?"

"Name's Asif," he grunted. He hesitated, then added, "Your Majesty."

The Queen rolled her eyes. "In private, you can drop the title. Call me by my name."

Reema's fists unclenched, her anger giving way to a strange sense of relief. Before she could ask or say anything else, Nisha held up a finger.

"Now, there's one more thing I need to know."

"What?"

Nisha's smile faded. She leaned forward, her face serious. "What was that bit about us not being alive for long?"

CHAPTER
TWENTY

When Reema told Nisha and Sher everything, her words hung in the air like a death sentence, pressing down on the room until it felt as though the walls might buckle under the strain.

Nisha went still, fingers steepled beneath her chin, thoughts swirling behind her gaze. On the dais, Sher Vasir stood with his arms crossed, his golden eyes narrowing as he exchanged a silent look with Nisha.

"A Djinn," Nisha murmured, her voice barely more than a breath. "Possessing Kaiden Damaris. Come to destroy the city."

"Not *a* Djinn. *The* Djinn," Reema said, her throat dry as sand. "He's already destroyed my village, Mirash."

For a long moment, the Queen said nothing, her gaze drifting as if she saw something far beyond the palace walls. Slowly, she turned her attention back to Reema, her expression hardening into something fierce and unyielding.

"Tell me again," she commanded, her voice slicing through the tension. "I want to hear his demand."

"He wants you to surrender to him in person. If you refuse ... he'll burn this city to ash."

A grim silence followed her words.

Reema glanced between Sher and Nisha, her brow furrowing as the silence lingered. "Alaric said *you* killed the Angel. Is that true?"

The Queen grimaced, sinking back into her throne. "It is."

Even though she'd heard the Angel was dead from the Djinn's own lips, it was hard to believe Nisha had been the one to kill him. Even if Alaric was right, she couldn't imagine how someone so mortal could kill a divine being capable of shaping the desert.

"How?" Reema asked. "How did you kill him?"

Nisha's eyes flicked to Sher, who stepped closer to her. "That's not something we talk about."

Reema ground her teeth. "Not something we talk about?" She jabbed her finger toward Kaiden's army, where she could feel the sense of doom emanating. "You have the Djinn on your doorstep, and you don't want to talk about how you killed the only being capable of fighting him?"

Next to Reema, Asif growled his own frustration. He'd been quiet all this time, but it was clear that dark thoughts brewed in his mind. He crossed his arms and said, "Are we sure the Angel's really dead?"

The Queen's face twisted in anger, and she slowly rose from her throne. "The Angel *is* dead."

"I'm just saying, the only proof we have is the word of a Bloodlined and the Djinn."

"You'd doubt Alaric?"

"What Asif's saying is, we want proof," Reema interjected. "Show us *something*. Prove you're not a—"

The black diamond ring exploded with crimson light, threads spooling together as they rushed toward Reema and Asif. Before they could so much as draw another breath, crimson spears hovered inches from their faces. They froze, jaws slack as they stared.

"Enough." Sher's voice was heavy as it echoed across the ballroom.

The Queen rested a hand on her Consort's arm, and the threads of light dissipated. Asif drew a shuddering breath, shaken by the sudden display of true power.

"As I said," Nisha uttered in a solemn tone. "The Angel is dead."

A savage glee rose up within Reema as her eyes fixed on the black diamond ring. The Queen had lied, or rather, misconstrued the truth. The Angel might be dead, but *she* hadn't killed him.

Reema looked into Sher Vasir's golden eyes, suddenly convinced he had killed the Angel. After all, the ring rested on his finger. Not hers. With power like that, they had a chance against the Djinn. Everything she'd done could be *undone*.

Except …

"Why haven't you used that to wipe out Kaiden's army?" Reema asked, gesturing to the war room tables covered with maps and plans. "Why waste time on this when you can end the war with a wave of his hand?"

Nisha's eyes flicked to Sher, his face a grim mask. She spoke for him. "There are lives in this city we care about, innocent lives. And we won't risk them until we're sure we can force Kaiden to submit."

"Damn this city!" Reema snarled. "Don't you get it? This is more than just about Kaiden and Zareen now."

The Queen and her Consort exchanged a glance.

"This isn't just any war," Reema said. "This is extermination."

Before Reema could say more, Nisha lifted a finger, silencing her. She took a deep breath, exhaling slowly.

"I get what you're saying. I do. But there are ... things for us to think through."

Reema's fists clenched, but she stayed silent, exhaustion creeping in. The savage glee from moments before flickered out, replaced by a dull, hollow ache in her chest.

"Believe me when I say we know what's at risk. We'll talk it through. But for now, get some rest," Nisha said.

"Time's running out. The Djinn won't wait forever."

"I know," Nisha said.

Reema wanted to argue, to convince her to end the Djinn now before she lost someone else she cared about. But as much as she hated to admit it, she was exhausted, her body trembling with the aftershocks of adrenaline and grief from Ra'ad's murder. She doubted she would sleep easily, not with the nightmares waiting the moment she closed her eyes. But she would try. Something big was coming, and she knew she'd need her strength for it.

At that moment, the ballroom doors creaked open, and Sedra reappeared, her expression as sharp as ever, though there was a subtle softness in her gaze when she glanced toward the Queen.

"Sedra, just in time. Find someone to guide these two to their rooms—the comfortable ones."

Sedra dipped her head in acknowledgment. "Yes, my Queen."

"And Alaric?" Reema asked.

"He's comfortable where he is."

Reema bristled, but Nisha leaned forward, her gaze softening. "But Sedra will make sure you have the keys to visit him. He's fine. You'll see."

Reema settled with a quiet grumble.

Nisha turned toward Sedra. "You can take them now."

Sedra dipped her head again. "Of course, my Queen." She hesitated.

"What is it?"

"She said before that she had an army positioned behind Kaiden Damaris's? Was she lying?"

"I don't think she was."

Sedra breathed a quiet sigh of relief, the corners of her mouth quirking up into a soft smile. "That's good to hear. I'll take them now."

She turned back to the doors, expecting Reema and Asif to follow. But Reema stayed put, casting one last glance toward the war tables. It all felt more like a distraction, when the solution rested so plainly on Sher's hand.

She sensed his gaze and, meeting his golden eyes, found the same grim resolve that had been there from the beginning.

"Rest, Reema," Sher said quietly, his voice carrying an unspoken promise. "We'll face this war together, but only when we're all ready."

With a final, reluctant nod, Reema let herself be led away, Asif at her side. As they passed through the doorway, the Queen's voice echoed softly behind them. "Well, shit."

The ballroom doors closed heavily behind them.

TWENTY-ONE

Reema and Asif walked alongside Sedra, following a palace servant through a crowd of Bloodlined and Commonborn. They'd been waiting in a nearby chamber to return to the war room, and as the trio passed, soft murmurs passed through the crowd. No doubt they wondered what had been said between the Queen and the mine slaves.

There wasn't a smile to be seen, and why should there be? Things were grim, with an army surrounding them, armed with enough men and relics to break the walls down. But Reema could only imagine how they'd react if they knew they stood against the Angel's oldest enemy.

They marched down hallway after hallway, the silence heavy and brooding. Reema noted each turn, mapping the palace in her mind as they went deeper inside. She wasn't sure why Sedra was still with them, but she noticed a certain pep in the guard's step. Maybe it was because she was finally in the palace and not out in the Glass District, or maybe she was just glad to be out of the sun. Whatever the reason, Sedra seemed in a good mood.

Sedra's voice echoed down the hall as she leaned in. "I have to admit, I thought you might be lying. I mean, could you blame me? Some random mine slaves show up claiming they've got an army in the desert?" She laughed.

Reema grunted, knowing how ridiculous it sounded.

Sedra glanced at Asif, frowning. "What's wrong with you, old man?"

"What?" Asif asked, surprised she was addressing him.

"You're staring at me."

Asif blinked, then snarled, "I'm not staring."

Reema had noticed it too. Something was bothering him, but she knew now wasn't the time to press.

"So how do you know the Queen?"

"Me?" Sedra asked. "I don't."

"She knows your name."

"She tries to know everybody's name."

"Why?"

"I'd guess it's her job to know her people, isn't it?"

"You admire her, don't you?"

Sedra hesitated, then nodded. "She doesn't pretend to be some noble. She's Commonborn, and she makes sure people know it."

The palace servant led them through a final, winding corridor, the walls narrowing as they passed tapestries of the Angel on his throne, gazing toward the desert.

"She must think something of you though," Sedra commented. "I'm guessing that meant it went well."

"What makes you think that?" Asif asked.

She leaned in, her voice measured but tinged with surprise. "You're headed to the inner quarters."

Reema raised an eyebrow. "The inner quarters?"

Sedra nodded, her eyes fixed on the palace servant's back. "I guess that's what the Queen means by 'somewhere comfortable.' Lucky bastards, that's what you are."

As they neared another set of grand, ornate doors, two palace guards stepped forward to block their way, hands resting on their weapon hilts. Their eyes flicked between Reema and Asif, lingering a bit too long on their weathered appearances.

The palace servant signaled, and after a brief hesitation, the guards stepped aside. The doors swung open to reveal another corridor, lined with rich carpets and golden lanterns that cast a soft, inviting glow. The difference between here and the rest of the palace was noticeable, with the grandeur and wealth downplayed into a sense of comfort. Strangely, it reminded Reema of the market district.

"If you please, this way," the palace servant said, leading them deeper in.

Sedra let out a soft whistle as they passed several open doors that gave glimpses inside. The palace servant stopped near the end of the corridor, in front of two doors.

He gestured to the rooms. "Your quarters, Miss Reema and Mister Asif."

Asif looked at her. She looked back.

"It's just Reema."

The palace servant nodded. "Is there anything else you require, M—Reema?"

"No."

The servant trailed away, leaving the three of them alone as the sound of his soft footsteps faded into silence.

Asif grunted, his eyes darting around the hallway as if he still expected trouble. Reema couldn't blame him. It felt wrong to be here in such comfort, with Zareen surrounded by death.

Sedra spoke again, her tone dropping to something more serious.

"Listen," Sedra began, locking eyes with Reema. "I don't know what the Queen has planned for you, but if there's a way I can help, you tell me."

Reema narrowed her eyes. "Why?"

Sedra hesitated, then shrugged, though her expression remained earnest. "Because I don't want to be just another sword standing watch in the Glass District. I don't want to be fodder if Kaiden decides to make a move. I want to be where things matter. Where decisions are made. And it seems like you two are at the heart of it. Makes sense to attach myself to you as best I can."

Reema studied her for a moment. "You can start by giving us our shivs back. And the Queen mentioned a key?"

Sedra blinked, confused for a moment. Then her eyes lit up. She withdrew their shivs from where they'd been stowed inside her armor and passed them over, along with an iron key the Queen had given her.

Reema breathed a sigh of relief at the feel of wrapped linen around stone. She'd spent countless hours carving the damned thing. It had kept her alive, served as her tool of revenge in the deep dark. It'd be a shame to lose it now.

Asif tucked his shiv away without much thought, his hand returning to stroke his beard as he considered Sedra.

"Well?" Sedra asked, a hint of desperation in her voice. She hungered for more, for a way out, a way *up*.

"My pickaxe?" Reema asked.

Sedra grimaced. "I'll have that delivered to you. One of my men has it."

Reema hoped the man didn't open the bag. Otherwise, she doubted she'd ever see the pickaxe again. After all, it wasn't exactly common to stumble across a priceless relic, certainly not one capable of carving through the earth.

Sedra must have noticed the worry in Reema's expression because she lifted a reassuring hand. "Don't worry. My men are smart. They wouldn't be playing with what's not theirs."

If they were so smart, why were they stashed in the Glass District as the meat between Kaiden's army and Reema's? Reema didn't voice that thought. But whatever Sedra's ambition was, Reema doubted she could help kill the Djinn.

Just as she was about to refuse Sedra and let her go, Asif interjected.

"Let's walk. I know I won't be sleeping, and I could use some conversation."

Sedra nodded, her expression softening with relief. "Alright."

Asif didn't meet Reema's eyes as he and Sedra walked away, their hushed voices fading down the hall. Shaking her head in surprise, Reema entered her room.

The room was simple but elegant. A low-burning lantern flickered on a small wooden table near the door, casting a soft amber glow across the room. The smooth walls glowed warmly in the fire's light. A large window, framed by heavy curtains, allowed a sliver of daylight to spill onto the floor.

Reema ignored the massive bed in the center of the room and went to the window, throwing the curtains wide and squinting against the sudden burst of light. When her eyes adjusted, she stared out beyond the palace spires, beyond the minarets rising over the homes of the Market District and past the red sandstone walls to the rising smoke over the army stationed outside.

The hairs on her arms rose as goosebumps spread over her skin, a cold chill running down her spine. It was foolish to think it, but she swore she could feel the Djinn's eyes on her, a whisper of his cackling laughter echoing in the back of her mind. Quick as she could, she drew the curtains closed, knowing it was stupid to think they could protect her from the Djinn.

With a deep sigh, she went to the bed and rested a hand against the mattress. It was plump and inviting, stuffed with feathers and wrapped in soft, clean linen. It was the kind of bed someone could lose themselves in for days. She pressed her palm into the mattress, feeling how easily it gave beneath her hand. It felt foreign, too soft, like it could swallow her whole. She was used to cold marble, the unforgiving stone of the mines, the hard ground beneath her back—and damn the deep, she was starting to miss it.

Her eyes caught on an embroidered blanket draped at the foot of the bed.

It was too much.

Reema closed the door, the silence broken only by a soft click. She leaned her head against it, letting out a slow breath, her body still buzzing from the tension and adrenaline of the past few days.

As the full weight of everything that had happened crashed down—Omar and Ra'ad's deaths, seeing Kaiden again, the sliver of hope she'd gained—she fell to her knees. She held herself, allowing a single tear to fall from her hardened eyes. Her hand tightened around the hilt of her shiv, grounding her.

She wasn't sure how long she stayed like that. Minutes dragged or hours flew as she became lost to time, lost in thoughts and feelings. Numb, overwhelmed by it all.

She glanced at the bed, imagining a long night awake, tormented by the image of her immolated parents, frozen in their endless scream; Ra'ad lying in the sand, blood at his lip, his head beneath the heel of the man who murdered her sister; or Omar, rotting at the bottom of a dune. Worse yet, she would be haunted by visions of what was to come.

Before she knew it, she had risen and left the room,

blood and air roaring in her ears as she raced down the hall. She reached the palace guards, words unknowingly spoken past trembling lips, directions given to the dungeon where she could find her one place of solace.

Hallway after hallway blurred by until she found herself in a dim, shadowed place, the walls bare of the decorations that adorned the rest of the palace. All that stood before her were flickering torch flames and a heavy wooden door fitted with a thick lock.

A single, muscle-bound guard stared at her, his face like stone. He must have been expecting her, as he didn't react when she moved to unlock the door.

Reema withdrew the key and fitted it to the lock. At the click, she hastily pulled the door open. A narrow staircase spiraled down into the earth, and as she descended, peace returned to her heart, as if knowing she was closer to home—not the home where her parents lay ruined, but where the unyielding white marble remained untouched.

Her footsteps echoed off the walls. The air was cooler, damp with the scent of sandstone and earth. It was strange. She had expected to hear the distant clank of chains and the shouts of men sentenced to a lifetime in the murky depths. But to her surprise, it was dead silent. In that silence, the shadows grew heavier, darker, as she hurried down the stairs. Just as she wondered if she should have grabbed a torch from above, the stairway opened like the maw of a beast.

To her surprise, the dungeon was well kept, with wooden doors instead of iron, the darkness held back by mounted torches. Every cell, except one, was empty, a dusty scent suggesting they had been vacant for a very long time. Maybe the ruler of Sundara before Nisha had preferred his enemies dead, rather than rotting away in his shadows.

Reema made her way to the single locked door, fitting a different key into the lock. The key turned, and she pushed the door open.

The first thing she noticed was the smell of a lit candle, its sweet scent instantly filling the space. It smelled sweet, like she imagined flowers would. She frowned, craning her neck to get a better look inside.

Reema released a breath she hadn't realized she was holding. The warmth of the fireplace seeped into her skin, chasing away the chill that had clung to her ever since she left the comfort of the room above.

The small cell was surprisingly well-furnished— more like a modest chamber than a prison. A low table sat beside the fireplace, holding a half-burned candle that filled the room with its sweet, floral scent. Beside it, a bookshelf lined one wall, sparse but stocked with a few carefully chosen volumes. It seemed more like a scholar's retreat than a dungeon cell.

Alaric stood in front of the flickering fire, the soft glow casting shadows across his face. His brow was slick with a faint sheen of sweat, and Reema realized it must have been sweltering for him in this small, confined space. Yet his expression remained calm, his glowing brown eyes meeting hers. The tension that had knotted her chest unraveled at the sight of him.

"There you are," Alaric said, his voice low and steady as the corner of his lips lifted into a smile. His hand rested on the cover of a book tucked beneath his arm, fingers tracing its spine absentmindedly. "I wondered how long I'd have to wait."

Reema stepped inside, letting the door swing shut behind her with a soft creak. She glanced around the small space, taking in the unassuming coziness of it. It felt so different from the harshness of the world outside, like an escape from everything. When her eyes landed on Alaric again, she felt the first stirrings of calm.

"I—" Reema faltered, unsure how to explain why she had come. Why she had fled the comfort of the quarters only to end up here in the dungeon with him.

Alaric didn't press her. He simply waited with that damned, butterfly-inducing smile. Her eyes flicked down, suddenly—and strangely—too shy to meet his gaze. But when she did, memories of the desert flashed before her, when hope was bright and easy, before they'd reached Sandspire and realized how foolish they truly were. Her cheeks burned as his clothes faded in her mind, replaced by the memory of him above her, naked and warm, with the moon shining down on them.

His grin widened, sparking a deeper fire in her core. Somehow, he knew exactly what she was thinking.

She cleared her throat. "Wait for what?"

"What?"

"You said you wondered how long you'd have to wait."

"Oh," he said, lifting the book expectantly. "To read with you, of course."

"To read?" she asked, her voice barely above a whisper.

For a moment, she just stood there, taking in the sight of him—his disheveled hair falling across his forehead, the quiet strength in his gaze, the way he remained so calm despite everything looming over them. The weight of the world felt lighter when she was with him, especially here in the depths of the earth.

He turned the cover toward her. "Two Ruthless Men." He flipped the cover open, his eyes scanning the pages. "I haven't read this before, so I don't know how good it is. But it's well spoken of, and judging by the description, you should like this one. It's about revenge, *real* revenge, and—"

She rushed toward him, throwing her arms around his neck and pressing herself against him. He seemed genuinely surprised by her sudden display of affection.

A half-second later, he dropped the book and wrapped his arms around her, holding her tight. They held each other, not caring about the sweat in the sweltering heat, because in each other's arms, they found peace from the monsters lurking in the shadows of their minds.

She let out a soft sigh of relief and allowed herself to relax. For a moment, it felt like the world above, the slow demise of her gang, the Djinn—none of it existed. In this pure moment, it was just her and Alaric.

Reema knew she didn't deserve this. The feelings he had for her, however deep, could never grow into something more. Not until she fixed everything. Not until the Djinn was gone for good. And as she stayed in his arms, she knew there were things they should talk about, like her conversation with Queen Nisha and her golden-eyed

Consort, or the state of the sundamned world above. But she knew that trying would ruin this safe place. Besides, she wasn't even sure where to start. She shook her head and pressed herself deeper into him, breathing him in.

She let his scent calm her.

Eventually, the moment passed, and they pulled away from each other. With a satisfied sigh, she bent down, picked up the book, and handed it back to him.

"Read to me," she said.

"Funny. I was thinking you'd read to me."

Reema settled into an old wooden chair in the corner, kicking her legs out and folding her arms over her stomach. "I'm tired. Read."

"As you say, boss," he smirked. With no other chairs in the room, he settled on the floor in front of her, crossing his legs. He brushed his disheveled hair out of his scarred face and opened the book.

He began to read, but soon, over the crackle of the fire, his words blurred together, indistinguishable except for the peace they brought her. She closed her eyes, leaned her head back against the chair, and breathed easier than she had in a long time.

And before she knew it, sleep took her.

CHAPTER
TWENTY-TWO

The door creaked open.

Reema jolted awake, gasping as she tried to remember where she was. At first, it felt like she was back in the mines, the earth pressing in on all sides, and the warmth of the torchlight battling to keep the shadows at bay. But as her eyes adjusted, the torchlight revealed itself as the dying fire in the hearth, and the white marble walls shifted into the dark sandstone around her. Then, she remembered.

Alaric lay on his side at her feet, one hand holding the book half-open, his finger marking the place where he must've fallen asleep, while his other hand rested near her foot.

And above him, standing in the doorway, was the Queen of Sundara.

Nisha smiled, her short dark hair framing her face as she entered with a roll of warm bread in her hands. Reema's stomach rumbled, suddenly hungrier than she realized.

"You look better," Nisha said, stirring Alaric's sleeping form. "But you remind me of myself when I lived in the Glass District, nothing but skin and bones. Here." She tossed the bread into Reema's hands, grinning at some memory as Reema gave in to her hunger and tore into it.

"Save me some," Alaric groaned, rolling onto his back. He pulled his glasses from his face and rubbed his eyes.

"Did you sleep well?" Nisha asked, her dark brown eyes gleaming with humor.

"Fine," Reema answered. In truth, she had slept great —no nightmares, no dreams, just a sweet, peaceful void. And her body didn't ache nearly as much as she'd expected. She imagined it was because she was more used to sleeping in uncomfortable places than comfortable ones.

"No," Alaric grumbled.

Her eyes flicked to him. "You're soft."

"I'm not."

"Yes, you are," Nisha said, frowning as he rolled over to face her. That's when she saw how much he had changed since he left Zareen.

Her eyes traced the scars: the burn mark left by the steel band forged over his eyes, the stab wound through his palm, and countless whip marks peeking through the top of his partially open tunic.

He straightened, resting his back against Reema's knees. With his eyes fixed on the Queen, he spoke to Reema. "Do you know the first time I met Nisha, she was trying to sneak into the King's ball?"

Reema shook her head.

"I thought it was the strangest thing. A Common-born, wearing a Farrakhan-made dress. She told me she was there to steal from the King and needed me to escort her in," he said with a chuckle. He gestured toward her. "Look at her now."

"What're you saying?" Nisha asked.

"He's saying that you've changed," Reema said, studying Nisha closely. "You don't seem like someone who'd need an escort into the ball now."

Nisha nodded, eyes shifting from Reema back to Alaric. "I have changed. But I'm not the only one. When I met Alaric, he had a lined beard, skin without a speck of dust on it, and if *that's* not enough, he wore *glasses*."

"He told me," Reema said. "They seem like they'd fit him."

Alaric chuckled, running his hands through his rugged beard. "I do miss my glasses. Reading was so much easier with them." He paused, his brow furrowing. "I think I've got a second pair laying around my rooms, somewhere."

"About that..."

Alaric's smile faded.

"Your home in the Peak District is gone. I emptied it out to make space for some of the Commonborn who are helping me."

"Oh."

"You were gone for so long, I thought you were dead."

Alaric sighed heavily. "It's fine."

But Reema could tell the news made him sad. She rested a hand on his shoulder.

"I suppose the Bloodlined and the Commonborn both pressured you, with my father marching on Zareen. What's the point in keeping space for the enemy's home?"

"Yeah."

Trying to change the topic, Reema asked, "I know I've said this before, but time's running short. Did you and your Consort talk things through about how we're going to stop the Djinn?"

"We did."

"And?"

Nisha clenched her jaw, flexing her hand as she met Reema's eyes. "There's something you need to know."

Reema's stomach sank. "What?"

"The magic that we used to kill the Angel, it doesn't exist anymore."

"I don't understand. I saw Sher use it—he summoned the spear from light."

"That ring is mortal-made. It's not a relic, or at least not in the way you think. The one we used to kill the Angel was similar, but different. That ring's gone now."

"What happened to it?" Alaric asked, his expression tightening. Reema felt his shoulders tense beneath her hand. "Did you lose it, or did—"

"I destroyed it."

Her words hung in the air, heavy with the weight of doom. Reema's chest tightened as she struggled to breathe.

"Why would you do that?" Alaric whispered.

"It's a long story. But it was necessary."

Reema's hand trembled as she removed it from Alaric's shoulder and stood. He rose to stand beside her, both of them realizing the grave truth.

"There's no way to kill the Djinn."

Nisha stared into Reema's eyes, unblinking, her stony facade unmoving. Then, in a soft, grim voice, she answered, "Maybe."

For a long moment, none of them spoke. The heaviness in the air pressed on Reema's chest like a tombstone crushing her ribs. She glanced down at the bread, her appetite gone. The once-warm loaf now sat cold and forgotten beside her. Alaric's shoulders were stiff, his muscles coiled like a spring, ready to snap. She could sense his anger building, slow and silent like the smoldering coals of the dying fire. Just like back in Sandspire, it felt like hope had been stolen from them again.

The silence stretched, thick and suffocating. Reema felt it creep around them, like shadows gathering in the corners of the room. Her heart pounded in her ears, each beat echoing with the realization that there was no way to kill the Djinn.

No way to stop him.

She opened her mouth to speak, to ask Nisha to explain, but the words never came. Instead, it was Alaric who broke the silence, his voice cold and hard.

"You destroyed it?" he whispered, his eyes narrowing. There was no humor in his tone now, no warmth. The Alaric Reema had known was gone, replaced by someone else.

Nisha stood. "Alaric, it wasn't—"

Alaric's jaw tightened. "What about your vault? There must be countless relics stored there. There must be something that can help."

"The vault's empty. The relics, the gold—it's all gone."

His face went slack, as if he was struggling to understand what possibly could have happened. Then his face slowly twisted into something darker, more ruthless. "So you destroyed the only thing capable of saving us?"

Nisha remained silent.

"You destroyed it!" Alaric repeated, his voice rising. His fists clenched, knuckles white. "You destroyed the one hope we had." He stepped forward, his presence suddenly overwhelming. "Do you realize what you've done?"

Reema felt the tension in the room spike as he advanced on Nisha. She had never seen Alaric like this— never seen the calm, composed man lose control so completely. The change was terrifying. Even Nisha, who had regarded him with familiarity, now looked at him with shock and caution.

"Alaric..." Reema said, her voice a soft plea for him to calm down, to return to the man she'd fallen for. But he didn't seem to hear. His eyes were locked on Nisha, burning with fury.

Nisha's jaw tightened, her gaze flicking to Reema for a moment before she spoke. "I had no sundamned choice, Alaric."

"You're telling me that the Commonborn thief, brave enough to try and steal from King Razhan, the one clever enough to take the throne for herself, couldn't find any other way?" Alaric's voice was venomous. "You've left us with *nothing*."

"Nothing? There's still hope, Alaric."

Reema's heart stuttered at that. "Hope?"

"Yes, Angel-damned hope. When you said there's no way to kill the Djinn, I said maybe. The mortal-made ring that Sher wears is more powerful than any relic I've seen. So there's still a chance."

Alaric let out a bitter laugh, his glowing brown eyes dark and wild. "You expect us to pin our hopes on a maybe?"

"Yes, I *do*."

Reema felt the words hit like a punch to the gut.

Alaric went quiet, his anger fading into something that scared Reema. He shook his head, and when he met her eyes, he whispered, "Then my father will win again."

Reema understood all at once. He'd lost his mother to his father, and now, with the Djinn possessing Kaiden, he was about to lose the city he loved.

"We're not giving up," Nisha said as she went to the door. "You've changed too much, Alaric. I hope, for your sake, that you find yourself again."

Then she left.

Reema stared at Alaric, her heart pounding. She didn't know what scared her more—the reality of the Djinn's power in Kaiden Damaris, or the person Alaric was becoming in the face of it.

"You should go," he whispered.

"Alaric..." she said softly.

He turned away from her. A simple movement that shattered her heart, confirming her fears—he couldn't love her until she fixed everything. It was her fault. She'd been the one to release the Djinn. The sight of his back nearly brought her to tears. She reached for him, but her hand froze in the air, trembling as she tried to bridge the gap, knowing this gap could only be bridged one way.

Reema let her hand drop and left the cell, the door creaking shut behind her. This was something that only the spilling of blood could solve.

She quickened her pace, flying up the stairs and bursting into the palace hallways. Just ahead, the Queen walked, her head bowed in thought.

"Nisha!"

The palace guards exchanged a glance at Reema's informality, but she ignored them as she approached. Strangely, she was out of breath by the time she stood across from Nisha.

"You think there's really still a chance?"

"I'm not promising anything."

"I know. I'm just asking if there's a *chance*."

A beat passed.

"There's a chance."

Reema clenched her jaw and nodded, forcing herself to come to terms with it. "You said you were concerned about the people of Zareen. I get that. Even if we fight the Djinn, Kaiden's army is still a threat."

Nisha nodded.

"Well, what if I could take care of them?"

Nisha's gaze flickered, her sharp eyes narrowing as she studied Reema. For a moment, the Queen said nothing, weighing her words. Then, she said, "Come with me."

Without another word, the Queen turned and walked down the dimly lit corridor. Reema hesitated for only a moment before following, her heart pounding. Before, deep in the mines, that pounding would have ignited the inferno of revenge, burning through her veins. But now, she felt only a cool peace, knowing this wasn't about her. It was about Alaric. For him, this needed to be done.

And with that, she carried no fear of failure.

CHAPTER
TWENTY-THREE

The massive doors to the ballroom-turned-war room slammed shut behind Reema as she stepped out, letting out a deep sigh. Hours had passed since she first entered with the Queen, poring over maps and discussing strategies. The advisors had been appalled by her plan at first, but Reema noticed the glint in Nisha's and Sher's eyes— they saw the potential.

There were still many unanswered questions, especially about the Djinn, but the plan was as solid as it could be.

Her body ached with weariness as she moved through the palace, entering the nearest chamber. Her mind was sluggish, barely registering Asif and Sedra seated together, waiting for her. There was a spark in Asif's eyes she didn't recognize, and her gaze flicked to Sedra with curiosity. What was his interest in her?

"There you are," Asif said, groaning as he pushed himself up from the chair. "I tried to get into the war room, but it seems you need the Queen's permission for that. And well..."

"She was busy," Reema nodded, her tone flat.

"Honestly, I expected you'd be down in the dungeon with Alaric, not up here."

"You went to see him?"

"A while ago, yeah. But the Bloodlined's in a dark mood."

"That's putting it lightly," Sedra grumbled. Asif grunted in agreement.

"So, boss, what happened in there?" Asif asked.

"A plan's been made," she said. Her eyes fell on Sedra, narrowing as a strange sense of familiarity struck her. She dug deeper into the feeling until a thought came to mind. "Go find somewhere else to be, guard. I need to speak with Asif alone."

"Guard?" Sedra arched a brow, chuckling. But her chuckles disappeared when she realized Reema was serious. Her lip curled. "I don't get to hear the sundamned plan?"

"Sedra, give us some space," Asif said, his tone firmer.

With a shake of her head, Sedra rose to her feet and walked off, leaving the two of them alone. Reema took Sedra's seat, sinking into the feather-stuffed chair with a sigh of relief. She leaned her head back, closing her eyes.

"You weren't going to tell me?" Reema asked.

Asif drew back, surprised by her intuition. But he shouldn't have been. It was that same intuition that had kept them alive all those years in the mines. That, and her reputation as the Ifrit.

"I wasn't sure," Asif said. "I'm *still* not sure."

"Say it out loud, Asif. I want to hear it."

It was hard for him, she could tell. But he got the words through his teeth. "Damn the deep, I think she's my daughter."

A silence hung between them. Reema knew Asif had long believed his daughter was dead. How could he not, after slavers left her on the doorstep of piss-drunk addicts? If she didn't die from their incompetence, she surely would've fallen prey to emberdust or the knife of some poor bastard in the Glass District desperate for coin.

Reema opened her eyes and stared at him. "How long have you known?"

Asif's jaw clenched, and he leaned back in his chair, letting out a breath that seemed to carry years of tension. "I'll be honest, I didn't want to believe it at first. It seemed impossible. But the more I look at her, the more I feel ... something. A pull, I guess. Like a thread connecting us."

He paused, rubbing a hand over his face, as if trying to erase the weight of his words. "Sedra. That was the name my wife picked out. I wanted something different, *softer* if you'd believe it. But now ..." He shook his head, his voice barely a whisper. "Now it feels right. It feels like her."

He chuckled, but his voice quickly strangled into a choked sob. Reema leaned forward, her chest tightening at the rare display of emotion.

"She even looks like her," he whispered. "She's got the same eyes. It's like I'm seeing a sundamned ghost."

"I think she looks like you."

He glanced at her, his eyes glistening. "You think so?"

"It's unfortunate, isn't it? That someone has to look like you out of all people?"

He burst out into laughter, and when it subsided, he looked at her and said, "You're a real asshole, Reema."

She smiled softly. "I know."

A quiet moment passed between them. Reema leaned back into her chair, staring ahead at the painting hanging on the wall. It was a desert scene, with rolling dunes beneath a bright sun. It was masterfully painted, the strokes so vivid she could almost feel the broiling heat on her skin.

"When're you going to tell her?" Reema asked.

"Never."

Reema didn't flinch out of surprise. She suspected it already. "You're afraid of her finding out who you are."

"Something like that." He drew a deep, shuddering breath, and out of habit, his hand went to his beard, stroking it as he spoke. "People like us don't get happy endings, Reema."

"We don't know that," she said, her voice hollow. But in truth, his words struck straight through to her heart. Nobody in her gang had ever been so deluded to think that they would live to old age with people they loved. Each one of them had always known that their stories would end in the tragedy of flames, and none more so than Reema and Asif themselves. But they were all too happy for their stories to end that way, so long as they got their revenge on the bastards who'd ruined them.

"Promise me you won't tell her," Asif asked quietly. "I have a feeling that somewhere deep down, she hopes her father is out there, trying to make his way back to her. I don't want her to know that I thought she was dead, to know how I'd given up on her. I don't want her to know what an Angel-damned miserable bastard I am."

Reema looked at him, and he looked at her, more vulnerable than she'd ever seen him.

"Please."

She'd never heard those words cross his lips.

"Okay," she answered. "I won't tell her."

He breathed a sigh of relief and relaxed in his chair. "Good." He paused. "Thanks."

An awkward silence settled between them, and Reema shifted uncomfortably in her seat. It was clear that neither of them were used to such heavy topics that didn't center around revenge or what cruelty had happened to them, and neither knew what to do afterwards.

Asif cleared his throat, "The plan?"

A slow, dark grin spread across Reema's lips. "You're going to like this."

His eyes gleamed and he matched her dark grin. "I'm listening."

TWENTY-FOUR

The sun broke over the horizon, its first light spilling across the desert like molten gold, setting the sands ablaze in orange and red. The air was still, and the city silent. It was the early hours of morning, but Reema doubted that anybody still slept. How could they, having felt the earth tremble and heard the heavy footsteps of soldiers outside their doors?

The Queen of Sundara stood at the outer gates of Zareen, alone except for her Consort. Their shadows stretched long, nearly reaching Reema as she watched from atop the city walls. The air was charged, like the moment before a sandstorm, where everything was still but the promise of chaos loomed on the horizon. She could feel it deep in her bones, the weight of it nearly suffocating. It was *here* that her actions would determine the fate of humanity.

Standing a short distance away, Kaiden Damaris and his army waited like a wall of death, rows of Bloodlineds armed with swords, spears, and the occasional relic, the glint of steel and armor catching the sun in flashes of silver. In front of them stood the Commonborn, plain in tattered clothing, their bodies valued only as meat shields.

Reema's breath tightened as the wall parted for the Lord of Sandspire. He crossed the desert slowly in a black thobe embroidered with gold. His long dark hair slicked back, beard meticulously shaped, and eyes depthless black. Though they were far apart, she felt his eyes flick up to meet hers. Thin lips spread wide into an evil smile.

Reema of Mirash.

As the whisper of her name passed through her mind, she froze, gripping the sandstone ledge. It would be a lie to say she wasn't afraid. She was, because despite the masterful plan they had laid out, in the back of her mind was the knowing that all of this was meant only to give them a *chance* at stopping the Djinn.

"It's finally happening, isn't it?"

She glanced over her shoulder at Alaric, climbing the steps to the top of the wall. They had to wait until the Bloodlined and Commonborn were gone from the palace before freeing him from the dungeon. But even then, he had to stay hidden—checkered fabric wrapped around his face to obscure him from wandering eyes—just until the day was over. Once the sun set, their fate would be decided.

Alaric approached her on the wall, his eyes serious as he stared out at his father in the distance. When he stopped, she couldn't help but notice how stiff he was. Neither had said a word to each other since the day before, only glancing at each other in passing. Asif had been the one to share the news of their plan, and if Alaric had any issues with it, he didn't make them known. Instead, he gave them a firm nod, content with his role.

Reema felt a tug in her chest as she studied him, realizing that this was it. Things were finally coming to an end. It felt foolish to let what happened yesterday linger between them in these final moments.

She drew a breath, and just as she was about to speak, he looked at her.

"Don't," he said. "Focus on that rage inside you, and save your words for after we've dealt with the Djinn and my father."

Reema frowned, but before she could speak, fire-made visions appeared beside the Djinn, terrifying screams pouring from them as they showed the city turning to ash.

Reema and Alaric watched in horror as children clawed for their mothers, merchants rolled aflame, and the golden-domed palace crumbled atop fleeing guards and servants. The few guards stationed along the wall stumbled back, faces pale with fear. In the city, people emerged from their homes, frightened but too curious about the screams in the air.

Kaiden Damaris's voice, layered with the Djinn's, boomed over the city. It shook sand from the walls and roofs, drawing screams and sending people into panic.

"Queen Nisha, have you come to surrender?"

Reema leaned in, straining to hear Nisha's response. They had made a pact that there would be no surrender to the evil bastard and the darkness possessing him. But

Reema knew things were different when you stood before the enemy.

"Come to surrender?" Nisha's voice was sharper than Reema expected, stabbing through the distance with surprising clarity. "I don't think so."

A thrill coursed through Reema.

Kaiden's dark smile inched wider. "So you've come to watch your city burn then."

Reema watched the Queen step forward, chin raised in defiance. Before, she had wondered how a thief from the slums of Zareen had become Queen, and how the Bloodlined allowed it. But watching her now, she understood. Like Reema, she had a will of stone.

She grinned as the Queen spat in Kaiden's direction. For a moment, the Djinn's control over Kaiden slipped, and the Bloodlined's face turned red with anger. He pointed a finger at Nisha.

"You'd spit at *me*, you Commonborn *dog*?"

Kaiden's eyes flickered, a trace of human rage twisting his features before they softened under the Djinn's control. A sinister smile spread across his face, cold and calculating, as if he'd expected this defiance all along.

"So I'll have the pleasure of watching you struggle against the flames," Kaiden's voice, twisted again by the Djinn's dark tone, said. He sounded almost gleeful as the air around him shimmered with heat. "You must know that surrender was never an option. This city, these people ... they were doomed the moment I returned."

The sand behind Kaiden and his army rippled as a towering wall of fire erupted from the earth. It roared over the horizon, circling the city and shining its hellish glow on every shadow. The sound was deafening—a crackling storm of fury that sent waves of heat slamming into the walls of Zareen.

Reema stared at it in shocked awe, the hopeless screams of people behind her rising in pitch. This was what she had dreamt for so long of subjecting the surface world to. She wanted them to feel this heat, to burn in this world and the next. Faced with the Djinn's dark magic, she knew she'd been wrong. Not even the worst of humanity deserved this cruel fate.

A ball of flame appeared over Kaiden's outstretched hand, and it arced toward Nisha and Sher.

Reema gripped the parapet, knuckles white, heart lurching, her body screaming at her to act, but she couldn't. Just like Nisha and Sher, she had her role to play in this battle. Her time had not come yet.

Before the fire could consume them, Sher raised his hand. A brilliant wall of crimson light erupted, shimmering with raw power as it clashed with the flames. The forces met with a thunderous crack, sending shockwaves across the battlefield. The air hissed and sizzled as fire licked the light, but Sher stood firm, his face grim with concentration as he held the Djinn's power at bay.

Nisha strode forward, her teeth bared as she screamed, "Is that all you have?"

Kaiden's smile widened, his dark eyes flashing with near-glee. He stalked forward, raising his hands, the black robes of his thobe fluttered from the force of his magic.

An inferno shot forth, smashing into the crimson

wall of light with enough force to send Sher to his knees. The light cracked, and with a roar, Sher summoned more light, sending it forth to reinforce the wall. But Reema wasn't sure it would be enough.

In the blink of an eye, Nisha withdrew a dagger and hurled it. It spun through the air and smashed into Kaiden's chest with a dull thud. His flames faltered, and the light wall appeared again.

Sundamned hells, where had the Queen learned to throw like that? She glanced at Alaric. Hadn't he said she was a thief?

Kaiden slowly pulled the dagger from his chest, his face stoic as he tossed it aside. Reema watched the wound in his chest heal over with fresh pink skin.

"I get it now, why the Angel made you his bitch," Nisha's voice reached Reema. "You're too easy of a target."

That finally seemed to get a rise out of the Djinn. Still possessing Kaiden, he raised his arms and the flame wall surrounding Zareen flared higher, the heat intensifying. Reema's clothes clung to her skin, beads of sweat rolling down her forehead. Even the desert sun had never felt this suffocating. A thought Alaric seemed to share as he freed the cloth wrapped around his face.

Kaiden's gaze caught on Alaric's, before shifting to Reema's.

Reema allowed a small grin.

That seemed to do the trick.

With a ground-shaking roar, Kaiden unleashed an inferno on Nisha. She scrambled back through the sand, reaching Sher just in time for him to draw the crimson light back in on themselves.

Some unspoken signal passed between Kaiden and his men, and a moment later, their roars matched his as they charged, weapons aimed at Zareen. Arrows rained through the air, whizzing past Reema to strike the city itself.

Those who'd been foolish and curious enough to step outside the safety of their homes raced back toward shelter. Not everyone made it. Blood trickled down the alleys and streets from the fallen, a dark promise that petrified those who made it to safety.

Nisha looked back at Reema, her eyes wild as she screamed, "Now!"

Reema reached for the relic pickaxe at her side, hidden from view. Power thrummed through her fingertips as she gripped the shaft, and with a pounding heart, she raised it over her head, the ancient metal gleaming in the inferno's glow.

She locked gazes with the Djinn, and his eyes widened.

She let out an explosive shout and slammed the pickaxe into the city wall. A resonant chime sliced through the screams of the dying, the roar of flames, and the shouts of men determined to spill innocent blood. Like the clear ring of a bell, the sound vibrated through the air, and the ground beneath her shook violently.

A crack formed in the sandstone wall, running down into the sand. Alaric held her steady as the wall beneath them crumbled to either side, the desert pitching into the earth.

They watched as Kaiden Damaris's entire army plunged into its depths, the murder in their eyes giving way to fear. They screamed as they disappeared into a cloud of rising sand.

But the will she'd imposed upon the earth did not stop there. The earth continued to part far behind Kaiden's army, reaching a place where a hundred miners waited.

Kaiden watched his army disappear into the earth with a twisted grimace, and for a moment, the fire walls faltered. The flames calmed, and the blue skies returned.

Reema doubted the fall had killed everyone in his army. But that wasn't her goal. She simply wanted to incapacitate them long enough to make a difference.

A new roar echoed, and like a sandstorm, Zareen's army charged through the gaps in the wall. They raced not toward Kaiden but into the gaping earth to eliminate their enemies. And on the other side of the desert, she heard a familiar roar rise to meet it, filled with the deep growls and shouts of miners.

"No!" Kaiden shouted, his layered voice cracking as control shifted between him and the Djinn. But the Djinn ended up with control, his eyes swallowed by a deep blackness filled with rage. He turned back to Nisha and Sher and unleashed the full extent of his power.

The sand between them turned to jagged glass, incinerated by the approaching flames. It slammed into the wall of light Sher summoned with a heavy boom that sent a shockwave through Reema's bones.

"Come on!" Alaric shouted, drawing Reema's attention. He was already climbing down the section of the wall they stood on. Reema glanced at Nisha and Sher, adrenaline pumping through her veins as they struggled for their lives.

This was her doing, and for the first time in a long while, fury consumed her. She hated herself for it, so much so that it made her shake with uncontrollable rage. She lifted the relic in her hands, seeing the reflection of her own eyes in the ancient metal pick. Her brows furrowed, her eyes hardened.

She had fulfilled her role, eliminating the army that threatened Zareen and leaving the Djinn to Nisha and Sher. But she knew, deep down, that the Ifrit who survived the mines wouldn't stand by, letting them do battle on her behalf. She would be in the thick of it, doing everything she could to plunge the relic pickaxe into the Djinn's chest.

Baring her teeth, she lowered the pickaxe and unleashed a scream that echoed through her soul. She raised the pickaxe again, an image fixed in her mind, and slammed it into the wall.

Alaric jumped off the wall just as the section beneath her crumbled, the damage enough to finally collapse it entirely. But she did not fall into the ruins. Instead, she slid down a groove that delivered her onto the sands, where she hit the ground running.

The wind roared in her ears as she charged toward Kaiden. Adrenaline surged through her with every pounding footstep, and the sounds of the dying in the tunnels faded to a dull backdrop. All she could see was the man who'd murdered her sister and the Djinn who'd murdered her parents.

Kaiden's dark eyes locked on hers as she ran past Nisha and Sher, his mouth twisting into a cruel sneer.

"Come to suffer the same fate as your parents?" He paused his attack on Nisha and Sher and turned to Reema. "Very well, Reema of Mirash."

He pointed a single finger toward her.

"Burn."

Flames erupted from his finger as she skidded to a halt and struck the sand with her relic. Another chime sang through the air, more violent than before, echoing the rage she felt in her core.

The flames vanished as he plummeted into a hole of collapsed sand, and the desert rushed to fill it. He cried out as sand dust clogged his airways, coursing down his throat and up his nose.

Reema dodged the plume of fire that erupted and swung the pickaxe straight for his skull, fixing her will to carve the way through the Djinn's soul.

Kaiden's hand shot free from the sand, a pulse of raw power bursting from his palm. Before Reema could react, the blast hit her square in the chest, the force of it sending her hurtling backward. She flew through the air, body twisting violently as the world spun. Flames erupted across the front of the armor Nisha had given her, licking at her skin beneath the metal. A strangled scream escaped her as she plummeted into the dark tunnels of dying men.

CHAPTER
TWENTY-FIVE

Reema crashed into the newly opened tunnel, darkness swallowing her in the swirling sand dust. Her body slammed into something solid, the impact knocking the air from her lungs as she crumpled into a heap.

All around her, the screams of Bloodlined, Common-born soldiers, and miners echoed off the cavernous walls, the sounds of battle and death reverberating in the oppressive dark.

Dazed, she covered herself in sand, snuffing out the flames on her chest. She groaned, the searing pain in her chest making it hard to breathe. The smell of scorched metal and leather filled the air.

Through the haze of pain, she lifted her eyes, watching as men clashed, swords against pickaxes. She pushed herself up, aware that Kaiden and the Djinn were still above. She needed to stop them. Needed to—

Glowing grey eyes emerged from the throng of bodies. One of Kaiden's Bloodlined saw her prone, and with a sneer, he started toward her.

Reema scrambled backward, searching frantically for the relic pickaxe. Her hand found only sand, and as her back pressed against a wall, her muscles locked in fear.

This was how she would die. Not in the mines, beneath collapsed marble, not in the blaze of the Djinn's dark magic, but at the feet of some unnamed Bloodlined.

Suddenly, a white marble shiv pierced the Bloodlined's neck, splattering blood across Reema's face. Tasting blood and wiping her face, she saw Renfri standing over the Bloodlined's body.

"I'm going to hold this over your head forever, Ifrit," Renfri smirked as she offered Reema her hand, already sticky with blood.

Reema grumbled as she took it, pulling the sword from the Bloodlined's body. His fingers were locked around the hilt, something she fixed with a few cracks.

She let out a heavy sigh. "Can't believe I'm saying this, but it's damn good to see you, Renfri." She searched the darkness behind her. "Where's Asif?"

"Killing, I'd guess. But he's got that new guard by his side. She seemed capable enough to keep his back."

Reema nodded. "I need to get back up top."

Sand swirled nearby, and a sudden scream echoed off the walls. A Commonborn—one of Kaiden's—slammed one of Nisha's soldiers into the craggy wall and wrapped his hands around the man's neck.

Before he could choke the life from him, Reema slashed the sword across his neck. The body collapsed at her feet, and the soldier panted his thanks before jumping back into the fray.

Reema looked at Renfri. "I can't waste time down here."

"The Djinn?"

She nodded.

Renfri grimaced. "Can't escape from here. But on the other side of this tunnel, there's a section that's collapsed more. You can probably climb up from there."

"Then let's go."

Reema and Renfri moved as one, cutting through the chaotic throng of bodies, their weapons flashing through the swirling sand dust as they stumbled over the sand-covered dead. The clang of steel, the slick of her marble shiv against flesh, the cries of pain along with the thick stench of blood surrounded them as they hacked their way through. Reema surrendered to the Ifrit, letting the rage consume her and guide her through the nightmare.

Wherever she went, the miners rallied around her, helping her push through the enemy. But as they neared the tunnel's edge, Reema caught a glimpse of something that made her stomach drop. In the midst of the battle, she saw Asif and Sedra, side by side, cutting through Bloodlined and enemy Commonborn with a brutal efficiency that made them seem almost like mirror images. Sedra's strikes were swift and precise, echoing Asif's as if she'd inherited not only his blood but his instinct for battle.

Asif caught her gaze mid-swing, his face smeared with blood, but his eyes gleaming with pride. He grinned at her, like he knew what she saw. Before she could return the look, a flash of movement at his side made her heart lurch.

A Bloodlined lord with a long beard and shining green eyes jumped from the shadows and brought his blade down in a savage arc. Reema screamed as the blade sliced clean through Asif's wrist. His severed hand hit the sand with a sickening thud, fingers still twitching.

Asif roared in pain, blood spraying from the stump as he staggered back.

The Bloodlined lord stalked toward him, face hidden in shadow as he spoke. "Remember the name Farhat as you cross into hell—"

A blade slashed through his neck. The Bloodlined came to an abrupt halt, mouth half-open in surprise. Then his head rolled from his body, and the body collapsed at Sedra's feet. But she barely registered it, her eyes fixed on Asif, horror and rage swirling in her expression as she dropped to his side.

Reema and Renfri pushed through the throng, breaths ragged as they reached Asif. His face was pale, but there was a fire in his eyes that hadn't dimmed, even as blood poured from his arm. While Reema and Renfri fought to keep any other enemies away, Sedra grabbed him under the shoulders and dragged him toward a safe corner of the tunnel. A violent curse escaped him as more sand spilled from above.

When it seemed they had a moment to themselves, Reema went back to Asif. Before she could speak, Renfri leaned over him, wrapping his stump tightly with a torn piece of linen from her top.

"You sundamned idiot," she growled, tying a second linen strip around his arm, tightening it to reduce the blood flow.

As she did, Asif hissed in pain. "I know, trust me."

"Is he going to be okay?" Sedra asked, jaw clenched, eyes scanning for enemies.

"He'll be fine," Renfri said, tightening the strip again, prompting another howl of pain from him.

"I'd be fine if you'd stop doing that!"

Renfri clamped a hand over his mouth. "Stop screaming, or you'll draw attention to us."

He looked up at her, and she looked down at him. Then, in a rush of movement so fast it caught Reema off guard, Renfri kissed him. It was a rough kiss, full of passion and worry, lasting no longer than a second. But when Renfri drew back, a grin spread across Asif's face, as if he hadn't just lost a hand.

Reema crouched over him, patting his shoulder. "You're done now. You've done your part, and we can't lose you."

He understood what she meant. He had purpose now, not just for Sedra or Renfri, but because Reema needed him. Besides Alaric, he was all that remained of their gang.

He nodded. "Go on, then. End this."

"Sedra," Reema barked.

Sedra looked over her shoulder.

"You let this man die, you won't have a father anymore. Understand?"

Asif's smile disappeared, his gaze snapping to Sedra's. Sedra frowned, blinking in confusion. With a curse, Asif raised his good fist and shook it at Reema for breaking her solemn promise.

All Reema could do was fix him with a look and a shrug that said, don't die.

Together, Reema and Renfri went back into the chaos, cutting their way through with reckless abandon.

When there was a lull in the action, Renfri shot Reema a sideways glance, brows furrowed in confusion. "Did you just say he's her father?"

Reema grunted and narrowly dodged a man charging with a blade aimed at her side. She hurled her shiv into the attacker's chest, dropping him like a stone. She planted her foot on his chest and yanked her blade out with a sickening *squelch*. "Yeah."

Renfri blinked, her movements slowing for a heartbeat as she processed the revelation. For once, she was stunned into silence.

They pushed onward until the tunnel walls began to narrow, the light from above grew faint but still revealed a collapsed section ahead, where jagged chunks of stone and sand formed a rough slope leading back to the surface.

"There," Renfri pointed, her voice tight. "There's your way out."

Reema nodded, wiping sweat and blood from her brow. "It's steep, but I can climb that."

"It'd disappoint me if the Ifrit couldn't."

Reema moved toward the slope, her gaze fixed on the faint light of the surface. Just as she reached the base, she stopped and turned back to Renfri, who stood still, looking toward where Asif and Sedra had remained. Reema could tell how she ached to return to him.

"What happened to choosing love or power?" Reema called out.

Renfri laughed. "I'm not a gang lord anymore. What power is there to have?"

Reema gripped Renfri's arm. "Keep your back covered."

Renfri smirked. "I always do."

Without another word, Reema turned and began to climb, shaking off a desperate man who clung to her foot with a heavy kick. She pulled herself over loose stones, scrambling past sliding sand, her body aching with every move.

As the sounds of battle faded, her focus narrowed to the light above. She didn't look back—she couldn't. She had to get to the surface. She had to end this.

CHAPTER
TWENTY-SIX

Back on the surface, things had taken a turn for the worse. The flames conjured by the Djinn spread along the city walls, and beneath a cloud of smoke, screams pierced the morning air.

Kaiden Damaris stood before Nisha, Sher, and Alaric, his face twisted in a dark grimace as he battled the power emanating from Sher's black diamond ring. Nisha and Alaric, stolen blades in hand, slipped in and out of combat, stabbing at him whenever they could, trying to shift his focus.

But they were slowly losing—Reema could see it in the exhaustion in Sher's golden eyes and the sluggishness overtaking the other two. No matter how hard they fought, they couldn't stop him.

Reema raced toward them, mind churning for a plan—something, *anything* to stop him.

A pillar of fire erupted from Kaiden, sending her skidding to a halt as she shielded her eyes. The flash blinded Nisha, Sher, and Alaric, giving him the edge he needed.

Two fireballs sent Nisha and Alaric flying, landing with heavy thuds. They scrambled, rolling in the sand to extinguish the flames licking at their skin.

The darkness in Kaiden's eyes deepened, and with a slow smile, he turned his full attention on Sher. An inferno poured from his hands, the searing heat pounding against Sher's summoned shield of crimson light.

Sher grimaced, growling as the power against him became overwhelming. He fell to his knee, squeezing his eyes shut, loosing a soul-rending scream before Reema heard a sudden crack. It was a small sound, but she felt it in her bones.

The crimson light faltered, motes of it fading as brilliant light escaped the ruined black diamond ring. Sher fell back onto the sand, jaw slack as he stared at the broken ring. It still gleamed as if it held magic. But when he held it up and attempted to summon its power again, nothing responded. Instead, motes of light drifted from the black diamond, quickly lost in the air.

Kaiden stood over Sher, his black thobe in tatters, dripping with blood from healed wounds. He lifted a hand, watching as flames danced over his fingertips.

"A valiant effort, Lord Vasir," Kaiden said, his voice layered with the Djinn's. "But in the end, you are not enough."

His hand dropped toward Sher.

"Kaiden Damaris!" Reema shouted, her voice cutting through the screams and chaos behind her.

Kaiden paused, turning his gaze upon her. "The Ifrit still lives. I am pleased. Now you can watch as I fulfill this dark unspoken wish of yours. The world you so despise will *burn*, starting with him."

Reema stood her ground, her breath shallow, tasting ash and smoke on the wind. The world around her burned, but she didn't care. Not anymore. She glared at him, watching the flames dance in the black pools of his eyes.

"You're right. It *was* my wish to see the world burn. But I was supposed to be the one to take my vengeance, so I could hear the screams of men like the one you possess now."

The words were ice in her throat, her heart betraying her, but she pressed on, forcing the challenge out like a blade. She had no relic, no armor strong enough to shield her. All she had was herself—and she had to hope that was what the Djinn wanted.

"Give me one more chance to make my wish."

Dark eyes narrowed before the flames snuffed out over his hand, and hollow, cruel laughter broke through the burning city. A fresh wave of panic swept through the screaming people of Zareen.

"Very well, Ifrit. Make your wish."

"Reema, no!" Alaric's voice tore through the chaos, raw and desperate. He stumbled forward, eyes wide with horror. "Stop this! You don't have to—"

Reema lifted her chin, forcing the fear twisting in her belly to drown beneath the rising flames of her rage. She fed that fire, let it devour her fear, devour every part of her, until nothing was left but the Ifrit.

She locked eyes with Alaric, staring deep into the

soul of the man who'd pulled her from the dark. She hoped he understood why she had to go back into it.

"I wish to take my vengeance."

The ice-blue glow returned to Kaiden's eyes, and he collapsed to the ground, gasping in the wake of the Djinn's power. Beside him, the Djinn materialized in his true form: a towering figure born from the very essence of the seven hells. The heat radiating from his form forced Reema back a step, the sand beneath his feet turning to glass.

With his face twisted in dark malice, the Djinn surged forward. A cloud of violent flames roared toward her like a sandstorm, and before she could draw another breath, it slammed into her chest.

To her surprise, the moment the heat touched her skin, it vanished, replaced by a suffocating cold that wrapped around her heart. It squeezed the life from her lungs. The world blurred. She felt her body drop to the ground, her knees buckling under the weight of the Djinn's presence. Her thoughts turned to ice, her mind spiraling into a freezing void as the Djinn seeped into her soul.

She screamed, but the sound was swallowed by darkness, erasing the screams of dying men, the roar of flames devouring the city, and Alaric's desperate voice.

The world collapsed inward as the Djinn invaded her mind. Reema spiraled, her thoughts splintering as if her soul were being shredded by darkness. Cold tendrils wrapped around her, his hatred twisting her memories and emotions. She heard her sister's laughter before it warped into a dull thud—the sound of her body hitting the ground at the Hole. She saw her parents smiling, their eyes twinkling with love, before their screams echoed as they turned to ash.

Every attempt she made to protect the precious parts of herself failed. When he found the depths of her love for Alaric, he laughed, his laughter rising when he realized she had never told him.

She could feel him pressing into the core of her being, trying to consume her, trying to bend her to his will, to make her his puppet as Kaiden was. She fought the unholy merging of their souls, clawing to protect her buried truths. But she was failing. The void tightened around her, strangling every whisper of a thought.

And then, all at once, it stopped.

She floated, drifting in the nothingness. It was there that she heard his voice. And it sounded like her.

Let us make your wish come true.

CHAPTER
TWENTY-SEVEN

A grip tightened around Reema like a vice, holding her still in the endless void. An image of herself appeared, walking toward her with eyes black as night.

All around her, men and women appeared as ghosts. She watched their lips curl, their eyes gleaming with dark intentions. She felt the cruelty radiating from them, like everything they touched turned to ruin. *These* were the men and women who crushed others beneath their heels simply because it pleased them.

Watch them, Ifrit. See the evil they do.

One man raised a fist, his face twisted with hatred as he began to beat some poor innocent soul. Over and over, he rained down blows, lost in the depths of his fury. But only when his fury ebbed and he reached for the joy of power over the other did Reema see him at his worst.

Elsewhere, a woman stood over a child, wearing a mask of disgust. The child sobbed, hands outstretched as he begged for mercy, but she kicked him like he was trash. The sickening crack of bone echoed in Reema's mind, followed by the woman's laughter as she walked away, leaving the child writhing in agony.

Their ghosts faded, another vision bleeding into her consciousness. This time, a man stood over his lover, his hands wrapped around her throat. Her lips turned blue, feet kicking helplessly as he grinned, watching the life drain from her eyes. Her hands clawed at his arms, desperate for breath, but he held her fast, savoring every second of her suffering. The satisfaction on his face was unmistakable, as though he had found peace in her slow, agonizing death.

The Djinn's voice slithered through the void. *Do you remember? This is what you wanted to rid the world of.*

Reema tried to dig deep, to find the resolve she needed to survive the mental assault. But no matter how deep she searched, she found only hollow emptiness. A deep, unsettling truth whispered in her ear. In the deep dark, there were no good souls, for the darkness blinded them all.

Except ... there *was* one man who, despite every reason to submit to the darkness, persisted in kindness and compassion. Even when he had been blinded and dumped into the mines of Sandspire.

An unbidden image appeared before her, not of the Alaric she knew now, but of times past. She watched as he suffered beneath his father's whip, rising again and again to comfort his mother in her pain and despair. She watched him give coin and bread to those in need, finding joy not in their thanks, but in knowing he eased their burden. She watched him stand over Salman, pulling back from darkness to offer mercy. She watched him sit in a dark cave, patiently teaching the most violent of gang lords how to read.

As Reema studied the vision, the ghost of him turned to meet her gaze. Slowly, a splotch of color poked through the grey; a subtle brown glow, no brighter than the dimmest candle. But it was bright enough.

The Djinn's grip tightened, squeezing her in the vast black void, as if he was trying to snuff out that brown glow. But no matter how hard the Djinn squeezed, Reema didn't tear her eyes from it.

Her body trembled, tendrils of rage stirring. They coiled first in her chest, then spread through every part of her, boiling her blood.

The Djinn's voice slithered through her thoughts, low and insidious. *You wished for this, mortal. Submit to me, and I will turn the world to ash, so we can create a new one. A better one. You want this. I know you do.*

Reema shook her head, fighting the voice, fighting the pressure.

Give. Yourself. To. Me.

But as she stared into Alaric's eyes, she saw the truth she needed. It didn't matter to Alaric that she had endangered his home or caused so much pain and horror. He loved her, and she didn't need to hear those words to know it. His eyes said it for him.

It was in his gaze that her fury reignited. Not with the blind rage of vengeance, but with a deeper fire, forged from the need to do what she had always done.

Survive.

The void trembled as heat pulsed within her chest, the Djinn's icy grip loosening. The Djinn growled, trying to take control of her again, trying to force the breath from her lungs. But Reema drew upon the molten core inside her and roared.

The sound that escaped her was primal, a battle cry echoing through every memory, every tunnel in the mines of Sandspire. Far in the distance, she felt white marble collapse, and as it did, the darkness around her cracked, splintering like glass.

Reema's power surged. The Djinn reeled, his dark eyes widening, filled for a brief moment with panic. Then fire erupted in the void as the Djinn prepared to attack her.

But this time, it was she who attacked him.

Time ceased to be a concept as she clashed with him, her fire against his, her rage against his malice. And despite the fact that every breath was a struggle, every moment a fight to hold on, she refused to be crushed.

This wasn't about undoing what she'd caused, but about doing what others could not.

She was the Ifrit, the named gang lord over the miners of Sandspire. And this place inside her ... *this* was where she'd end this war.

CHAPTER 28
ALARIC

Days had passed.

Beneath the golden domed palace, hidden in the Queen's vault, Alaric sat in a simple white thobe. His beard and hair had been hacked away at the Queen's order to clean himself up. He stared at Reema as she lay unconscious, her body writhing in fits on a bed carried here just for her.

His hands steepled beneath his chin, his knee shaking nervously.

It felt wrong that the city had already begun to recover from the battle. Stonemasons were shaping sandstone blocks to repair the collapsed walls, merchants were back in the streets shouting their wares, and thieves were stripping fallen soldiers of everything, down to their tattered, bloodied shirts—anything worth a soft penny.

Word spread across the Kingdom of Sundara that the Commonborn Queen had vanquished the great Djinn.

But Alaric wondered what they would think if they knew it was all a lie.

What would they do if they knew the Djinn was still alive, trapped inside a mortal hidden beneath the palace?

Alaric pressed his hands to his temples, dragging his fingers through his hair. "Stay with me," he whispered. "Stay with me."

Reema let out a soft moan, and his head snapped up. Flames licked across her skin, the acrid scent of burnt flesh filling the air, only to extinguish a moment later and leave fresh, smooth skin behind.

The first time he saw it, he had panicked. They all had—Nisha, Sher, Asif, and his found daughter, Sedra. They thought the Djinn was overcoming Reema, that the end was upon them. But to their surprise, the flames died out, she healed, and nothing changed—not that hour, not that day, not even the next.

But that wasn't even the most terrifying part. When the healer examined her, he pulled back her eyelids and jumped back in terror. He had seen a battle in her eyes— a warring of brown and black, each fighting for control.

When Alaric touched her, sheer heat radiated from her body, as hot as the desert sun. It scorched his fingers, leaving them raw and aching. Sundamned hells, he craved to touch her, to run his hand through her dark hair, kiss her forehead, and let her know he was *there*, like the last time, when they had fallen to their near-certain death. But he could not.

Alaric muttered incoherently, digging his nails into his scalp. He felt the tiniest flicker of pain, but it wasn't enough to pull him from the misery of watching her. He was so tired, so exhausted. And yet, he couldn't sleep. What if she woke and needed him and he wasn't there? That fear gnawed at his bones.

He closed his eyes, a sweet cool relief washing over him. His body begged him to leave, to lay down and sleep. But he refused.

"Come back to me," he croaked, his shattered voice barely a whisper. "You survive, and I'll grant you a magical wish, sprinkled with my very own special marble dust. Okay?"

That was the first promise she had ever made to him, the one he had held her to, and the one that had reshaped his entire existence.

He waited for her to answer. Of course, she did not.

Clearing his throat, he opened his eyes, wincing at the burning sensation creeping through them. He narrowed them, hoping it would help, and continued to stare at her.

She was beautiful. *Achingly* beautiful.

"I fell in love with you before I ever even saw you. Do you know that?"

Her lips parted, ever so slightly. He paused, hoping she'd wake with brown eyes, that the black void would be gone. That *somehow*, inside that small but terrifying miner, the Ifrit would eat the Djinn.

When she stilled, he continued.

"I felt it for the first time when you came back for me after leaving me as bait. But I didn't know it for certain until later, when I heard your voice, reading that title so damn slowly."

He let out a heavy sigh, his eyes welling with tears.

"Beneath the Sands of Sorrow." A tear slipped from the corner of his eye, trailing down like a single grain of sand sliding down a dune. He knelt beside Reema, holding his hands an inch from her burning skin, hoping she could feel his presence. "I promise you, Reema, if you come back, I'll whisper how much I love you every sundamned morning, noon, and night."

He shook his head, his expression twisted with pain and grief.

"No, not whisper. I will *shout* it. Scream it so the moon and stars will hear." He pressed his hand to hers, clenching his teeth against the searing pain as tears streamed down his cheeks. But the pain grew too much, and he pulled his hand away, sobbing as he pressed his head against the edge of her bed, his heart throbbing as painfully as his hand. "Please, just come back. I beg you. *Please*."

Alaric didn't move from his place beside Reema's bed, his chest heaving with every broken sob. The burning in his hand spread, pulsing like his blood was aflame, but it was nothing compared to the hollow agony in his chest. He stayed there, forehead pressed against the cool metal frame of the bed, desperate to stay connected to her in any way, even if it meant drowning in pain.

The silence in the vault was thick, broken only by the occasional hiss of Reema's breath. Then, through the stillness, came the steady click of boots against stone.

"Alaric."

He lifted his head, meeting Nisha's eyes as she neared. She stopped just behind him, saying nothing for

a long moment. Her gaze swept over Reema's unconscious form, then down to Alaric, huddled on the floor,
broken and small.

"Nothing new?" she asked quietly.

He shook his head.

"I see you burned your hand again."

He didn't answer right away, just stared at Reema.
Nisha had to lean in to hear him when he whispered. "I
was horrible to her, in the end."

Nisha's brow furrowed in confusion, but then she
remembered the time in the cell, when he'd let his anger
get the better of him. She sighed and sank into a chair,
dropping into it without her usual grace.

"Do you know how Sher got all those scars?" she
asked, resting further into the chair and interlacing her
fingers.

Alaric shook his head again, too tired to even guess.

"I shoved him into a pit of glass-sharded sand."

He glanced up at her and blinked. He hadn't heard
that before.

"I told you that day you escorted me into Razhan's
ball that I was going to rob the King. But I never told you
what I was stealing."

"I just assumed it was gold," he mumbled.

She smirked. "There *was* a lot of it. But no, I was
trying to steal a magic lamp, capable of granting any
wish I desired."

Alaric drew a deep breath, suddenly realizing how
Razhan had simply disappeared, and she'd been the one
to take up the throne. Did she succeed in stealing the

lamp? Was that what she wished for, the crown to rule the desert?

Nisha lifted a finger. "Don't look at me like that. I know what you're thinking. I've got far more valuable things to wish for than a sundamned crown." She shifted in her seat. "Anyway, I wasn't the only one trying to steal it. Can you guess who else?"

"Sher?"

"I'd fallen for the golden-eyed fool, even though we were both after the same sundamned thing. When it came down to it, at the end, I shoved him into the pit."

Alaric stared at her, stunned into silence.

"It sounds heartless, I know. And it *was*. Well, he asked me to do it, but let's stay on track. Do you get what I'm trying to tell you?"

He stayed silent.

"This stuff happens. Especially when you've got an all-powerful Djinn on your doorstep, threatening to turn the world to ash. You both had a lot on your shoulders. You think I haven't fought with Asher while your father's been setting up camp outside my walls? You have to cut yourself some slack, my friend."

Alaric's breath caught, the weight of his guilt and fear easing slightly. He looked back at Reema, watching as her head twitched to the side and her lips drew back in a momentary, painful grimace.

"My whole life, my father has won every battle I've seen him in. You see, he has this power, a way of making others bend to his will. I already lost my mother to him, and I was—I *am*—afraid of losing Reema too. So I thought I could beat him the way he beats everyone else. With a ruthless, iron will."

"You tried fighting fire with fire."

Alaric nodded, his face solemn and grave.

"Some people are lucky enough that fighting fire with fire works for them." Nisha sighed and stood. She walked over, placed a hand on his shoulder, and leaned in. "But you're not one of those people, Alaric."

He hated that she was right—it only made his mistake clearer. He should have told Reema the truth: that he loved her more than he hated his father.

Nisha started back toward the secret passageway, the click of her boots echoing through the chamber. When she reached the entrance, she looked back and said, "I came by to tell you that your father's asked to see you. *Again.*"

Alaric closed his eyes, his blood running cold. This was the third time he'd heard his father's final request as a man on deadman's row. Each time before, he'd ignored it, choosing instead to stay where it mattered. This time would be no different.

"It'd be a mistake not to meet him," Nisha said, seeing his face.

"I'm needed here."

"You're not. You're needed with him."

He turned to her, seething. "And why should I care about my father's needs?"

Nisha gave him a soft, melancholic smile, her eyes heavy with understanding. "It's not about what your father needs," she said gently. "It's about what *you* need."

Then she was gone.

Alaric stayed frozen where he was, staring at Reema. He wanted to stay, to be here for her. But deep down, he knew that no matter what he did here, it wouldn't change the battle she was fighting. And it wouldn't change the one he'd been afraid of his whole life.

His hand hovered over hers. He had never felt so helpless, watching her teeter between life and death. The fear in him twisted tighter, urging him to stay, so that nothing would happen when he looked away. But his gaze drifted toward the door, Nisha's words lingering like sand dust. They peeled back something inside him, forcing him to confront the truth.

He needed to see his father one last time.

With a long, heavy sigh, he looked at Reema once more and, in a soft voice, said, "I see you. You are much stronger than even I ever knew. So keep surprising me, Reema. Keep fighting."

He rose to his feet. He half-turned to go but hesitated, his chin trembling as he glanced back at her. Gritting his teeth, he forced himself to go, his footsteps heavy as he left the vault.

Lost in the monotony of his sandals tapping against stone, he fell into his thoughts. A whisper haunted him, having long ago weaved its way through every fiber of his being.

Let's see who you are.

He flinched at the crack of a whip, looking up to see where it came from, only to realize it was imagined— memories pulling him back to the days spent under his father's whip. He squeezed his eyes shut as he walked, trying to push the image away, and instead, was met with the sight of his half-beaten mother, screaming and begging for Kaiden to stop.

Only outside the palace doors did he come back to himself, drawn by the sight of the city. It was still half in ruins, the streets of the Peak and Market Districts lined with broken stone, shattered arrows, and crumbled remains of buildings that had caught fire. For a moment, the city mirrored the ruins of his soul: some parts beautiful and majestic, others blackened ash.

His eyes drifted to the place in the distance, its cells filled with murderers, rapists, and worse: his father. His heart thudded in his chest. He hated that he had felt fear when he saw his father in the camp. Hated that he felt fear even now.

Let's see who you are.

Fists clenched at his sides as he forced himself to cross into the gold-specked sands. The long walk blurred against the backdrop of his racing heart, and before he knew it, he stood at the prison gates.

He drew a deep breath and passed through, ignoring the lost souls imprisoned in open-air cells. He ignored their cries for help as the relentless desert sun cracked their lips and burned their backs.

When he reached a small building at last, a guard seated at a desk waited for him. The guard's eyes widened at the sight of Alaric, his face now famous both for its banded scar and its likeness to the man who had carried the demon in his soul.

The Angel's name slipped from the guard's lips, as if

it might protect him from the Damaris son carrying the same evil as his father.

"I'm here to see Kaiden Damaris," Alaric said in the heavy silence.

The guard blinked. He would have already been prepared by the Queen's messengers, informed that Alaric was one of the few permitted to see the Lord of Sandspire.

He nodded numbly and waved him down one of the corridors.

Alaric followed the path, the air thick with sweat and hopelessness. The cries of Bloodlined and Commonborn, both awaiting trial, echoed through the dimly lit corridor, silenced as he walked past their cells. His leather sandals echoed against coarse sandstone, his heart pounding harder with every step.

At long last, he reached his father's cell.

A tiny window high on the wall let in just enough light for Alaric to see inside. His father sat with his back against the wall, one hand draped over a knee, his usual black thobe replaced by the sturdy linen worn by slaves. Despite the linen and his long black hair falling over his rugged face, there was no mistaking who his father was, or who he'd *been*.

His glowing ice-blue eyes lifted to meet Alaric's, and for a moment, that deep-seated fear spiked. He felt like a child again. And Kaiden knew it. The corner of his lips twitched into a smirk.

"My son."

Alaric's nostrils flared as he stepped forward and gripped the bars. He could feel his father's invisible whip poised above him, but just like before, he stared defiantly into his father's eyes, as though welcoming the challenge despite the paralyzing fear.

With slow, measured movements, Kaiden Damaris rose to his feet and faced Alaric on the other side of the bars. He held his hands behind his back, his chin lifted as though Alaric was the one imprisoned, not him.

His father's eyes swept over him, studying him. "Do the people of Zareen know that the Djinn is still here, living on in your slave mistress?"

Alaric surged against the bars, his wrist stinging as it slammed against iron. The iron clang echoed violently through the room, and his father's eyes lit up.

"You do not get to speak about her, father. Not a single fucking word," he growled, his grip tightening on the bars, his body trembling as he stared into the face of the man who had haunted him for as long as he could remember. The air between them was thick and suffocating, heavy with every sundamned lash, bruise, and wound Kaiden had ever inflicted. Rage pulsed through his veins, in tune with the now violent drumbeat of his heart.

His father cocked his head, his eyes piercing through Alaric.

"I must admit, I was surprised to see you. I thought you lost to the mines," Kaiden's voice slithered through the ensuing silence. His eyes glistened as shadows and pride twisted his face into something monstrous. "I wondered how my weak son could have crawled out of that place alive. But now ... now I see. You are not weak. Not anymore. I was wrong."

272 • Z.R. ABADDI

Alaric's teeth ground together, his jaw clenched so tight it ached. He wanted to scream, to roar, but his voice felt trapped in his throat, choked by years of terror and hatred. His father took a step closer, his towering frame casting a shadow over Alaric, just as it always had.

"You're what I made you," Kaiden whispered, his words stabbing into Alaric like a dagger. "Perhaps it was the mines, yes. But it was my hand that forged you, wasn't it? Every lash, every scar, shaped you into this. Despite your mother's coddling, despite her weakness, you've become something worthy. Something I created."

The words snapped something inside Alaric. His breath came in ragged, shallow bursts, his vision swimming as his hatred boiled over. Before he could stop himself, he lunged forward, his hand shooting through the bars and clamping around his father's throat.

Kaiden didn't flinch. His eyes widened—not in fear, but in pleasure. His lips curled into a grotesque smile, his head tilting as Alaric's fingers dug deeper into his neck. The man didn't resist. He leaned into the grip as though savoring Alaric's rage.

"Do it," he rasped, his voice strained but full of pleasure. "Let's see who you are. Prove to me that you're mine."

Alaric felt his father's pulse jump beneath his hand. Every breath Kaiden struggled to take was like music, every gasp a sweet reminder that he could *finally* end it here. Right now. The cruel bastard who had stolen his childhood, who had stolen his mother, who had ruined every Angel-damned thing in his life—he could snuff him out like a flame.

Alaric squeezed tighter, his nails biting into his father's neck as Kaiden's face changed color. The veins bulged in his temples, his eyes bloodshot, yet he never looked away. He was smiling. Smiling as Alaric strangled him.

Kaiden's lips twitched, mouthing one last word as his voice faltered under the pressure: "Good."

Alaric's vision blurred with tears that had welled up inside him since childhood. He wanted to kill him. He had to.

But then an unbidden memory came forth, dragged from the darkness of the mines. Words unknowingly branded into the walls of his mind.

You're nothing like him.

He squeezed his eyes shut, shook his head as if he could free himself of Reema's voice. But instead, her words came again, reverberating inside his head.

You're compassionate. You're merciful. You like to read, for Angel's sake. What kind of bad man reads books?

He opened his eyes, his breath coming in gasping sobs, his body shaking with the desire to keep squeezing. But deep down, he knew this was what his father had wanted all along. This was his final cruelty. To turn Alaric into a monster—just like him.

Alaric's grip tightened, a violent tremor running through his arm. His nails dug deeper, blood beading at his father's throat, and Kaiden's eyes glistened with joy.

You are a good man.

Something shattered inside Alaric, a scream of defiance ripping through his very soul. With a sob, he wrenched his hand away, staggering back from the bars.

The air left his lungs in a broken gasp, his hand falling limp at his side. His father coughed, the red welts on his neck standing out like brands.

"You were wrong, Father. I was never weak."

Kaiden's smile faltered, confusion knitting his brow as he struggled to catch his breath. "What are you—?"

"I'm strong because of *her*. Because of my mother. Compassion *is* strength. Mercy *is* strength. I'm not like you. I never was."

Kaiden's expression crumbled, a flicker of disbelief crossing his features. Alaric saw fear for the first time.

Alaric leaned in, and with a whisper, twisted the dagger of truth. "You're as weak as they come. You'll know it the day you hang, when you can't find me in the crowd to watch you take your last worthless breaths."

Alaric straightened, adjusting the sleeve of his thobe. He met his father's ice-blue eyes one last time.

"Goodbye, Father."

He turned and strode down the corridor, finally free from the shadow of Kaiden Damaris.

"Where are you going?" Kaiden called, his voice frantic as he pressed himself against the bars, peering through them with panic. "You have to finish this! You have to kill me!"

But Alaric didn't stop. He didn't look back. His father's voice echoed down the corridor, growing fainter with every step until it finally blended with the voices of the other condemned.

CHAPTER
TWENTY-NINE

Reema drew a gasping breath and opened her eyes for the first time in a week. Raw power thrummed through her blood, her bones, the very fabric of her soul. It was hard to explain, but she felt ... *divine*. She could sense the heartbeat of the man asleep beside her, feel it calling out to her. She could hear the soft footsteps of people above, walking the halls of the palace. She could even feel the sun's heat beating down on the earth, as though she stood under it herself.

She sat up, every muscle painfully tight. She was caught off guard by Alaric's appearance, his hair free of the disheveled mess and his face clean-shaven. But then he breathed out, and she felt his warm breath in the air.

She craved to touch him, to feel his comfort against the monster imprisoned in her core, who still roared and fought for release. But she could barely move, her veins straining along her throat as she struggled to control her body. She could taste his malice, feel his rage. And it terrified her.

"Alaric," she whispered, pushing her voice through gritted teeth. "Alaric!"

Alaric jolted awake, his eyes shooting open. At the sight of her sitting up, his eyes flooded with joy and his mouth spread into a smile. He rushed toward her, arms wide open for the hug she so desperately wanted. But she was on the verge of breaking, unsure how long she could hold the Djinn.

"No!" she shouted in a shaky voice.

He froze. His smile faded as he realized the danger that still lurked. He knelt by her bed. "What do you need? Tell me."

"Get the Queen."

Alaric shot to his feet and raced away, the pounding of his leather sandals echoing harshly in the wide emptiness of the vault.

A sharp pain stabbed through Reema's mind and she lay back, holding her head in an attempt to stem the headache. She squeezed her eyes shut, clenched her jaw, and pressed her palms against her skull as she fought to control the mounting pressure inside her.

It wasn't long before the sound of voices reached her. A few moments later, Alaric arrived with Nisha, Sher, Asif, Renfri, and Sedra in tow. The marks of war were on them all, from the small burns covering Nisha and Sher to Asif's mending stump and Sedra's broken nose. Even Renfri bore an angry slash across her throat, as though someone had been an inch away from putting her in the grave.

"Shit," Asif and Renfri said, seeing right away the struggle Reema was in.

"We need to evacuate the city," Nisha breathed as she turned to Sher. Her voice dropped lower. "We need to get Auri away from here, while we can."

Sher leaned in, quiet and reassuring. But Reema suddenly couldn't hear him. All she could hear was the Djinn's uproar.

An argument broke out around her, Nisha, Sher, and Sedra on one side, Alaric, Asif, and Renfri on the other.

Their voices mixed with the Djinn's endless roar, splitting her head. All she wanted was to make it stop.

"Shut up!" Reema screamed, slicing through the tension, and for a brief, Angel-blessed moment, the Djinn fell back. She drew a breath and fixed each of them with her gaze. "Shut your sundamned mouths and *listen*."

She was back in her element as gang lord, and though this vault belonged to the Queen, it belonged to her now.

She lifted her hand and tapped into the stolen power thrumming through her. Fire erupted along her hand, and the others stepped back, light dancing from the flickering flames onto their stunned faces.

"I can see into his mind now, as infinite as it is," she said. The clash between them had revealed much about the Djinn's cruel nature, how he had grown jealous of the way mortals adored the Angel. She could not delve too deeply into his essence because she knew he would drown her with all that he was. But there was one thing she'd uncovered, a deep fear he tried to hide from her. "There's a way to construct a new prison for him, even with the Angel gone."

The light of hope sparked in Alaric's eyes, and he moved forward, his hands twitching, wishing he could take hers. And damn the deep, she wished he could. But not yet.

"How?" Nisha asked.

"The Angel left parts of himself here. Many parts."

"The relics," Sher stated.

She nodded. "The relics. They still hold some of the Angel's power. If I melt them down, I might be able to shape it into something new." She looked up and met Nisha's gaze. "We'll need all the relics you can gather."

"I'll get you all the relics you need. Don't worry."

Reema glanced at the fire covering her hand, feeling the pressure inside her rise again. With a grimace, she added, "I don't know how long I can control him. So *hurry*."

The Queen cursed and turned on her heel, Sher at her side. Reema could hear hushed mentions of the Faithful and an associate of Sher's, a man named Laith.

"Asif, Renfri," she called, watching Nisha and Sher disappear into the passageway.

"Yes, boss?" they asked almost simultaneously.

"When I fell into that sundamned tunnel outside the walls, I dropped the relic pickaxe. I need it."

Sedra ran a hand over her buzzed head. She looked nervous.

"What?" Reema asked.

"You've been unconscious for a long time. The scavengers and those rat thieves from the Glass District, they've had time to go through the battlefield."

"Then *find* it," Reema snarled, flames licking higher

on her hand. "I don't care what you have to do. Bring me my Angel-damned pickaxe."

Sedra frowned and opened her mouth, but Asif gripped her wrist, silencing her.

"We'll find it," he said, giving her a firm nod.

He dragged Sedra away, and Renfri followed with a backward glance. Soon, they too were gone.

Alone at last, Alaric kneeled beside her, his expression gentle and soft. "I don't suppose you heard anything I said while you slept?"

Reema couldn't tear her eyes from him, even if she wanted to. She stared into his deep, glowing brown eyes, remembering how they had pulled her from the depths of despair. Someday, she'd tell him about how he was the reason she overcame the Djinn. Someday, she'd tell him—

"I love you."

His whisper cut through her thoughts, stilling the flames coiling around her hand. It stilled the Djinn's pressure and stilled her racing heart. Her chest tightened as she forgot how to breathe.

Though she knew Alaric loved her from the way he looked at her, hearing it aloud sent a wave of warmth through her. Renfri had once told her she had to choose between love and power. But in this moment, she knew Renfri had been wrong. Love was power.

Reema reached for him, and he flinched. She paused, a mixture of emotions threatening to overcome her.

He held up his hands. "I tried to touch you several times while you slept, and each time, you burned me."

Her eyes dropped to his hands, and she saw his

fingers and palm were an angry red. She shook her head, drew the Djinn's power back, and felt the cool air brush her skin.

"I won't burn you now."

She grabbed him by his clothes and pulled him close, her lips crashing into his with a fire as wild and consuming as the flames she'd just drawn back.

In that moment, all that existed was the fierce, aching pull between them. Her fingers curled into him, holding him like he was the only thing tethering her to this world. And in a way, he was.

She kissed him with everything she had, pouring into it all the emotions she'd buried: fear, pain, longing, and most of all, love. The kiss was searing, desperate, as they both wanted more, *so* much more.

For a brief, heart-stopping instant, the Djinn within her surged, trying to break through the mental prison she had forged. But she held him back, not for herself, but for Alaric. She forced him back into the place where she'd kept her rage for years and leaned into the kiss.

When she finally pulled away, her breath came in ragged gasps, her heart pounding in her chest. Her eyes locked onto his, and an unbidden memory whispered through her mind.

I see you.

"I love you," she whispered back. "Just as you are."

Alaric's lips curled into a slow, knowing smile. He reached up and brushed his thumb across her cheek. "I know," he said, his voice soft, teasing, but the glimmer in his eyes betrayed how much her words meant to him. "So, *boss*, what do you need?"

Reema leaned back with a scowl. "Oh, piss off."

His smile deepened.

"Got a book?" she asked.

"Not this time."

She shook her head. "No, stay with me. Read 'Beneath the Sands of Sorrow.'"

"Very well." He put a hand over hers. "Where should I start?"

"At the start." She grimaced as the Djinn's fire rushed through her again, the pressure twice as strong as before. She pressed her hands to her chest as if it could keep her heart from pounding out of it. She squeezed her eyes shut, fear gripping her as she heard the Djinn's slithering voice echo through her mind.

Alaric quickly pulled his hand back at the sudden rush of heat. A flicker of worry crossed his eyes, but he knew there was nothing else he could do except read to her.

He cleared his throat, and as he began to recite the book from memory, she clung to his words, to his voice. Slowly, the Djinn's voice fell back into the deep dark.

"This is the story of Faisal and Tasneem."

Reema lay still, eyes closed, breathing shallow and measured. She felt the Djinn lurking beneath the surface of her consciousness, clawing his way back into control, inch by inch. But she forced him back, using the sound of Alaric's voice to anchor herself and keep from being overwhelmed.

In the stillness, time became meaningless. Minutes stretched into hours, and the vault was filled with only Alaric's quiet reading and Reema's occasional labored breath as she fought to maintain control. The Djinn's fire flickered over her skin, burning with a dark promise of what was to come. She grasped the edges of the bed. As a mine slave, she was no stranger to pain, but this was *beyond* that. She burned from the inside out.

And still, Alaric read on, his voice low and soothing, as if the very act of storytelling could keep the world from crumbling around her.

After what felt like an eternity, the door to the vault groaned open. The spell of the moment was broken, and Alaric's voice trailed off as they both looked up.

One by one, trusted servants and guards entered, arms full of relics. Swords that would never dull, jugs that would never empty, even a painting of a great sea of water—its power so strong that Reema could smell *salt* from where she lay. Every artifact was unceremoniously dumped into a growing pile in the center of the vault, not far from Reema's bed.

The servants and guards glanced nervously at Reema as they worked, but no one spoke.

"Faster, you shit-covered scabs!" Nisha snapped, her voice echoing as she stepped into the vault.

Sher entered next to a man who was forgettable, with a soft jawline, brown eyes, and dark hair of medium length. He looked like any number of men walking the streets of the Market District. She heard Sher address him — this was the mysterious Laith of the Faithful.

Laith studied her with a curious, watchful eye. He

leaned toward Sher and whispered something as Nisha made her way to Reema.

"We've convinced the Faithful to give up their relics," Nisha said quietly. "I figured it'd be harder, given that they dedicated their lives to collecting them for the Angel's return. But our friend back there caught on quickly that there wouldn't be a world for him to return to if we didn't stop the Djinn."

Alaric looked up at her. "Do they know you—"

"*Quiet.*" Nisha glanced over her shoulder, making sure Laith hadn't heard anything. "No, they don't. And it'll stay that way, so long as you keep your trap shut."

Reema knew that if the Faithful ever found out the new Commonborn Queen had killed the one they worshipped, it would be her end. But that was only if they found out.

She watched as more and more servants and guards carried priceless relics in, her eyes catching on what looked like a loom. There was more of the Angel's magic in the world than she had realized.

"Is that Farrakhan's?" Alaric asked, referencing the loom.

Nisha nodded. "I've got men going door to door, taking anything that even *looks* like it could be a relic."

"I'm sure Dariush was upset."

"He was. But I won't take chances on this."

"Keep reading to me, Alaric," Reema said, feeling suddenly weary and spent.

Alaric looked alarmed when he faced her and quickly resumed his reading. Nisha remained for a while longer, listening, before leaving to see what else could be done.

Reema's focus slipped between the pain burning through her veins and the rhythmic cadence of Alaric's voice. But it wasn't enough. The pressure inside her continued to mount, a slow, insidious weight pressing harder and harder on her chest. The Djinn stirred beneath her skin, his whispers growing louder, more insistent, clawing at the walls she had tried so desperately to keep intact.

Then, it happened.

A sharp, searing pain tore through her body like molten fire, burning up her spine, and her breath hitched. Her fingers dug into the sheets, her knuckles white as the pain flared. The Djinn's voice slithered into her mind, low and vicious.

You cannot hold me forever, Ifrit.

Her vision blurred, her heartbeat erratic, as she felt a crack in her mental walls. The Djinn's presence surged, trying to break free. She gasped, clutching her chest as if it could keep him from taking her.

This man you love will suffer. He will scream and wish that he had never met you.

Alaric stopped reading, his eyes wide with concern. "Reema?"

She groaned, the pain twisting in her gut, a feeling like her very soul was splitting apart.

"It's time," she managed through clenched teeth, every word scraping her throat. "We have to do it now."

Nisha's head snapped toward her, eyes narrowing in alarm. "Sher," she called, her voice tense. "Get them out. All of them."

Sher moved quickly, ushering Laith and the

remaining servants and guards from the room, leaving the vault eerily silent. The door slammed shut behind them, the echo ringing in Reema's ears as Nisha and Sher stood at the threshold, their expressions grave.

Nisha stepped forward, her face tight with worry. "There are more relics on the way. Should we wait?"

"No," Reema gasped, her body trembling as the Djinn's power surged inside her again, pushing at the edges of her control. "There's no time. Where's the pickaxe?"

"The pickaxe," Alaric said, his voice edged with panic. His eyes flicked toward the pile of relics. "Was it dumped in that pile?"

As if summoned by their words, a pounding came from the door, echoing through the vault. They turned in unison as the door creaked open, and there, standing in the entrance, were Sedra, Renfri, and Asif, panting as they sought to catch their breath.

Asif held the relic pickaxe in his one good hand, its ancient metal gleaming faintly in the dim torchlight. He raised it up. "I've got the damned thing."

Relief flooded Reema, though it was short-lived as another wave of agony ripped through her, the Djinn's presence beginning to overpower her. "Hurry," she rasped, her strength waning. "We don't have long."

Alaric wrapped the fabric of his thobe around his hands to keep them from getting burnt and helped Reema to her feet. She took the pickaxe from Asif and motioned them back, knowing if this went wrong, it was better they weren't close.

She staggered forward on unsteady feet. It took all

her strength to hold the heavy pickaxe with trembling, tired hands, as the heat of the Djinn's fury rippled through her veins, threatening to tear her apart. Every breath she took felt like swallowing fire, scorching her lungs and burning through the last of her strength.

Her vision swam as the Djinn's voice filled her mind, louder, more insistent.

You dare think you can cage me? You are nothing.

She clenched her teeth, forcing herself forward, each step agonizing as the Djinn clawed at her, his hatred seeping into her very bones. Behind her, everyone stepped back, knowing they were powerless to intervene.

Her gaze fixed on the pile of relics, knowing it was their last hope. The Angel's power lay dormant within them, waiting, sensing her need. And the Djinn felt it too. His rage ignited, swelling inside her like a rising sandstorm. He lashed out, trying to consume her from the inside, to seize control before she could strike.

Her knees buckled beneath the weight of his will. But she was the Ifrit. She had survived the mines, survived the cruelty of dark men with darker intentions. She would not give in.

With a snarl of defiance, she reached deep into the well of power the Djinn sought to regain control of and used it against him. She harnessed it, molded it in her mind, and an inferno erupted from her fingers, casting a wave of fire so great it engulfed the entire vault.

The heat was unbearable, hotter than the desert sun, and sweat poured from everyone's skin. The air shimmered as the flames licked the relics, melting them into a pool of molten energy that vibrated with raw, untamed power.

The Djinn screamed within her, a sound of primal terror and rage. He knew what was coming.

With a final, furious cry, Reema raised the pickaxe high above her head, closing her eyes and imagining a white crystal prison, filled with the evil contained within her. That image fixed in her mind, she slammed the pickaxe down with all her strength.

The pickaxe struck the molten relics with a resounding chime, and the energy locked within them burst forth, filling the room with a brilliant, blinding light.

The Djinn's furious roar echoed, and the others in the room clamped their hands over their ears, squinting into the blinding light. They watched the molten essence pool upward, forming a pillar twice as tall as Reema.

As the pillar slowly expanded, whips of light lashed out toward her. They passed through her body, wrapping around something deep in her soul, tearing a scream from her throat—a scream that pitched higher as the Djinn dug his claws into her.

Their screams intermingled as he fought against the pull, but it was too late. Reema had pushed her will down into the shaping prison. The Djinn's claws scraped through her being before they finally broke.

His fiery form appeared in the air, arms pinned to his body by the light coiled around him. He continued to struggle, his black eyes filled with fear. The light dragged him backward until, with a final echoing shout, the Djinn was sealed away.

Reema collapsed to her knees, the pickaxe slipping from her hands as the room fell into an eerie, scorching silence. She gasped for breath. She searched herself for any remnant of him, any lingering trace of evil. But there was only sweet, hollow nothing.

Arms wrapped around her, nearly squeezing the breath from her lungs as Alaric whispered, "It's over."

The brilliant glow of the formed prison slowly began to dim, and as it did, Sedra let out an incredulous laugh as she, Asif, Nisha, Sher, and Renfri came forward to study it.

Now, the prison stood before them as a towering pillar of gleaming white crystal. It shimmered, as pure a light as Reema had ever seen.

And best of all, she could see nothing of the Djinn.

Behind her, Asif turned toward Renfri with wide eyes. Before he could speak, Renfri pulled him into a sudden, passionate kiss. Asif leaned into it, wrapping his arm around her, the tension in his shoulders gone and at ease.

Sedra, watching from the side, broke into a wide grin, an expression Nisha and Sher matched as he took her hand, their fingers intertwining.

Reema leaned back against Alaric, her strength gone, her bones exhausted, but her soul infinitely lighter. His arms tightened around her, and the rhythm of his heart-beat matched her own.

The quiet settled over them all like a blanket of peace. And for the first time in a long while, Reema felt like she could breathe.

Reema stared out over the sea of sand. The dunes rose and fell like mountains, the desert sun beating down as if nothing had ever changed. Weeks had passed. If anyone asked, Reema would say it was because she needed time to recover. But the truth was, she dreaded what she was about to do—one final moment of pain.

Beneath her, the camel shifted. She patted the animal awkwardly, unsure how to put it at ease. The camel they'd ridden from Sandspire had been far more agreeable than this temperamental beast. He spat and pulled roughly to the side, jolting the relic pickaxe from where it hung.

"Alaric!" she called, looking back over her shoulder.

Sher glanced away from his conversation with Nisha and Alaric, and seeing her unease with the camel, burst into laughter.

Alaric paused, turning to see what was so funny. His lips spread into a deep smirk.

"Don't tell me the Ifrit's afraid of a camel!" Asif's

laughter cut through the air as he, Renfri, and Sedra walked through the gate.

Reema scowled, keeping silent, knowing there was nothing she could say. The three of them approached her while Alaric wrapped up his conversation with the Queen and her Consort.

"Got everything, boss?" Asif asked.

"I do," she said. She locked eyes with him. "You sure you don't want to come?"

"To Sandspire?" He looked back at the city of Zareen, and she followed his gaze.

Her eyes scanned the slums of the Glass District, the golden-domed palace surrounded by a thousand spires, and the towering sandstone walls boxing it all in. Then she looked up at the Angel's throne, resting atop the red, flat-topped mountain. It was beautiful.

Asif's expression filled with deep sadness as he looked back at Reema. He was probably doing the same as her: thinking about all the years they'd spent beneath the earth, watching each other's backs.

"I don't think so," he said. "This is home now."

Reema nodded, full of understanding. This had always been home for him, before he'd found himself in the mines of Sandspire.

Alaric finished speaking with Nisha and Sher, then approached Reema, ready to mount the camel. But for a moment, the air between them was still. It was a strange kind of stillness, a pause before the parting of old friends, before the sands of fate split them on different paths.

Reema's eyes met Asif's again, and this time, she saw a rare display of emotion in the lines of his face. It wasn't something she was used to seeing from him, and it made her feel the tug of what they were leaving behind. All those years surviving together, those painful, violent days in the mines—those memories were etched into her soul as deeply as they were into his.

"Goodbye, Asif," she said, her voice steady, though her heart was heavy.

"Goodbye, Reema," Asif murmured back, nearly choking on the emotion.

Alaric climbed onto the camel behind Reema, his fingers tightening around the reins.

"One last thing," she said, tilting her head toward Asif.

"What's that?" Asif asked.

"I made you a promise. Your rage is mine, and mine is yours. Do you remember?"

"Of course I do," he answered.

"Here's my gift to you. When you watch the slave master hang, you'll see a pair of slavers beside him. You might recognize them. They were sentenced for stealing years from a father and his daughter."

Asif swallowed hard and exchanged a look with Sedra. For a moment, it seemed he might say something more, but instead, he gave a tight nod, his gruff demeanor cracking under the weight of genuine sadness and gratitude. His calloused fingers brushed his chin, searching for the last ounce of strength in his silence.

His silent thanks hung in the air, full of everything they weren't saying aloud: that they had survived together, that his pain had been hers, and in some ways, always would be. It was a bond stronger than any vow of blood or brotherhood. It was something forged only in the shadows of the mines, in the grip of a pickaxe.

Reema shifted her gaze to Sedra. "Take care of him, Sedra."

Sedra grinned, trying to keep the mood light. "I'll watch over the old man."

Asif let out a snort, shaking his head, but there was a softness in his eyes as he glanced between Sedra and Reema.

"And Renfri?" Reema asked.

"Don't worry, Ifrit. There'll be no graves dug any time soon. Not for him."

Reema nodded, the corners of her lips twitching. "Good."

She raised her hand in a final farewell, having already said goodbye to the Queen and her Consort. With that, Alaric gave the reins a tug, and the camel began to move forward. Just before she looked away, she saw a tear slip from the corner of Asif's eye and trickle into his thick beard.

Neither Reema nor Alaric looked back. Not until they heard Asif's voice call out after them.

"Take care of her, you Bloodlined bastard, or I'll hunt you down."

Alaric chuckled and waved farewell to Asif.

The desert stretched before them, golden dunes rolling beneath the blinding sun like an endless sea. As Reema and Alaric rode in silence, the wind whispered softly across the sands, carrying with it a promise of new beginnings.

Reema felt the steady rhythm of the camel's gait

beneath her, the desert sun pressing down on them both. Alaric's chest was warm against her back. His arms rested loosely around her. She closed her eyes and reveled in the brush of his breath against the back of her neck.

Her heart twinged with the pain of the final goodbye, but she knew it had to happen. She and Asif had to move on, though knowing that didn't make it any easier. After all, they'd walked the same path of fate for so long—long enough to lose all their brothers.

Behind them, Zareen faded into the distance, its golden domes and towering spires slowly swallowed by the horizon. There was no need to look back; they had said their goodbyes, and now their path led toward the city of Sandspire, where Alaric would take up the mantle of Lord Damaris.

"You know," Alaric said, his voice low and gentle, "you still haven't told me what you plan to do with that pickaxe."

Reema smiled, her eyes fixed far beyond the horizon, to where a spire of slave-mined marble pierced the sky.

"You're right. I haven't."

ALSO BY Z.R. ABADDI

The Desert of Wishes Series

Thieves of Zareen Duet

A Wish So Lost

A Wish So Wanted

Slaves of Sandspire Duet

A Wish So Dark

A Wish So Free

Champion of Morswen Trilogy

Rage to Ruin

Curse of Midnight

Whisper of Deceit